AT FIRST I WAS AFRAID

DISCO DIVA MYSTERIES
BOOK 1

MARTY LUDLUM

BABYLON
BOOKS

A DISCO DIVA MYSTERY

AT FIRST I WAS *Afraid*

MARTY LUDLUM

CHAPTER ONE

Tuesday 9:10 a.m.

IF I HAD KNOWN I would be blown up today, I wouldn't have wasted time on my hair.

I hate my bank. The teller line moved at glacial speed, and the lobby was packed. On top of that, the freaking ATM ate my card—again. Technology was my curse.

I was running behind today, so I ate my convenience-store breakfast while in line. I had a giant, waxy bag full of those little chocolate-covered donuts. My mouth was in a state of ecstasy, glazed in the smooth, thick coating left behind by the confectionary delights. The first four just made me want more. I should have bought two bags.

Two nicely dressed women stared at me open-mouthed as I pushed in another. I grinned. "I have a metabolism issue."

"Sorry," the first woman said. "We didn't mean to stare."

"It's okay. I'm starving all the time. I eat like two teenage boys."

"Yet you stay so petite."

My almost-five-foot frame sported my ninety-seven pounds. I easily could pass for a junior high boy. "My metabolism runs wild. I can't turn it off." I gave them a grin.

The second woman smiled. "I hate you, just a little bit."

I nodded. "I get that a lot."

I inched forward every few minutes in this velvet-roped Skinner box. Maybe at the end of the line I would get a piece of cheese. Great, now I was hungry for cheese. And maybe some wine? It was too early for wine. Besides, I was on duty. The Las Vegas Police Department looked poorly on drinking while on duty. Law enforcement was my dream job. In elementary school, I wore my plastic badge proudly on the playground. Now, I have a real badge, which will suffice until I get my dream job, a karma delivery service. I waited patiently for that opportunity.

The bank lobby décor was over-the-top with marble every-where: marble tables, marble pillars, marble everything. They tried too hard to impress. The bank had built a small coffee boutique in the corner, making the wait slightly more tolerable. Ah, the sweet smell of java. My caramel mocha latte was a little cup of heaven. I took another sip.

I loved to people-watch, and my unassuming hometown, Las Vegas, Nevada, provided the perfect place. A nice-looking man directly in front of me abandoned his place in line. I flashed him a grin so he would not see the chocolate flecks coating my teeth, but he didn't acknowledge me. His loss. At least the line moved.

A kindergarten-age girl approached me. She wore a simple, angelic, red dress with white ruffles and a matching bow in her hair, lacy socks, and shiny shoes. That was how people used to dress. What happened? *Seriously. What happened?*

"My name is Penny. Can I have one?" She smiled, displaying a missing front tooth.

I looked into my bag and counted quickly. Six, no, seven. Seven left. "Yes," I smiled.

Her mother appeared at her side. "Penny, no." Looking at me she mouthed, "Sorry."

"No problem." I held the bag down for easy reach. She took a donut with her left hand, and we exchanged smiles. Then her right hand darted into my bag and grabbed another one.

"Thank you," she said as she scampered away.

"Sorry," her mother repeated. The mother looked like a super model. Her hair and makeup must have taken a team. And she had kids?

I smiled politely, but I really wanted those donuts back. I was starving. I checked the bag again. Only five little chocolate donuts left. I should have bought two bags. Next time, I will.

During the last four bites of chocolate bliss—I measured time in donuts—my bank line moved approximately eight inches. I hummed "You Should Be Dancing" by the Bee Gees to make the time pass. I was a serious disco junkie. *Saturday Night Fever* was the soundtrack of my life. I tapped my foot to the rhythm, hoping time would pass faster. It did, temporarily. The joy of people-watching had evaporated. The lobby had ten spots for tellers, but only one teller was working, of course. One. Just one. Freak. Why have ten spots for tellers if you only had one? If it weren't for my latte, I would be upset. I really hated this bank.

My brother, Robin, approached. "Finally found a valet." Robin wouldn't park his shiny, new sports car in a regular parking spot. Of course not. Men and their toys. Spying my bag of heavenly treats he said, "Mind if I have one, sis?"

"Yes, I mind." Sharing with siblings was overrated.

"But I gave you a ride here."

Ouch, guilt from my brother. "Okay . . . but just one."

The Vegas heat and my body temp had made the tiny

chocolate rings of happiness melt a little, and my hands were sticky. I needed a napkin, but of course none were in sight. I could have wiped my gooey icing on my pants, but these were my good black slacks, the only ones that really fit. I pulled Robin's deposit slip from his hand and used it as a napkin.

"I need that," he protested.

"You can get another." I gave him a mischievous smile, as siblings do.

An old man at the front of the line argued with the teller. "Your bank is run by idiots."

The complaining man had the worst toupee in the history of the world. His real hair was several shades lighter and separated from the toupee by a quarter inch of pale white skin. I supposed one day it had fit, but not today.

"Please calm down, sir," the teller said. "These brochures describe our fees—"

He slapped the papers from her hand, and they fluttered to the floor. "Fees are revolting. Four dollars to mail my damn statement to me? Do I need to come back there and show you how to do *your* job?"

Really? Toupee Man was picking a fight over four dollars? Hmmm. I supposed I agreed with him, but why fight with the teller? She couldn't fix anything. Time and place, Toupee Man, time and place. Nine more people before I got to the front.

The talking toupee kept shouting at the teller and got more agitated with each sentence. I guessed I should intervene before violence ensued. I handed the nearly empty bag to Robin. "I have two donuts left, right?"

Robin nodded.

"Say it out loud. I have two donuts left, and I will have two donuts when I return." I gave him a stern look, required when dealing with older brothers. I stared holes into him, and he finally relented.

"You have two donuts left. Both will be here when you return. I promise to guard them with my life. Two donuts."

"Thank you. Your dedication is appreciated." Money can't buy happiness, but it can buy chocolate mini donuts, which was kind of the same thing.

I unhooked the velvet rope, stepped out of line, and approached Toupee Man from behind. "Is there a problem here?" I asked in my softest voice. Soft voices help deescalate the situation, as my police training indicated.

Toupee Man jerked his head in my direction, and I swore the toupee shifted. The part in his hair now appeared in the middle of his head. The hairpiece compelled me to stare. "Get out of my face."

Why would he say that? *I'm a police officer. See my badge?* I looked down. I wasn't in my police uniform, my usual attire. Yesterday, I was promoted to detective with the Las Vegas Police, thank you very much. I was the third in my family to reach detective status. I was so proud I could burst. *Donna Wyznecki, Super Detective: solving crimes and breaking hearts.*

I stared at the toupee. "Please, settle down, sir. We can resolve this, but you need to settle down." I spoke softly and slowly with no sudden movements, a perfect model of deescalation. My first full day as a detective and already solving the world's problems.

He eyed me with contempt. "Shouldn't you be at school?"

This guy made being nice difficult. "Please, sir. I'm a police officer."

"You?" He sneered at me. "You're too short to be a cop."

I remembered my training. Control my tone of voice, even softer this time, and always agree with something said. "Yes, I'm short. I'm five foot adjacent, but Las Vegas doesn't have a height requirement for officers."

He shoved me and my delicious latte hit the floor. Every

sweet, wonderful drop puddled on the marble. Flailing, I caught my balance but not before I heard a ripping sound and a sudden draft on my derriere. Freak. I instinctively covered my exposed rump with my hand. These were my good black slacks, the only ones that really fit! Ugh.

"This is none of your concern. Go back to junior high, kid."

"What did you just call me?"

"None of your concern . . . *kid.*"

I was ready to scream. My anger boiled as I fisted my free hand. *Let's rumble, Baldy.* I wanted to knock that toupee right off his empty head. He was so close, I could smell his chili breath, and from the aroma, it was yesterday's chili.

A security guard wedged between us.

"Everybody, stop," the guard said. "Just stop."

We stared each other down like boxers waiting for the bell. Then, the security guard, the teller, and Mister Toupee froze and stared at me. I looked around, confused. What happened? Why had everyone turned silent? I followed their gaze. They stared at my service pistol on my belt. My gun. People usually froze when they noticed a gun. "It's okay." I flashed my Las Vegas detective's badge in a circle for all to see. "It's okay. I'm one of Las Vegas's finest." Their expressions relaxed.

Mister Toupee returned to his original mission. "Listen, keep your damn nose out of my business."

"I'm making this my business." And you owe me six dollars for the latte, jerk. Did I say "jerk" out loud?

The teller scooped up the papers. Mister Toupee snatched them, still staring daggers at me. "Don't stick your nose where it doesn't belong."

We stared at each other, neither blinking. Heat rose in my face.

He reached out with his greasy hand to push me again, and I stepped aside at the last moment, still covering my exposed tush. Toupee Man lost his footing on the latte-slick-ened floor and hit the ground hard. His toupee skittered away and landed a foot from his shiny head. His wrinkled pants absorbed most of my latte puddle. I didn't know what animal they had used to make that toupee, but it looked dead now.

"Damn you," he groaned, reaching for his hairpiece.

"You okay, sir?" The security guard winked at me. The guard was on my side.

Mister Toupee adjusted his rumpled, latte-soaked clothes. His face glowed bright red. "My suit is ruined. This is an expensive suit."

"I doubt that."

"You'll be sorry," Mister Toupee said.

"I'm already sorry I know you, jerk." Did I say that out loud? Oops.

Another security guard emerged from the crowd and helped Mister Toupee steady himself.

"Oh, my back," Mister Toupee said, in clearly feigned pain. His acting was terrible. The guards escorted him to the door. "You'll be hearing from my lawyer."

"Is he in the Hair Club for Men too?" My mouth usually got me into trouble. I should be quiet, but I was on a roll.

Mister Toupee departed, then the strangest thing happened. Everyone clapped for me. Really. After the brief applause, and my quick bow, my hand strategically placed to cover my drafty rump, I got back in line. I probably should have curtseyed, but I wasn't sure if I remembered how.

My brother whispered to me, "Your panties are exposed," in the kind way only a brother could.

"What color?" I asked, as I could not remember getting dressed this morning.

He glanced at my rear. "Purple."

"Please tell me they're solid fabric and not see-through lace."

He stared straight ahead, fighting to stifle a laugh.

This day was not going to be a winner.

The world returned to normal. Well, half-speed normal. Despite the many bank employees, no one took a teller spot. No one. Nine empty teller spots and a line of customers. Was I the only one who considered this a tragedy? I really hated this bank. I finally got my turn at the counter.

"Have a Second United day," the teller told the departing customer.

Second United sucks.

"Welcome to Second United of Nevada. How can I serve you?"

Serve me? Really? How about getting more than one teller? That would serve me. Wait. Dammit. Why was I here? I wanted to scream. After all this, I couldn't remember why I was here. Then it hit me. "The ATM ate my debit card again."

"Your name please?"

"Donna . . . Donna Wyznecki."

"How do you spell that?"

"W-Y-Z-N-E-C-K-I. It's pronounced Wizz-neck-ee. It's Romanian."

The teller nodded and clicked the keys on her computer. "Your full name is Donna Summer Wyznecki?"

I nodded. She gave me a questioning stare, so I explained, "My father is a big disco fan."

The teller started singing, "She Works Hard for the Money." I had no choice but to accept that challenge and join her. Neither of us was a strong singer, but we enjoyed the distraction from the workday. A third voice joined, and we stopped singing, realizing we were easily outclassed. My brother, Robin, was a professional singer and musician, part of the Las Vegas gig economy. He had all the talent in our family.

"Your voice is beautiful. Are you a professional?" the teller asked with a coy smile.

"Robin Gibb Wyznecki, at your service." He gave a quick bow. "Named after the Bee Gees singer. My dad is a big disco fan."

"We live for disco," I said.

"Those disco clothes—just awful," the teller cringed. "So tacky, I mean those patterned polyester shirts—"

"Don't forget the bell bottom rayon slacks in all the unnatural colors of the rainbow."

The teller shook her head. "Dreadful fashions. So glad it's history."

"Not quite. Our dad still wears disco clothes," Robin said.

I nodded. "Every day. Every single day. I told you, he's a big disco fan."

The teller mouthed, "Sorry." She smiled. "But I do love that music. Love to dance."

"Me too." I had to admit it. I loved the music and loved to disco dance. "Maybe I should be in some twelve-step program?"

Robin winked at the teller. "We should go dancing sometime. I'm going to get a deposit slip," and he moved towards one of the marble tables, still protecting my last two donuts.

I think the teller was smitten with my brother. When she returned her attention to me, she asked, "Are you still at . . ." and she rattled off my address. I nodded. She clicked a few more keys and frowned. "I see this is your . . . oh, *fourth* replacement card in twelve months. There's a thirty-five-dollar fee for a second card. And I see that fee has been waived twice already."

"Technology and I don't get along." Crap. How much was

left in my checking account? My voracious appetite gobbled up my budget. I shouldn't lean on Robin. He'd already bought my latte and shuttled me here. My car wouldn't start. I wasn't sure why. This was only the second day the gas tank showed "E." I had at least two more days before I needed to fill up, three if I pushed it.

A manager approached wearing a nice suit with a nametag that said "Valerie." She had a Cartier watch and a humungous marquise solitaire on her left hand. I couldn't see her shoes from behind the counter, but I bet they were expensive.

"This is Ms. Wyznecki," the teller said.

"*Detective* Wyznecki," I corrected.

"Yes, sorry . . . Detective Wyznecki."

The teller tilted her computer screen so the manager could view it. The manager asked, "Are you the person who dealt with Mr. Higgins?"

Higgins? Who was Mr. Higgins? I shrugged. The teller pointed to the top of her head. Ah, Toupee Man had a name, Mr. Higgins.

"He's been a thorn in our side for a while. Mr. Higgins is our most dissatisfied customer. He has made a scene every day this week. Every day. He gives me a migraine." Turning to the teller, the manager said, "Get Detective Wyznecki whatever she needs. No fees for Las Vegas's finest." She handed me her business card. Valerie McAlister, Vice President of Operations. Another victory for women. "And here's a courtesy card for our coffee bar. Please enjoy with our compliments."

"Thank you." I looked at the card, a twenty-dollar gift card. Hot damn. I loved this bank. I might live here. Hallelujah, this will be a wonderful day. I needed my two doughnuts. I was thirsty too. After the doughnuts, I would get another latte and an almond croissant. Okay, two croissants. I deserved them. A girl must keep up her strength.

The teller interrupted my daydream about caffeine and almonds. "Mrs. McAlister, line four for you. The caller must urgently speak to *the man* in charge."

Really? *The man* in charge?

Valerie tapped the speakerphone on, and I was close enough to overhear. "This is Valerie McAlister, the Vice President of Operations. How can I help you?"

A man's scratchy voice arose. "A woman—really? I shouldn't be surprised. You kept me on hold for too long."

"Sorry, sir. The bank is quite busy today. How can I help you?"

"There is a bomb in the bank. I wanted to give you more warning, but you kept me on hold. The selfish will be punished. The selfish will be punished . . ."

"If this is a joke . . ."

"No joke. There is a bomb in the bank. It will go off in . . . less than one minute. The selfish will be punished. The selfish . . ."

What? A bomb?

Blood drained from Valerie's face.

I sprang into action. "This doesn't sound like a joke. Get everyone out!"

Valerie acted like a pro. "Evacuate the building!" She tapped into the building intercom. "Everyone, please exit the building immediately. This is not a drill."

Employees scattered toward the exits. My fellow patrons remained in the velvet rope maze, looking perturbed. No one wanted to lose their place in line. "Evacuate, now!" I shouted. The queued customers didn't move an inch. "Dammit, people, get out! There's a bomb in here!"

That got everyone moving. Customers ran, shoved, and climbed over each other like they were at a Black Friday sale at Wal-Mart. I barked orders. "Get out, now!"

Penny, the little girl with the ruffled dress, stood alone in the lobby. Her mother, the super model, twenty feet away, was pushed to the ground in the panic. The mother reached out, but her child was too distant. The little girl teared up. She didn't know what to do. I scooped her up and ran for the exit.

My brother stood at the marble table, deposit slip in hand, wide-eyed with confusion.

"Robin, run—" I shouted.

Then it happened. I didn't hear it so much as I felt it. A blast of hurricane-force wind threw me across the floor. My equilibrium was gone. Every scrap of paper and every speck of dirt in the room blasted my exposed skin. Ceiling tiles fell like heavy chunks of plaster raindrops. My ribs connected with a marble pillar, squeezing the air from me. I screamed but heard nothing. My lungs fought to expand. Glass shards fell off me like glitter.

My ears registered a deep hum, like a church organ stuck on one note. I saw every movement but heard only the hum. Disheveled people scrambled in slow motion in every direction. Lights flickered. The monotonous tone impeded my concentration. What had happened? The velvet ropes were gone. Dust discolored the marble walls. Pieces of ceiling littered every surface. A dangling computer screen swayed, suspended by its power cord. The cracked screen still displayed my account information from a moment ago.

Nothing made a sound. The little girl shuddered under my weight. Was she okay? Was I? I tried to stand. I had no feeling in my legs, like they weren't there. My whole body tingled. Was I on fire? Was I dying? Where was Robin? I tried to call for him but couldn't hear my own voice.

The cold marble floor stung my face. Dust filled my nostrils and mouth and an acrid smell wafted through the air. Was something on fire? Singed papers mixed with ceiling plaster scattered across the floor, like dirty snow. "Robin, where are you?" I spoke but could not hear my own voice. The persistent hum in my ears continued. My heartbeat pulsed in my chest, my arms, and my head. I was hungry. Why was I thinking of almond croissants? And cheese?

My hearing came back with a jolt. The cacophony of noise overwhelmed my ears: screaming, crying, yelling, shoes clattering on the marble floor, broken glass crunching beneath unsteady feet, all at the volume of a jet. I dislodged the little girl in the ruffled dress. The suspended computer screen sputtered images off and on as it swayed. The plug gave way and it crashed to the floor, sending a shot of adrenaline through my body. My heart pounced like it would explode.

I stood on wobbly legs. Ceiling dust fell off me. The searing pain in my back burned. A blurry security guard helped me up. "Something's wrong with my back." My ears rang and my eyes watered. I touched my back and winced. My hand was covered in blood, my blood. I didn't like seeing my blood. The room spun. *Where was my brother?*

"Robin?" I screamed.

Who freaking did this? And why?

And where are my damn donuts?

CHAPTER TWO

Tuesday 10:35 a.m.

THE AMBULANCE SHUTTLED me to UMC. My back
must have been seriously injured, but I wasn't in one of those
uncomfortable neck brace things. University Medical Center
was the big hospital in downtown Las Vegas, which meant I
would be well cared for. Hey, I might have a slot machine in
my room. The emergency room was like a bloody carnival,
sensory overload. I was rolled to a curtained stall as the more
seriously wounded flooded inside. The paramedics shifted me
to a bed, propped on my side.

A nurse stood beside my bed with a stainless-steel clipboard. "I need to see if any of your information has changed
since your last visit. Is your name Donna *Summer*
Wyznecki?"

"Yes." The nurse gave me a puzzled stare. "Dad loves
disco."

"Age twenty-eight?"

"Yes. I'm single, and actively looking."

The nurse smiled. "I'll post a notice on your door. Height, four feet, eleven inches?"

"I'll give you twenty dollars if you list me at five feet."

"Make it twenty-five and it's a deal." The nurse smiled. "Weight ninety-three pounds?"

I nodded and spotted my reflection off a stainless-steel cabinet. Not my best look.

"Any medical conditions I should add to your chart?"

"I have a metabolism issue. I must eat constantly."

The nurse smiled. "Lucky."

"I have the digestive system of a hummingbird guzzling espresso. Can I roll over onto my back?"

"You should not move because of your injuries."

Injuries? How bad was I? I finally got the courage to ask, "Am I going to die? And where is my brother, Robin?"

"You'll be fine. He's down the hall. You need to stay in bed, on your side."

The nurse didn't provide any details on Robin, but if it was bad news, she would have said more. Wouldn't she? My head swirled and my stomach throbbed, a sign my blood sugar was approaching zero. "I'm starving. Can I get something to eat? My metabolism . . ."

"I have a plate of bacon leftover from this morning."

My stomach did the happy dance. This day was looking up.

"I think it's turkey bacon. Does that matter?"

Mind if I pay the hospital in Monopoly money? Does that matter? "Hard pass on the turkey bacon," I said.

The nurse smiled. "I think we're having meatloaf today."

Are you kidding me? Hospital meatloaf? Was I being punished?

The nurse sensed my disappointment. "You're on an unrestricted diet. You can order something."

No hospital food, I had suffered enough. Where to eat near

UMC? I called Doña Maria Tamales, my favorite tamales place, and ordered six pork in red sauce and six chicken in green sauce for me and Robin. Wait. Was it sacrilege to order tamales on Taco Tuesday? Was Tamale Tuesday also acceptable?

My phone vibrated like a . . . well . . . it vibrated a lot. Messages streamed in. Vegas P.D. had an automated alert system. If any officer was injured on the job, the family members were immediately notified. Vegas police didn't want the family to learn about the injury from the media—or even worse, Facebook.

I had a big family, and my phone buzzed repeatedly. My parents called. Well, my mother called. My father never had much to say. Two of my brothers called. Not Robin, of course. Robin! No one told me any details. My blood pressure rose, and the monitor beeped a warning. My younger sister called. Six Wyznecki kids—we were a disco-themed version of the Brady Bunch from hell. We didn't have Alice the maid, but we needed a therapist on speed dial. I assured each one that I was fine. I needed to re-think who I listed on my family notification sheet.

My food arrived, and I chowed down on the tamales and homemade chips and salsa. I hadn't even ordered the chips and salsa. The folks at Doña Maria's knew me quite well. My metabolism made me a preferred customer at all the local eateries.

Word about my injury spread fast. My room became the busiest spot in Vegas outside The Strip. My fellow officers wanted to see me in the flesh. I dabbed red sauce from my face and green sauce from my hospital gown and IV tube. I was too hungry to be ladylike.

My boss, Captain Creek, entered my room. He usually held a cigarette, but not in a hospital. He was, to use the polite term, portly. His potbelly triumphed over years of failed diets. I could tell when he was within twenty feet of my room because he reeked of cigarette smoke and wheezed. "Thank God you're alive, Donna. What did you see?"

I described every detail I remembered: the teller, Robin, Mister Toupee, the security guard, Valerie, and the little girl in the red dress. I described the voice, raspy, saying "Punish the selfish banks," or something like that.

My mentor, Charlie Todd, scribbled furious notes. Vegas Police mentored the most senior detective, Charlie, with the newest, me. We made quite a pair. Charlie stood at nearly seven feet tall, a trim African American man, and I was just the opposite, short, pale, and female. Charlie was the perfect mentor, highly organized. He noticed every detail and kept meticulous notes.

"How's the injury list?" the captain asked.

Charlie checked his notes. "Twenty in the hospital with five in critical, as of eight minutes ago."

"Get me an update."

"Is Penny okay?" I asked.

"We'll check." Captain Creek nodded to Charlie, who whipped out his phone and moved to the corner of the room.

"What about Robin?" Their worried expressions answered my question.

The captain changed the subject. "Why were you at the bank?"

"Damn ATM ate my debit card again." I hated technology.

Charlie passed the captain a slip of paper, which he read and then folded back up and put in his pocket.

"What about Robin? And the little girl? Tell me something." This had to be unwelcome news. Dammit.

"You heard someone mention 'bomb'?" the captain asked. I

nodded. "Did you see this person?" The captain's hand looked naked without his signature cigarette.

"No, it was a phone call, but sounded like a male voice."

"So, he called to warn them before the blast. That's interesting. And then?"

"Pandemonium. Lots of pushing, then the explosion."

A steady stream of officers checked on me, making the room claustrophobic.

Captain Creek barked orders like a quarterback, one order for each member of his crew. "One of our own was hurt. No one goes home today." Everyone nodded in solidarity. "I want interview notes from everyone at the scene and at the hospital on my desk now. Get the bank's security video. You know they video everything inside the bank. They will cooperate. Trace the phone calls into the bank. Maybe we can get lucky. Get outside video from everywhere within a half mile of that bank. I want to see the faces of everyone leaving. Don't take any bull about needing a warrant. Get me a full list of all injured. Recreate where everyone was when the bomb went off, and I mean everyone, even those who work for the bank—I want a list of every witness inside the bank and out. Get help and start a background check on every one of them. Get a list of every car parked within two blocks—the bomber had to get to the bank somehow. Check with Parole Services. See if we released any bombers. Get my crime scene crew in there. No one takes a break until I get every damn fingerprint inside that bank. And the bomb tech guys need to earn their pay. Find out who made this thing. And before anyone leaves, remember our two goals." The captain wheezed. "First . . ."

"Catch the bad guy," everyone said in unison, myself included.

"And second . . ." the captain prompted.

"Don't scare the damn tourists," the chorus repeated.

I felt a warm rush as the pain medicine kicked in.

"I want to know every detail about this crime." The captain's voice boomed. "And I mean *now* people. Work like we have a purpose." The group departed like a football team breaking huddle. The captain lowered his voice. "Charlie, find out about her brother, and get with your friends in the media. Put out a story. No one needs to know about the bomb. Stop the rumor mill. Our narrative will be our advantage in the short term."

Vegas police were family—a big dysfunctional family, but a family—and someone had attacked a bank and injured one of the family. Me.

My bank branch sat well off the Strip, so the tourists should be unconcerned. Our visitors never understood that Las Vegas was a real city, with banks, parks, schools, and hospitals, ample doughnut shops, and wonderful tamales. I gobbled a bite of chicken tamale.

"We'll find the man who did this, Donna," the captain reassured me.

"Can you find out about Robin?"

His cigarette breath was giving me a tumor.

A scrub-clad male nurse sauntered into my room with a plastic shower caddy of medical supplies. Wow, he was dreamy but that might be the pain medicine talking. He was trim and handsome with a bright smile. I might require mouth-to-mouth resuscitation. How much pain medicine did they give me? My mouth might get me into trouble—again.

"Time for a little checkup," my future husband said.

"Do I need to leave?" the captain asked.

"I'll just be a second." The nurse took my wrist, taking my pulse. He had a gentle touch. "How's your pain, on a scale of one to ten?"

"Mostly one through the magic of chemistry," I replied.

"You have pretty eyes." I gave him my best smile. Someone was humming the wedding march. It might have been me.

"Thank you." He winked at me. "Do you know what kind of bomb it was?"

"No, not yet," I said.

"Any idea who did it or why?"

"Strange questions for a nurse," Charlie said.

"Just making small talk," the nurse said, staring at the monitors.

"Where's your identification card?" the captain asked.

"I must have left it in another room. I better go retrieve it." The nurse dropped my wrist and moved toward the door.

Why was he leaving? This relationship was promising. "You left your stuff." I gestured to the plastic caddy sitting at my feet.

The captain called out, "Grab that nurse!" After brief scuffling in the hallway, two large, uniformed officers hauled the nurse back into my room.

Charlie pulled the intruder's wallet and flipped it open. "Garrett, Zack. South Las Vegas address. Not a nurse. He's a reporter with the *Las Vegas Tourist Scoop*." The *Vegas Tourist Scoop* was a tabloid's tabloid. Rumors and speculation were too reliable for them. Pure garbage.

The captain approached Zack and eyed his wallet carefully. "Zack Garrett. That name is familiar, but not in a good way."

"The First Amendment protects me—"

"Not from impersonating a nurse," my captain interrupted, filling Zack's personal space with his protruding belly. "This is simple. You forget anything you think you heard here today, and I'll forget this trespassing incident."

Zack stood, still captive by the two officers. "All right, I accept."

Captain Creek moved in even closer, nose to nose. "I'm not asking you. I'm telling you." The captain looked at the officers holding Zack. "Now get him out of here." The officers half-walked, half-carried my half-boyfriend out of the room.

And just like that, my most promising prospect in a while left.

"Charlie, get working on the media." The captain narrowed his eyes at me. "Watch out, Donna, reporters will try anything. Be on your guard."

"I will."

"Anything else I can do for you?"

Curiosity burned inside me. "Penny? What happened to her? And my brother, Robin? Is he . . ." I couldn't say the word "dead."

I closed my eyes, not wanting to know if Robin and little Penny survived—or didn't.

Charlie reviewed his notes. "She has a broken arm, some bruises and scrapes, but she will be fine, because of you."

Relief filled my heart, and a couple of tears tumbled down my cheeks. "How about my brother?"

The captain sighed. "I'm afraid he's still unconscious. I'll let you know the minute we hear anything." He looked at Charlie. "How many injured?"

Charlie checked his notes. "Hospital has thirty-four admissions, concussions, broken bones, lots of lacerations and ear damage." I sighed in relief. Then Charlie continued. "Seven in critical care, brain injuries. Must have been close to the blast."

I closed my eyes. I didn't want to know, but at the same time, I had to know. *Don't make me ask.* "Any fatalities?" *Please say no.*

"No, again thanks to you," the captain said.

Charlie interjected. "The little girl you saved, Penny, is Steve Shale's kid."

"The mayor?" the captain asked.

"Shale? Mr. Politics?" I asked. "Is he with wife number four?" Shale, a shameless politician, got divorced and remarried every few years, each new wife younger than the previous one. Eventually he will have to marry a kindergartener.

"She is number five, actually," Charlie said.

Five, really? I must have missed one. Las Vegas was an interesting place.

"Anyway, dear wife number five took Penny on a shopping day, and they stopped by the bank. Wrong place, wrong time. They're grateful. They want to give you something."

"Can I get one of those giant gold keys that doesn't really open anything? I always wanted one of those."

"Probably not," the captain said, not appreciating my sarcasm.

"Suppose they had one made of chocolate? That would make a good gift. Thanks anyway. Maybe when I'm not wearing a hospital gown."

Captain Creek smiled. "Detective Wyznecki, anything you need?"

"No, just a little rest."

Charlie flashed his phone's screen to the captain. "I have good news," the captain said. "Your family is here."

"My family is here?" Freak. I should have felt the disturbance in the Force. So much for rest.

CHAPTER THREE

Tuesday 12:45 p.m.

HERE THEY CAME. A cluster of my siblings crowded into the room, talking at the same time, and all talking to me. I tried to interject into each conversation, but it became a jumbled mess of voices.

Then my mother arrived. Like the Red Sea parting, my siblings made way for the family matriarch. She wore a new hairstyle, a bob cut, now dyed reddish-brown. I bet Dad hadn't noticed. "Love your hair, Mom."

She pushed by everyone and kissed me on the forehead as she has done since I was in diapers. Mom always wore pantsuits. Recently she sported soft shades, today wearing light rose, accented with too much costume jewelry. "My baby, my baby, my baby. Oh my God, I was so worried about my baby." Mom spoke in an overly dramatic way that eclipsed William Shatner. "Is my baby all right?" She frowned and shook her head.

What could it be this time?

"Oh honey." She brushed my hair with her hand. Dust from broken ceiling tiles rained onto my pillow. "Your hair—" Besides being dramatic, she was a tad judgmental.

"Sorry, Mom, I didn't really plan this."

The circus was in town—in my room. Could I volunteer to get blown up again? My father walked in, silently skirting the back wall. Dad nodded to the captain who grunted in response. Dad retired from a lengthy career in Internal Affairs, which was not a way to make or keep friends. Dad's disco ensemble for today was an eye-catcher, a blue plaid shirt and orange patterned pants. He was impossible not to notice. Most officers stared. Dad muttered, "Shouldn't have gotten hurt."

I waited for more, but that was his entire commentary. Thanks, Dad. Four whole words. He was a regular Hallmark greeting card.

Mom brushed my hair with her hand. "Elaine is with Robin. The neighbor is watching the kids." Robin and Elaine had two little ones. This wasn't how life was supposed to go. I had to think positive thoughts. Robin was going to get better. He had to.

"Detective Wyznecki?" the doctor asked as he entered with a nurse in tow. "Can I speak with my patient alone?" No one moved. So much for my privacy.

Charlie confirmed his identification. We wouldn't fall for that old trick again.

The captain, the officers, and the rest of my family paraded out into the hallway, all except my mother. She didn't move an inch.

"How are you feeling?" The doctor shined a light in my eyes. "Does anything hurt?"

"Does anything hurt, baby?" my mother echoed.

"Most everything hurts," I said. "My back is still numb. A real bitch of a headache."

"That's to be expected, being so close to the blast," the doctor said. "Probably a mild concussion."

"Donna, don't talk like that," Mom said. "It's not lady-like."

"Yes, Mom, but I did just get blown up. I think I'm entitled to cuss a little." Maybe a lot, depending on the pain medicine. "Any word on my brother's status?"

"We had to medically induce a coma to allow his brain swelling to mitigate."

Medically induced coma? Brain swelling? That couldn't be good. *Positive thoughts, Donna.*

"We're doing everything we can. We really won't know anything until he wakes up. He has the best neurologists in Nevada working on him."

"He's a musician. His hearing is important . . ." I choked up.

"For the moment," the doctor said, "we need to focus on you."

What was wrong with me? I felt crappy, but was I going to . . . ?

The doctor reached into his coat pocket and removed a bloodstained baggie, which contained a black piece of plastic and a silver chain. "You know those bank pens, the kind chained to the table?"

I didn't like where this was going.

"The blast shoved one of those bank pens into your—"

"Back?" I asked, dreading the answer.

"Buttock."

Laughter erupted in the hallway. *Freak. Impaled in the ass with a bank teller's pen.* This was a disaster, and now my colleagues and family knew. The butt jokes would never stop.

CHAPTER FOUR

Tuesday 2:15 p.m.

"GET SOME REST, DONNA," the captain said. "Officer Services will contact you."

Crap on a cracker. Officer Services handled on-duty injuries. That meant I had to get a mental evaluation. I didn't want to sit on the sidelines and talk to some psychiatrist. I wanted to track down the guy who hurt my brother. I was pissed. Did the captain expect me just to sit on the couch while my brother's killer— Wait. Killer? No, no, no. My brother would pull through this.

I couldn't rest until I'd seen Robin myself. Eventually, the nurse brought a wheelchair and helped me into it. Charlie offered to take me to Robin's room. The nurse agreed awfully quickly.

I whispered to Charlie, "These pain meds are making me loopy. Did I say anything inappropriate to the nurse?"

He smiled. "I think you two are engaged now."

Oh boy.

Charlie pushed my wheelchair down the hall while I tried to balance on one butt cheek. Robin was in much worse shape than me. A ventilator breathed for him. His nurse told me he was in a medically induced coma. I had heard that term twice now and hadn't liked it either time.

I looked at Charlie. "Get me out of here." Charlie helped as friends always do, even if it was against my doctor's wishes. After a little cajoling and a lot of promises that I'd rest, he got them to release me.

I got dressed and shoved my minimal belongings into a white plastic bag. I had to get out of this place. Charlie wheeled me out of the E.R. entrance and ran to get the car.

I struggled to stand with the cane the hospital gave me. Every time I moved, pain shot through me. The cane took the weight off my leg, and kept me from flexing my butt muscle, which I had never noticed before. Charlie shuttled me to the precinct with only one reply of, "Yes, Miss Daisy."

"I was worried about you." Helen D'Angelo came around the entrance desk to hug me, which hurt, but I needed physical contact. Helen controlled all incoming and outgoing police assignments, regulated the entrance into the precinct, and was everyone's unofficial mother figure. She looked like Bea Arthur from *The Golden Girls*—she was tall, broad, and never took crap from anyone. No one went into the station without Helen's approval. "I've added your brother to my prayers."

"Thank you," I whispered.

Helen shuffled tarot cards on her desk. She was also a part-time psychic or medium or something. I didn't know if Helen believed in that stuff or not. She worked in carnivals before joining the police force, so I had doubts about her clairvoyant skills.

"Would you like me to do a tarot reading for you?"

"Maybe later," I said.

Helen looked out for me and the few other female detectives. She was our guardian angel. I asked Helen to call me the instant she had any updates about Robin. She would. We were police sisters, working together in a sea of testosterone.

I limped to the detectives' division with Helen on my heels. Something was up. Well-wishers greeted me. Maybe they wouldn't tease me about being stabbed in the rump. Wrong again. I hobbled through a group of gentle pats on the back and mild teasing—and plenty of butt jokes. I finally got to my desk and cut off the plastic bracelet from the hospital. A cake box sat on my desk. Freak. I sat down tenderly. "Another bomb?" I teased. Please let it be a bomb so the butt jokes will stop.

"Don't be silly. We got you a cake." Sandy was one of the few other female detectives, and she looked like Shirley Temple. Not Shirley Temple as a little girl but what she might have looked like in her forties—a woman with a mound of blonde ringlets and a perpetual smile, always happy and upbeat.

A crowd gathered around my desk. I didn't know if they wanted to check on my health or get a piece of cake. I assumed the latter. I flipped open the cardboard box. Sandy cleared her throat as though she was about to read a royal decree. "May I have your attention, everyone. On behalf of the Disco Divas, for extreme valor under fire, I award you, Donna Summer Wyznecki, the Order of the Purple Butt."

A smattering of overzealous applause erupted from the small gathering. "Knock it off." I smiled. "You know you are getting some cake." I looked at my partner. "Oh, Sandy, you shouldn't have." And I meant it.

While Sandy cut and distributed the cake, I glanced over to the glass walls of the major crime conference room and noticed a beehive of activity. We called the room "the fishbowl" since it had glass walls on all sides. Having a case in the fishbowl was serious, and this was my case. My crime had priority. Las Vegas had lots of street crime and occasional violent crime—but bombings were rare. I wanted to think they were doing all this because of me, but I knew the two goals: first, catch the bad guy, and second, don't scare the damn tourists. Explosions were bad for tourism.

After the cake-induced sugar-fix, with two slices for me since I was recuperating, Sandy shoved paper plates and plastic forks into a trash can. Everyone congregated in the fishbowl. The walls had live television feeds of every local station and national network. In addition, we monitored outside each police precinct and eight screens showed the city's busiest intersections. The final product was half James Bond's lair and half Best Buy's showroom. It made me hungry for popcorn. I had to get inside. I needed to know who had hurt my rump and my brother and why.

Three detectives narrated their findings. My fellow officers had amassed quite a bit of evidence in such a brief time. Dozens of photos taken immediately after the blast showed the injured, including me. They had also collected diagrams of the bank building, a handwritten, lengthy list of suspects recently released from prison, and a timeline showed a minute-by-minute account.

I limped in without saying a word. Sandy offered me her seat. Walking with a cane had some advantages. Wait, the only one chivalrous enough to offer me a seat was a woman? Oh well. I had hoped to slip in undetected. Wrong again.

"Detective Wyznecki, so glad you could join us." Captain Creek nodded in appreciation, and I got a nice round of applause from my peers.

"Stop clapping," I said. "You're not getting any more cake."

Captain Creek changed the subject. "Who would do this? Who hates this bank?"

Voices interjected from around the room. Everyone on the force hated this bank. Officers commented on high fees for credit cards, high interest on car loans, being denied a mortgage. Second United was the preferred bank for city employees, which meant everyone had an account there, and everyone was displeased with their never-ending fees. I was going to mention my fee for a replacement debit card but remembered that Valerie liked me.

Captain Creek nodded. "Okay, everyone hates them. Me too." This admission got grumbles of approval. "But who hates them enough to blow up the lobby?"

The fishbowl turned quiet. The captain continued. "Well, somebody did, so let's find out who." He looked at me and spoke softly. "Donna, I need to see you for a minute."

The captain whisked me away to a small interrogation room with chipped paint and a lingering scent of nervous sweat. This could only mean one thing, my Officer Services notification. The department required a medical release and psychological counseling for officers injured in the line of duty. Until cleared, I couldn't find the man who hurt Robin and my tender tush.

This sucked. I would have to meet with the department psychiatrist and talk about my feelings and my fears, blah, blah, blah. Crazy people crap. My family didn't go to psychiatrists. We needed it—oh my, did we need it—but we didn't go. I eased into one of the metal chairs bolted to the floor. In these interrogation rooms, everything was metal and bolted to the floor, for good reason.

The door opened, Lynn Parsons entered, and my feminine confidence left. Lynn was beautiful, with tanned skin and wavy, long, dark hair, plus the big smile and the shapely body of Jennifer Lopez. My envy roared. Every man's eyes followed her. Every woman was jealous. Lynn was the union lawyer for any officer charged with a discipline issue. Most officers never knew their union lawyer, as you only met during complaint hearings. Lynn and I were best friends. I supposed that meant I had my share of complaints. It wasn't my fault. I had a problem dealing with crazy stupid people. Don't put me around crazy stupid people, no problem.

"Hey, Lynn," I said, as we hugged. We made a good pair, like Cagney & Lacey, Rizzoli & Isles, Tacos & Margaritas, Batman & Robin. Of course, I was Batman, and she was Robin.

Robin? That reminded me of my brother's predicament.

Captain Creek sat down, and, since he was unable to scoot his chair back, his immense belly rubbed against the table, his unlit cigarette in his left hand. The small room magnified his cigarette breath. My eyes stung. He plopped my file on the table between us. Most of the officer's files were five or six pages. Mine was about an inch thick. Crazy stupid people, lots of them, especially in Vegas.

"I want to be part of the investigation," I said.

"First you have to get cleared," the captain said. "We must do this by the book. You got injured."

"No need to remind me. I hear a butt joke every sixty seconds. The doctor said I was okay."

"The doctor said you could not leave the hospital or return to active duty in the field. Officially, you are on restricted assignment until cleared by medical and psych." The captain passed the written notification to Lynn, who scanned it before handing it to me for a signature.

"Besides, you're too close to this. Your brother is a victim. How is he?"

"Still unconscious . . ." I couldn't utter the words "medically induced coma." It sounded too hopeless. I scribbled my signature and passed the form back.

The captain examined the form. "Your task until further notice is to review the bank's employees for any criminal ties."

"That sounds like scut work for rookies."

"It's a longshot, but it needs to be done. And you can do it from your desk."

I sighed. "It *is* scut work for rookies."

"Donna, don't leave your desk without permission." The captain smiled.

"What if I have to pee?"

"You have a trash can at your desk," the captain chuckled. "Donna, I'm serious. No fieldwork until further orders."

I nodded in agreement.

"Besides, he nearly blew your ass off." He laughed and wheezed simultaneously. Another butt joke, and this time from my captain. No safe space for me.

"At least let me know when you solve the case."

"You will be the first to know." The captain left, content with his signed form.

Lynn glowed. I wondered why. "How are you, Donna? How's your love life? Seeing anyone?"

What was the polite word for dead, hopeless, lifeless? Hmmm. My social calendar gathered dust. "Not bad. How about you?"

Lynn thrusted her left hand in my face so fast I got PTSD. A shiny gold band with a big fat diamond on top. "I'm engaged." She shook her left hand, so the diamond sparkled. "I'm getting married."

Freaking crap. Lynn was getting married, and I hadn't had a real date since . . . my longest relationship has been with Little Debbie. "I'm so happy for you." I really was happy for her. We hugged. The ring sparkled and illuminated the room.

"I needed to tell you so . . ."

Oh, no. Please don't say it. Please don't ask me to . . .

"I want you to be one of my bridesmaids."

Great, great, great. She was getting married, and I couldn't get a date. *Freak*. On top of that, I would have to wear some ridiculous dress, standing next to a bunch of supermodels. My life was a train wreck.

We hugged again and I smiled. "Thank you so much. I'd love to."

We made a date for lunch, which meant salad. I already felt hunger pains. Salad wasn't food. We fed salad to cows so they could become hamburgers. Half the world tried to blow me up and the other half tried to starve me. I would drop by In-N-Out Burger for a double-double on the way to lunch with Lynn.

Great, just great. A bridesmaid, again.

CHAPTER FIVE

Tuesday 3:45 p.m.

COULD my life get any worse? Of course it could. Stuck with scut duty, reviewing bank employee files for criminal behavior. I might as well search for unicorns or casino patrons who won millions. I shuffled to my desk, each step stinging my sore rear. At my government surplus metal desk I sat down gingerly and brushed off cake crumbs. I noticed a bite-size clump that had been dropped in the sugar frenzy. I wheeled my head around to ensure no one was watching, then dropped the icing-covered delicacy in my mouth. Delicious, just like I expected.

I should buy a birthday cake. It's not my birthday, but the bakery never checks. It's kind of an honor system.

Valerie, the bank manager, arrived at my desk, followed by a uniformed officer carrying a large stack of paper files. We exchanged hugs, limited by my groan. Valerie was bruised and scraped, still wearing the same sharp suit, a little dusty. I checked. I was right, expensive shoes, Louboutin heels with those bright red soles. Wow, Valerie knew her shoes. You go girl.

Valerie plopped the giant stack of paper files on my desk. The tower of paper stood at least a foot high. Freak. I could feel a wave of boredom crashing against me.

"I'll be right back. I have more files in my car."

More? Ugh.

I started the mind-numbing task of searching for a criminal in a group of well-paid and well-behaved office workers. It was pointless. Of course, bank employees are not really your typical criminals. I typed name after name into our extensive database for background checks. Nothing, time and time again.

I almost jumped for joy when I found one employee, Katheryn Bradley, had a speeding ticket. At least that meant the database search was still working. What next? Finding one of the bank's employees was late for choir practice?

I shifted my weight in my chair without a thought and felt a blast of pain rush through me. All I could do was shut my eyes and let it pass.

I had to train my mind to focus on not shifting around. No movement, no matter how small. Think frozen, like the statue game we used to play as kids, to see how long we could remain motionless. Statue was an interesting game until I realized that mom had invented it to keep her collection of disco-named children still for just a few moments. Smart move, Mom, smart move.

I got into a routine, typing in the full name, then staring at the screen until "No record indicated" appeared. I repeated the process, again and again.

Valerie returned with a banker's box filled with more employee paper files. "One more box to go," she said. Another box? I might retire doing this same boring task. These people sounded like honor society applicants, not criminal masterminds.

Name after name, no record indicated. Roy Hinkley, no record indicated. Jonas Gumby, no record indicated. A trained monkey could do my job. Mary Summers, no record indicated. Faces blended together. Bank employees were a consistent lot, lacking criminal incentives.

Bank employee 3257, a slight exaggeration, was Raymond P. Soames. Instead of my typical "No record indicated," my computer screen filled with text.

Bingo.

Our Mr. Soames had one, two, no three restraining orders. He had been a busy bee. It was a leap to go from restraining orders to bomber, but not impossible. Anyway, he was the only person in my search that had anything more than a traffic ticket.

I printed off the two-page summary of each protective order and put it into Mr. Soames' file. I continued my less-than-exciting task for what seemed like days but was only a couple of hours. Halfway through the last box, I noticed the clock had finally moved a little. It was 5:15 p.m. I needed to leave. I was bored, and tired, and in pain, and hungry. Besides, nobody gets overtime until we had a real suspect.

A uniformed rookie took my desk and started typing in names with enthusiasm. Good for her. I showed her my results: a huge pile of rejects, no criminal ties, and my one and only positive hit, Mr. Raymond P. Soames.

CHAPTER SIX

Tuesday 5:35 p.m.

I TRIED to drive Robin's fancy new car, which was a bad idea. At first, the valet did not want to surrender the keys to me, but my badge and a nice tip altered his view. I had to move the seat all the way forward so I could reach the pedals. His car had a stick shift, which I never mastered growing up and still struggled with. My sore rump didn't help. I teared up trying to get out of the parking spot. After two blocks, I surrendered so I could fight another day and drove the car back to the same valet. I didn't ask for my tip back, and he didn't offer. I ordered a taxi and rode to my under-decorated apartment for a change of clothes. I checked my phone for messages about Robin's status. Nothing. I left a voicemail for Elaine, his wife, and tried to sound upbeat. I hoped my deception was credible.

Freak, I was starving. My cooking skills were limited to Frosted Flakes and the microwave. Neither sounded good. Even though today was Taco Tuesday, I had visions of Makino Sushi and Seafood Buffet. My tummy responded like Pavlov's dog. Makino's buffet would pay me to leave. Wait, I had family obligations. Mom had insisted on the blood of the Sacred Heart of Jesus that I I promised, promised, promised to come to her house for dinner. I knew better than to fight this battle. Mom was a Guinness World Record holder at insisting people bend to her will, and I fell victim repeatedly.

As my taxi pulled up to Mom's house, I remembered she had drawn similar religiously significant obligations from my siblings. Their cars lined the driveway and the curb out front. Mom wanted a family dinner to gain a sense of normalcy. However, my family was anything but normal. Once I arrived, all the witnesses were there, and the family circus could begin. What were my other options? I could check myself back into the hospital. Hospital meatloaf, could it be that bad? This event might be slow and painful, but at least the food would be great.

My mother, my dear, sweet mother, overdid everything. She over-compensated for the failings of others, usually my father. She over-planned every event, and over-decorated for holidays—even ones like St. Patrick's Day. We were Romanian, not Irish, but our house would be covered in shamrock-green decor. More importantly, she always made too much food, usually by a factor of two or three, just in case the cast of Cirque du Soleil stopped by for dinner. Mom's leftovers are my favorite food group. And she was overly dramatic, a common family trait. My father was emotionally detached, and his fashion sense had stopped cold in the disco era.

My siblings arranged the table just so, as per Mom's golden standard, and I watched, being injured in the line of duty. They bombarded me with a litany of butt jokes, a few of which made me chuckle.

Dad changed into his dinner ensemble, a green plaid shirt and orange rayon bell bottoms. I could almost hear the Village People singing. He plopped himself down at the head of the table and spooned out food. He didn't acknowledge me, and I didn't expect him to. He took a couple of bites, not waiting for anyone else to arrive, and having approved of the taste, took his plate to his commanding view in front of the television.

"Great talking to you, Dad." No response.

My family gathered around the table. All except Robin and my little sister Gloria, who was at his bedside, and yes, her full name was Gloria Gaynor Wyznecki, named after the disco matriarch. Did I mention Dad loved disco?

Before the blessing, Mom asked, "Should we wait for your father?"

"No, he's already got his plate and returned to the living room," I said. "Again, no regard for other humans."

Mom overcompensated again. "He told me he had a show he really wanted to watch."

"Really? He watches the same reruns repeatedly," said my oldest brother, Barry, and yes, his full name was Barry Gibb Wyznecki, after the Bee Gees' lead singer.

We were quite a group. The big people, me included, sat at the dining table. The grandkids sat at their own kid-sized table. Barry had twin boys, seven years old and full of mischief. Robin had a five-year-old girl and a three-year-old boy. They seemed subdued, not their normal rambunctious selves. The kids sensed something was wrong but were afraid to ask. I tried not to cry in front of them. They were too young to be without a father.

Robin's wife, Elaine, kept guard at the hospital. She would not leave his side. The hospital only allowed two visitors at a time, Elaine and one other, so we took turns. My little sister, Gloria, sat with her now.

Mom offered the blessing and mentioned Robin. Hearing his name made my heart drop. The kids cried. I hobbled over to the kids' table and embraced them in a big hug. Mom came over and kissed the head of each grandchild. We settled again and dried our tears.

"Well, I'm starving," I said. "How about you?" All four grandkids nodded.

Our family was as noisy as a small restaurant. Mom made her special spicy lasagna and for the less adventurous palates, fish sticks and mac-n-cheese. I wanted to devour about two pounds of Mom's lasagna, but I loaded my plate with fish sticks and mac-n-cheese. When in Rome . . . I enjoyed sitting at the kids' table. My feet touched the ground. This was much more comfortable. I might sit here for all future family dinners.

"Mom, did you get any updates?" I didn't want to say Robin's name again. It might start another cascade of tears. Mom understood.

"Nothing yet. I'm confident that with prayer things will be better soon."

We dined and had a lively discussion with Mom's cooking as the center of the world, and only an occasional butt joke. The kids had a great exchange about the merits of different cartoon shows, none of which sounded familiar. What happened to Pee Wee Herman and Scooby Doo? I brought up a family outing to our favorite Vegas amusement park. Circus Circus was like Disneyland, but with smaller lines and covered with a dome so it stayed a nice seventy degrees year around. From a parent's viewpoint, it was the perfect amusement park. I put a reminder in my phone to check on tickets. They usually had good discounts for locals, especially law enforcement.

The kids gobbled down every fish stick and noodle in sight and departed for the playroom. I stayed at the kid's table. I liked that my feet touched the floor. So comfortable.

The room turned quiet. Mom eyed me. "Donna, dear, I've been meaning to talk to you."

Freak. Please, someone change the subject. None of my

siblings stepped up to my defense. I gave them the evil eye. Admitting defeat I said, "What is it, Mom?"

"You know I've been worried about you. I was never excited about you choosing this career. It's just too dangerous. Your brothers joined the force, despite my objections, because of your father's urging."

I had heard this song too many times. "It's not that danger-ous," I said.

"I think it is. Look where we've been, in the hospital at your bedside worrying about your surviving. Our family cannot lose another . . ."

We fell silent. My brother had died on patrol, and despite our constant talking, we never said his name. We never talked about the empty chair at the table. Roll up your pant legs, the guilt tidal wave would be deep. "This was just a freak accident. This isn't normal for a detective."

"It only takes one accident for you to die, Donna."

I couldn't argue with that. Mom worried about me, and I wanted to avoid causing her pain, but being a detective was important. I worked so damn hard to get here. Being a woman detective in a mostly male police force was a huge accomplish-ment. Being an under-sized woman detective, I was practically a unicorn.

My mother's eyes shone with tears.

"Sorry, Mom. I'll try to be careful." If she only understood how important this was for me, to be recognized as an equal in a male dominated workplace. After years of work, I had finally achieved detective status; I would hate to quit my very first week out of fear. That would reinforce all the alpha male sexist nonsense I had fought my entire life. "Mom, do you want me to resign?"

"No, dear, I know this is important for you. I just worry." She stared intently at me. "Dear, maybe this is a sign?"

I wanted to be a detective. I needed to be a detective. It was part of my identity. I wasn't ready to give up after working so hard. Having a dad work in Internal Affairs made life difficult. He made enemies as fast as Tacos El Gordo made tacos. Quit? No, especially not now. Someone tried to blow me up and hurt Robin and countless others. I must fix it. I hoped that signaled the end of the dump-on-Donna train. Wrong again.

Mom continued, "Besides if you're out there risking your life, when are you going to give me some grandchildren?"

Great, great, great. When Mom wasn't worried about me dying, she worried about me not having kids. I couldn't win. Finally, my siblings jumped in and changed the focus of the conversation from my failings as a grandchild provider to the humorous side of getting my rump impaled with a bank pen.

Another brother, Maurice, full name Maurice Gibb Wyznecki, after the Bee Gees singer, went to the upright piano in the parlor. We all learned to play the piano on this weathered instrument. Mom gave us the basics, and then we took lessons after school from the music teacher, Miss Ivy, until we reached high school. We loved that old piano and the memories it represented, one of which was about to be repeated. Maurice put in a CD of disco classics and flexed his fingers over the piano keys.

Maurice sang the first verse of "How Deep Is Your Love," one of my favorite Bee Gees hits. I made it a duet by the third line. One by one, my siblings joined, and when my mother joined, my heart grew three sizes. We sang and danced to the medley of disco hits we grew up with, each song getting a little louder. What we lacked in talent, which was considerable, we made up for with enthusiasm and volume. Singing and dancing made it seem like Robin was here. Music drew us together as a family, all except my father. He never participated. Mom told us he was destined to be a musician when parenting snuck up on him and led him to a real occupation with a paycheck and benefits—law enforcement.

We discoed through our family favorites the way we'd done since we were children and had choreographed from repetition. A regular American Bandstand dance off. I tried to dance like my namesake, Donna Summer on *Bad Girls* when my rump reminded me I had been impaled with a bank pen. Tears stung my eyes, but I wouldn't be stopped. I sat down gently and continued with the family performance. After the dinner floor show, my siblings cleared the table. I tried to help but was politely rebuffed because of my injuries.

While the family von Trapp finished the dishes, I did a little research of my own. Mom's computer hadn't gotten a lot of activity. Was this Windows 95? Oh, when the dinosaurs roamed. I swore I heard a dial up connection. Did they still have those? I wiped a layer of dust from the screen.

I searched for details on the bank explosion. Pictures took forever to download, but the text was informative. The police had been tightlipped, so the media had few details. To make up for the lack of facts, the rumor mill went wild. Speculation from the *Vegas Tourist Scoop* ranged from mental hospital escapees to Middle Eastern terrorists to mobsters to religious zealots to drug cartels.

The police fought back with Charlie's official pronouncement, which described the explosion as "minor" and caused by the utility company tunneling a new water line. I didn't know if Charlie's deception would work, but it was worth a try.

Barry's voice echoed from the living room. "Donna, you've got to come see this."

I followed his voice. Breaking News had interrupted Dad's authoritarian control of the television. I wondered what it was about. I could give you a thousand guesses, but you would need only one.

CHAPTER SEVEN

Tuesday 7:41 p.m.

THE NEWSCASTER ADJUSTED his coiffed hair as his microphone came on. "At Channel 8 News, we have just obtained a video of the explosion inside Second United Bank. We have not confirmed the authenticity of this video. As a warning, this video is disturbing and graphic."

The black-and-white video had no sound, luckily. The camera gave an eagle's view. Customers and bank employees moved and chatted. The scene looked ordinary enough—the bank lobby, lots of marble. People plodded through the velvet-roped boundaries inch by inch. I spotted myself wearing my favorite black slacks, they fit perfectly. Ugh. My hair was a mess. Fortunately, the camera could not see my ripped pants and the black-and-white photo did not reveal my purple panties. I talked to the teller then along came Valerie, the vice president. Robin moved to the marble table for a deposit slip. Then the phone call. I shouted at the group. Customers stood frozen then darted in every direction looking for an exit. I scooped up the little girl and took two steps, then the screen went bright white—the explosion. The camera shook loose of its moorings but still recorded. Smoke and dust clouds impeded the camera's focus. Ceiling debris covered every surface. Everything had been scattered and damaged in a fraction of a second. The newscaster came back on the screen and repeated details on the number of injured and announced a press conference for later this evening.

Mom sobbed, "My baby Donna, oh my baby, Robin . . ." She retrieved her jacket and purse. "I'm going to sit by Robin's bedside."

My siblings and I arranged a quick schedule to make sure someone was always at his side. I was a night owl, so I volunteered to take the graveyard shift. Upon saying "graveyard" I felt queasy and said, "I mean the late shift."

I needed a breath of fresh air and wobbled to the back porch.

Dad sat in a porch chair, drinking wine and smoking a cigarette. Mom wouldn't let him smoke in the house. "Donna I need to talk to you." If this was Dad's heartfelt talk, it would be far too late, but I wanted to hear it. "You should quit. This job is dangerous."

I waited for more, but that was the entire speech. Seven words. I should quit? No. I wanted to be a detective more than anything, except a Dolly Parton look alike. On the positive side, Dad almost showed concern for me. "I'll be careful. Wait. You never mentioned danger before."

"You were safe when you wrote parking tickets."

I wasn't a meter maid, but that hardly made a difference now.

"Girls just are not competent to do this kind of stuff."

Competent? Really? Competent? Gee, thanks for the support, Dad. But I held my tongue, not my usual response.

Dad continued, "You're too small. That's why I didn't go to your commissioning. I didn't want you to be a detective. You're too little. Now, get me a lemonade. Your mother made some."

I was too stunned to move. What an ass. He should support me no matter what. I was his daughter.

My phone buzzed. I had a text message from my captain.

Come back to the precinct for a press conference. Bring your dress blues.

A statement, not a request. I hated wearing the dress blues. I didn't know why I was needed for a press conference, but this would not be a mystery for long. I put my phone in my unharmed rear pocket.

Dad stared at me again. Oh, right, the lemonade. I went into the house and kept going out the front door. I needed to leave before someone called the Department of Health and Human Services.

* * *

THE BOMBER PEEKED *through the boarded-up window of the downtown bank. The damage was impressive. Ceiling tiles were everywhere. Furniture was tossed around. The lobby looked to be in tatters. The bomber pushed aside the plywood and police tape and took a step inside. The bank lobby was a complete loss, but the bomb did not result in enough injuries. Next time, twice as much dynamite. The selfish will be punished.*

CHAPTER EIGHT

Tuesday 8:36 p.m

I COMPOSED my limited makeup and gave my hair a quick hand-comb in the rear-view mirror before I limped into the police station. I was presentable if we graded on a curve. I waved my ID at the badge reader, but the tiny light didn't switch from red to green. I tried again with the same result.

Helen looked up over her readers. "You're not cleared for duty."

I whispered, "I'm just here for the press conference."

"I'll buzz you in this time, in your unofficial capacity, girl-friend," Helen whispered under her breath. She dropped her book, entitled *Tea Leaf Readings for Fun and Profit*.

I stepped into the detective's area on the second floor, only to be greeted by a smiling Sandy. "Hey, Donna. Did you get cleared?"

Freak, was San Quinton guarded this much? I was screened twice just to get inside. I felt like James Bond, if James Bond was a ninety-eight-pound tomboy with unruly hair. "Just here for the press conference." But I was there to check on my investigation, unofficially, of course.

I received a hug from Charlie, my mentor, who asked about Robin. I tried to sound positive, but there was no way to spin "no improvement" in a clever way. As the detectives gathered in the fishbowl, I slipped in the back and sat down gently and quietly.

We usually had a quick meeting before any press conference, to make sure everyone was on the same page.

The captain gestured with an unlit cigarette to a hand-drawn layout of the bank. "Bomb techs are sure the explosion started at a trash can in the lobby. We have officers watching the video trying to find who placed it there. But the cameras were focused on the money." He wheezed a little but caught his breath. "Low resolution on the trash cans. Blocked images. Tedious stuff."

"Any report on who made the bomb?" Charlie asked.

"Someone who is good at making bombs," the captain said.

"I wouldn't go that far," a familiar voice said from the doorway.

The killer smile of John Rabine, LVPD's lead bomb technician, and formerly my high school sweetheart, lit up the room. John-Boy, my pet name for him, looked a little like John-Boy from *The Walton's*, tall and slim, with a devilish smile. But my John-Boy wasn't nearly as wholesome. That's why I married him. He walked through the crowded fishbowl towards me and winked at two different women along the way. And that was why I divorced him.

We were happily married for six months until one day I met his girlfriend at the precinct. Yeah, his skanky girlfriend. I just assumed he would stop dating after the wedding. Were all men pigs? I needed to knee him in the crotch for the women of the world.

"How are you doing, Donna? I was worried about you." John-Boy's raspy voice made me tingle. Damn him. After all this time he still made me melt. "Let me take care of you."

I knew what that meant, and I wasn't completely uninterested. No, no, no. I knew he still had feelings for that bimbo. Men were impossible to trust.

"I'm sorry I wasn't here for you. I just finished my ATF refresher training in Atlanta."

"Did you learn anything?" I asked.

"I was the instructor. Just got back."

"Call your family?"

"I don't have any family."

"I meant your skanky *girlfriend*."

"Her name is Brandy, and we're not seeing each other anymore."

Maybe she died of a terrible social disease? I didn't say that out loud, thankfully.

"I hate to interrupt today's episode of *The Dating Game*," the captain prompted, "but can we get back to the case?"

"Yes, sir." John-Boy straightened. "You see, a bomb has three major components: The explosive, the detonator, and the shrapnel. Obviously, the detonator and the explosive worked well."

If he made one ink-pen-in-the-butt joke, I would strangle him right here. He didn't. Wise move, John-Boy, wise move.

"The bomb was so intense because of the location. The marble interior of the bank magnified it. Really a miracle everyone didn't die from the concussive blast alone."

"Why not?" I had to ask.

"The walls were marble, but the ceiling was fake, so it absorbed the blast. If the ceiling had been marble, no one would have survived."

My heart skipped a beat. I was that close to death. My thoughts returned to Robin, still on the ventilator.

"Anything else?" the captain asked.

"This bomb didn't have any shrapnel. If he had packed the bomb with ball bearings, screws, or nails, he would've killed everyone in the building."

"Does that indicate an amateur made it? Not know what he was doing?" the captain asked.

"Unlikely. This bomber showed serious skills, a real work of art."

"Do you think he missed a step?" Charlie asked.

"He probably assumed the concussive blast would kill everyone. Explosion inside a marble room. Nothing to absorb the force but the people. He didn't know about the ceiling. That was a lucky break."

"Or maybe he just wanted noise but no killing?" Charlie asked.

"Possibly, but I don't know why he'd do that," John-Boy said.

"Maybe he *or she* never intended to blow it up?" I asked.

"A fake?" John-Boy asked. "Then why use real explosives?"

"Only the bomber can answer that," Charlie stated.

"A female bomber? That would be unusual," the captain said.

"But not impossible," I offered.

"Where did he *or she* get the explosives?" Sandy asked.

"There we got lucky." John-Boy beamed with pride from his discovery. "A fragment from a stick of dynamite, a coded label traced back to a mining operation out in the desert."

"Mines?" I asked, "Like *the miner forty-niner*? I thought they went the way of the buffalo."

"They still raise buffalos for food . . ." Helen added.

"Are there really a lot of mines still going?" Sandy asked.

"Buffalo? What do they taste like?" I wondered. "Is the meat tough?"

"They're good . . . lean meat . . ." Helen said. "You have to work it, mix with some fatty meat to make a good burger."

"I could go for a buffalo burger," I said.

The captain snapped his fingers. "Hey, hey, cooking show is over. Back to the bombing case. Remember it? The bombing? Let's focus, people."

Ben, our department techie and guru of everything nerdy, leaned back from his computer. "Mines are still going strong. Fifty are active in Nevada alone." Ben was always a fountain of trivia, usually it was helpful.

"Any explosives missing or reported stolen?" I asked, not wanting to know.

Ben tapped the keys at machine gun speed. "Twelve reports of missing explosives."

"So how much?" Sandy asked. No one wanted an answer.

Ben squinted at his screen. "Just over six hundred sticks of dynamite. Probably more. That's just how many have been reported."

"Dynamite has gone out of fashion," John-Boy explained. "Now they use more high-tech explosives, like gels, emulsions, and ammonium nitrate."

He lost me in this science lesson. "So, what do they do with their dynamite?"

"Throw it away. Bury it in an old mine. Sometimes just blow it up to get rid of it. The mines are a little careless with the stuff."

"Careless? With dynamite?" I didn't believe this.

John-Boy nodded. "They store it in remote areas in the desert and often don't check for weeks at a time. Remember, this is outdated inventory, stuff they don't need or use, like day-old donuts."

"Who doesn't like day-old donuts?" I asked. "Them's fighting words . . ."

The captain spoke up. "So can we feel confident in the six hundred missing sticks?"

John-Boy smiled. "I'm confident way more than six hundred are missing."

Charlie asked the question everyone dreaded. "How many sticks were used at the bank?"

The room got deathly quiet as John-Boy pondered. "Six. Maybe eight."

Eight sticks destroyed the bank lobby, and at least six hundred were missing? *Freak.*

Captain Creek fidgeted with his unlit cigarette. "I need a smoke."

We moved to the captain's unofficial office, the sixth-floor roof, where he and others could smoke. The city prohibited indoor smoking long ago, and the roof provided a place for the captain to get his nicotine fix. I liked to be alone on the roof. The air was clean, and I had an eagle's view of downtown Vegas. At night, the light show was a carnival for the eyes.

The thought of six hundred sticks of missing dynamite rattled me. How much was needed to destroy a building? An airplane? An airport? A casino? How many people could be injured or killed?

Charlie spoke up. "I think we should have a moment of prayer for seven people in critical condition." The captain nodded. Charlie looked at his notes. "Lord, we ask for your healing blessing for Raymond Soames . . ."

Raymond Soames? Why was that name familiar?

". . . Peter Malloy, a Jane Doe not yet identified, Robin Wyznecki . . ."

Hearing Robin's name was like a slap in the face. I was too

stunned to hear the remainder of the prayer or to move. I had to remind myself to breathe.

The captain doled out each officer's assignment. Some investigated the missing dynamite. Others searched for recent parolees with a history of using explosives. We had the usual suspects on the radar, a lengthy list. Vegas was also a retreat for retired criminals. The frustration showed on the captain's face. "Okay, we have a press conference starting in twenty minutes. Donna, you need to be in dress blues behind the podium."

"I hate the formal uniform," I said.

"Everyone does," the captain explained. "I hope your derriere injury won't prevent you from donning your uniform."

Several of my peers snickered, and I made a mental note of their names for retribution.

Charlie read his cell phone and showed the message to the captain. Both looked unsettled. The captain stomped out his cigarette. He spoke deliberately. "This case is now our top priority. Just got word from the hospital. This is now a homicide."

CHAPTER NINE

Tuesday 9:45 p.m.

HOMICIDE? Freak. I couldn't breathe. Robin? My brother? Tears trickled down my cheeks. I grabbed my phone and tried to call Mom, but my blurred vision and trembling hands prevented me. He was in the bank because of me and now he was dead. This was my fault. *I'm a terrible person.*

An eternity later, the captain continued, "The fatality was Will Ignacio, a sixteen-year-old boy cashing his first paycheck. An officer is on the way to meet with the family. Two of Will's family members are still being treated at the hospital. Wrong place, wrong time."

What? "Will who? Is Robin . . ." I couldn't complete the question.

The captain looked at me. "Your brother is still critical but stable, or I would have heard about it."

Critical. I hated that word. But it meant he was alive. I dried my eyes and called Mom. If Robin was still alive, I wanted to hear it from Mom's voice.

Mom confirmed Robin was still alive, not by much, but still alive. I needed that reassurance. Mom's voice brought me back from the cliff's edge.

I stepped onto the stage in the press briefing room. An army of reporters snapped photos of me in my dress uniform. Besides being itchy, my uniform was too snug in all the wrong places. The extra small men's jacket fit better than my last one. Every time I moved a millimeter the heavy tail of my wool jacket whacked against my sore rump, giving me a new experience in pain.

It was unusual to have a press conference so soon after the incident and with no arrests. But here we were, impressing the taxpayers and, more important, stopping the rumor mill. The only time I had been in the briefing room was when I was promoted to detective, just days ago. I had been too excited to notice the drab surroundings, plain walls, floor tiles, and rows of matching folding chairs. The only décor was cheaply framed photos of past captains. It screamed "government building."

Hopefully, this wouldn't last long, but I doubted it. My tush hurt even when I used my cane. My sutures pulled every time I flexed my leg. Every single time. The captain insisted I use the cane, to add to the dramatic effect. It also helped me to not cry.

Captain Creek gripped the podium, ready to engage the media. The story had become an obsession on the local news. He smiled and unfolded his notes. "I've asked you here for a special reason. Earlier today, Second United Bank suffered a devastating loss. The explosion was caused by Nevada Power and Water. The utility company excavated a pipeline tunnel, unaware they were directly beneath the bank. The workers thought they were under the street and about ten feet deeper. The utility company is being investigated for negligence. There were rumors that this explosion was a criminal act, related to a robbery. Those rumors are unfounded. I should repeat, this was not an intentional act."

I worked hard to keep a straight face. *Not intentional, my sore rump.*

"Many could have been killed. However, because of the quick and courageous actions of Detective Donna Wyznecki, the damage caused by the explosion was minimized. Detective Wyznecki was at the bank investigating another matter when she discovered the utility company had misplaced the excavation charges."

Investigating what? *How to get another ATM card?* Oh well, I was a hero now, time to keep my mouth shut. My stomach rumbled. Did we have a refreshments table set up? Coffee and donuts would be nice. Of course, I could skip the coffee.

"Due to Detective Wyznecki's quick thinking and decisive actions, many people were saved, including Penny, the young daughter of Mayor Steve Shale. Unfortunately, there was one fatality, Will Ignacio, a Las Vegas teenager, who was cashing his first paycheck. Several of his family members were also injured. At last count, twenty-two people are still hospitalized, including Detective Wyznecki's brother, Robin, who remains in critical condition."

My lungs seized at the mention of Robin. The itchy uniform didn't seem like such a significant worry. Guilt settled over me like a suffocating blanket. I fought back tears.

"Detective Wyznecki acted bravely, disregarding her own safety, and serves as a model for all our officers. As such, she is awarded this commendation for bravery."

Captain Creek handed me a plaque. The top line read, "Happy Retirement, Randy," but I doubted anyone in the audience could read the inscription. I continued the charade. We shook hands and the captain continued, "She was injured in the explosion, and we hope for her speedy recovery."

I nodded to acknowledge the polite applause.

The captain looked around. "I believe the mayor has a few words."

Steve Shale approached the podium. I didn't like him. He came off as half career politician, half game show host. He had a nice bright smile, but he was a constant womanizer, always looking for someone younger and prettier, even while married —especially while married. He turned and shook my hand. I looked at his face. His eyes were red and swollen. He had been crying.

"Detective Wyznecki, you saved my Penny. I owe you a debt of gratitude I'll never be able to repay." His lips quivered, and his eyes filled with tears.

This wasn't Shale's typical Chamber of Commerce speech. He acted like a real human with compassion, something I wouldn't have expected. He shook my hand again, more vigorously this time. Tears rushed down his cheeks. He hugged me, gently at first, but then gave me a full bear hug. My rump felt like a giant pimple being squeezed. I started tearing up from the excruciating pain. I should have taken a pain pill before this started. My bad. Both of us stood there crying, but for different reasons.

I had protected Penny, but I'd failed Robin. Knowing he was injured made my blood pressure skyrocket.

Penny sat in the second row, dressed like an angel, this time in baby blue, offset by the bright pink cast on her arm. She lunged toward me, but her mother grabbed her hand. They whispered to each other, then Penny rushed the stage, hair ribbon bobbing, and aggressively hugged me, causing more pain, but I didn't care. Shale orchestrated this whole endeavor for the media attention. He planned to run for higher office, everyone in Nevada knew it. He always wanted the spotlight. It worked. Tears made the story more powerful. Reporters soaked it up. Cameras clicked. I might be on the front page of a dozen newspapers. I should have spent more time on my hair.

Steve Shale regained his composure and pulled Penny close. "Detective Wyznecki, we've received a lot of calls about your injuries. How are you?"

Wait. I have to talk? No one warned me. I doubted that the mayor's office got calls about me. No one knew my name until now, but this was all part of the media dance we were performing.

Before I could answer, Penny spoke up, concern filling her face. "Daddy said you got hurt. Are you going to die?"

She was so innocent. "No, sweetie. I'm going to be fine."

"Where were you injured?" Steve Shale asked.

I smiled without saying a word. *Please. Don't go there.*

"Where?" he repeated.

"At the bank," I answered. A few chuckles came from the press corp.

"No, sorry. I meant what . . .? I believe your leg was broken?"

Freak. Please. Someone stop him.

Captain Creek approached and whispered that I had been injured in the butt. Whispered was the wrong word because he said it loud enough for all the reporters to hear. Several giggled.

"Well, even a butt injury is serious," Shale said. More giggles from the crowd.

Penny's eyes widened, shining with sheer delight. "You hurt your butt?" She covered her mouth.

Reporters moved from giggles to belly laughs.

"You can't be a good detective without a good derriere," the captain explained.

Freak. Television cameras got all of this. Everyone

laughed about my tush. It wasn't funny, and it did hurt. Crap, I wanted to hide. This was a nightmare. I didn't know which was more embarrassing, that in high school none of the boys looked at my rear end or that now everyone in my time zone stared at my rump and laughed. *God, if you ever wanted to answer a prayer, an earthquake would be nice about now. A power outage? A fire alarm? Locusts?* I waited. Nothing, of course.

Helen pushed open the door to the press conference. Halleluiah, she was here to rescue me. *Helen, please change the subject away from my butt.* Her voice cut through the silence, "Sorry, Captain."

Two red uniformed bugle players stood at opposite sides of the entry way and tooted "First Call"—a grand entrance. Instinctively, everyone stood.

What was this? I had no idea, but I wouldn't have bet a dollar about who appeared next.

A man entered, his bright white teeth seemingly two steps ahead of his body, with a twirling, floor-length white fur cape covered in sparkles covering his bejeweled tuxedo. He sported a pompadour with glitter in his hair and flashy diamond rings on every finger. Smiling Jim Reed, Las Vegas's premier Liberace impersonator entered the room as though floating on air. His sparsely clad dancers fanned around him.

"Ladies and gentlemen"—he spoke with a grand bow, sparkles blinding—"I have come to inform you that one of my dancers was injured in this terrible, terrible incident. As a result, I will donate the proceeds of this week's shows to medical expenses for those injured. Please come see my nightly show on The Strip."

Trumpets blared again, and he twirled out of the room, followed by his entourage and most of the reporters.

I loved my weird little town.

THE BOMBER CLICKED *photos of this garish display. A press conference for those he injured, for all his hard work, and now this piano player wannabe tried to steal the attention from his accomplishments. He was not happy.*

He'd pretended to be a reporter and confidently strode into the press conference room without anyone questioning him. Armed with a ball cap, blond wig, and glasses, and two cameras around his neck, he considered his attempt at deception pitiful. He was afraid someone would be looking for him. Not even close. The police were so inept. The investigation had not gotten that far yet. Lax security, if one could even call it security. He clicked photos of Liberace, Mayor Shale, and the police captain.

He focused several images on this short policewoman, Donna something. She saved the day? Please. His first attempt accomplished all his basic goals. A good start. His next one would be three times as powerful. But who was this little woman ruining his work? He needed to get her attention. He needed to stop her. His next bomb would. The selfish would be punished.

CHAPTER TEN

Tuesday 10:09 p.m.

BACK IN THE FISHBOWL, Captain Creek spoke first, wheezing a little. "We have a list of suspects that we should be screening." Sandy harded the list to the attending officers.

I eyed six pages of recent releases from jail, Vegas Police's own frequent flyer program. A lot of these names were familiar. I spotted two I had arrested. The list was impressive—fifty names and I was just on page four. Ugh. This was hopeless. And I was hungry. I couldn't concentrate when I was hungry.

The captain held up his hand to silence the group. "Charlie will give a report about our primary suspects. Charlie?"

Ben, our digital wizard, posted the information to the screens around the room.

Charlie stood with his notes in hand. "I have two suspects, but these seem like long shots. Our first is Garfield 'Gar' Vickers. Gar is the leader of a family of criminals. He's done three stints in prison." Gar looked like a man who had lived a hard life. He had a lined, haggard face and easily looked twenty years older than his real age. Prison did that to a man. Charlie continued, "Gar has supplied drug cartels and gangs with guns and explosives. But he's simply a profiteer."

This unsettled the fishbowl group. If Gar would sell explosives to drug cartels, he would sell them to anyone. His potential accomplices would include anyone with money.

"FBI wiretapping has revealed Gar is planning a large campaign."

My confidence dipped.

Ben changed the screen and Charlie continued. "Our second suspect is Ivan Kutner, aka Ivan the Terrible. He is a White Nationalist and a spokesperson for the American Nazi movement. An engineer by training with great technical skills, he has claimed credit for two dozen bombings. He has always defended himself, claiming the prosecutions were political."

"Ugh," I said under my breath. "I really hate Nazis."

Charlie continued. "Now Ivan has turned his attention to us. He got out of prison six months ago, pending a new trial. He posted an online video which shows him praying for the death of Vegas, ruled by the mud people and their Jewish overlords."

Ivan's photos showed grainy images of him always near Nazi flags, always holding weapons. Charlie continued. "Ivan Kutner is a serious threat. He has access to funds and a team of loyal supporters who would die for him and die for their cause. He is a domestic terrorist who is not afraid of retaliation."

Terrorism, the "T" word, stopped every side discussion, plunging the room into deathly silence. We weren't prepared for a White Nationalist attack. I could hear myself breathe. In law enforcement, nothing was worse than terrorism. It worried every police department in America. In a tourist haven like Vegas, terrorism was a constant nightmare, lurking in the shadows every single day. Was this the first step in a terrorist campaign?

"Why is Ivan mad at banks?" Sandy asked.

Charlie glanced at his notes. "He had too many large cash transactions, which the bank reported to the FBI. That led to an investigation, which led to his conviction. He's blaming the banks."

Chatter started, but the captain called everyone back to attention. "Donna has been reviewing files of the bank's employees."

I glanced at my notes. "Most, well nearly all the bank's employees are spotless. I only found one with a criminal record, Raymond P. Soames.' Ben flashed Raymond's driver's license photo on the screens around the fishbowl. "Mr. Soames had violated three different protective orders, all related to an old girlfriend, Audra Barkley, an employee of the bank. Soames was not angry at the bank, just at her, so not sure if he would be motivated to be the bomber. But he's the best suspect I have."

The captain stepped forward. "I want every officer to have a photo of these three suspects, now. Any questions?"

"Should we issue a BOLO?" Helen asked.

Captain Creek nodded. "An alert could help."

"But won't that make us look bad?" Charlie asked. "We just told everyone that it was a utility explosion."

"That was just to calm the tourists and confuse our suspect. I don't care about image," the captain said. "I want this guy caught."

I approached. "I have a question—"

"Donna, you are on restricted duty until cleared by O.S."

"Yes, but—" I protested. My phone vibrated before I could say anything that would have gotten me into trouble.

"You need to check on Robin," Mom said.

"I'm . . ."

"Donna, I don't care what you're doing, family comes first."

"I'm leaving now." Did this mean Robin was worse? Captain wanted me gone anyway. But fury boiled as I left. One of these three bums potentially injured Robin. I hated all three of them. I would not stop until I caught the one who was responsible—and then I'll break every one of his fingers.

CHAPTER ELEVEN

Wednesday 12:14 a.m.

ROBIN'S HOSPITAL room was deathly quiet. He was covered in purple bruises, black stitches, and red cuts, hooked to a rainbow of wires and machines. He resembled a science project, a robot half assembled. The ventilator wheezed rhythmically. I tried not to cry around his wife, Elaine, but I couldn't help it. She was still stunned, in a daze of denial. Talking to her was awkward. I tried to distract her, but every topic led to Robin and his condition. I couldn't leave, so I took my pain pill and curled up in a faux-leather chair for four solid hours. After my power nap, I was wide awake, a side effect of my metabolism.

The insomnia served me well but was demanding on the hospital's vending machines. While I read and reread the info on suspects, I munched an assortment of snacks, alternating between sweet and salty. A giant plate of nachos would be great. Did anyone deliver at this hour?

My three prime suspects sounded legitimate: a career criminal, Gar Vickers, a possessive ex-boyfriend, Raymond Soames, and a ruthless White Nationalist, Ivan the Terrible. Any of these men could be the guilty party. The history of each was meticulously detailed. All three had lengthy files with the Vegas Police.

I read the details of Raymond Soames' protective orders. All three involved him harassing and stalking the same woman, Audra Barkley, an employee of Second United. I read and re-read Audra's handwritten complaint.

Raymond Soames was also a bank employee. She and Raymond had a very brief relationship, which she described as "a couple of dates," when Soames became very possessive and angry, constantly staring at her while at work, following her after work, leaving notes on her car and her apartment door. She described the first few as being "sweet" but turning bitter when she ended their brief relationship. Notes morphed from demanding to threatening. Calls at all hours of the day and night. She would see him outside her apartment window, but he always disappeared by the time the police arrived. Raymond was moved to different shifts and different days, but he still found excuses to be at the bank, constantly following her. Raymond became very jealous of any male she happened to speak to, to the extreme of starting two fights at the bank—he was fired after the second one. The more I knew about Mr. Soames, the less I liked him. He was possessive and jealous, a real jerk. He was on the injured list at UMC. Both of his legs were broken in the blast. Did he get injured by his own bomb? It wouldn't be the first time.

Ben, our computer guru, compiled a list that contained twenty pages of additional suspects, our career deadbeats. To be candid, none of them had the initiative to blow up a bank. Someone had put in a lot of work to make this happen.

Someone was motivated to accomplish this, but motivated by what?

The nurse dropped off a breakfast tray with pancakes and turkey bacon for Elaine, Robin, and me. Woman cannot live by turkey bacon alone, but I had no other options. I didn't want Robin's tray wasted, since he was still unconscious, so I gobbled his down. Elaine only took one bite despite my urging. It was turkey bacon, but she still needed to eat. How could the hospital expect people to heal without donuts?

Maurice switched off with me at six in the morning. Maurice was an early bird, always was, even as a child, a status I considered to be a mental disorder. I wanted to stay, even though there wasn't anything I could do. Elaine sent me to work, insisted really. "Catch this guy, for Robin." Her eyes were bright with unshed tears. This was unreal, beyond anyone's nightmares.

I picked up a couple of donuts and a giant cappuccino on the way to the precinct. Nothing too fancy, two chocolate-frosted, two vanilla-frosted with coconut sprinkles, and a maple Long John, without the filling. I had to be calorie conscious. My body was a temple and all that.

I showered and changed into clothes stashed in my locker. I pulled my hair back into a ponytail, the best I could do with limited time and effort. I returned to the fishbowl and read all the notes added since yesterday. Truly shocking.

Ben washed down Advil with an energy drink. His eyes were shot with red spiderwebs, and his hands shook from too much caffeine.

"Any progress?" I asked.

Ben rubbed his bloodshot eyes. "I've been through the videos a hundred times in slow motion. Every second. Nothing."

"Nothing?" I repeated.

"No one put anything larger than an envelope in the trash can. But it had to happen. The screen is grainy, and the points of view are limited. I could have missed something. All the damn cameras are pointed at the teller. The trash can is barely in view. Most of the time someone stood between the cameras and the trash can, blocking any view." He lifted a clipboard. "I have eleven times noted where I can't see anything." Ben rubbed his eyes in frustration. "Too many people in the way. Any of these eleven times could have been the moment of drop-off. I'll watch them again."

I looked at his tired eyes. "Ben, how long have you been watching videos without a break?"

"He's been at it all night," Sandy said.

"The bank video shows nothing," Ben repeated.

"I hate this bank," I said.

Ben nodded. "Me too. They have ten teller booths but only have—"

"One teller working," we said in unison.

"Okay," I said. "Maybe, we are looking at the right place but at the wrong time."

Ben's eyes widened as he considered this possibility. "I only looked at the video during business hours. I assumed someone posing as a customer dropped it in the trash can while the bank was open. Maybe that was a mistake."

"Someone broke into the bank at night and left the bomb?" Charlie asked. "That seems unlikely. More like impossible. No one breaks into a bank to *leave* something."

Ben worked more magic and restarted the video from midnight. He fast-forwarded and time raced by on the screen starting at midnight, advancing with no action. At 4:05 a.m. the bank lights came on. A group of five men entered the lobby. All wore white jumpsuits with the Royal Janitorial logo on the back. The janitors moved in comical fast-forward, like a Benny

Hill chase scene. The crew swept and mopped in superfast motion. No one got near the trash can in the lobby. The clock sped by. The janitors emptied trash cans and stacked the loaded trash bags on a giant cart. One janitor approached the trash can that held our attention. Ben slowed the video to normal speed. We collectively held our breath. The janitor scanned the room to make sure no one was watching, then he removed the full trash bag and threw it on the cart. He dug into the bottom of the cart, pulled out a package with wires and a timer, and set it gently in the garbage can. He then whipped out a trash can liner and covered his crime.

That was it. *Freak.* A janitor had put the bomb in the trash can. My breath quickened. We'd found the bomber. Relief spread among our detectives. We found him, now we needed to catch him.

Ben found a frame that focused on the janitor's face. We printed off full-screen images of the bomber. His face was plain —a white man, probably fifty years old, clean-shaven, skinny. Nothing remarkable about him. Did I really expect him to have horns and a pointed tail? He looked ordinary, too ordinary, so ordinary he wouldn't be noticed, and that worried me. And he didn't look anything like our three main suspects. Crap.

CHAPTER TWELVE

Wednesday, 8:15 a.m.

WE SHARED our discovery of a lead with the rest of the team —the janitor who placed the bomb in the bank. We high-fived each other in a brief celebration of success. The captain tapped his unlit cigarette on the table. "Let's wait to pop the champagne. Celebrate after this bastard is in cuffs. And not one word to anyone outside this room."

The captain parsed duties to capture the janitor. I had to be included. My ribs still ached from hitting that marble column. My tender tush . . . well, it hadn't improved, and Robin . . . time for payback. "Donna."

I nodded.

"You're still on restricted duty, so stay in the car." Then the captain winked at me. I wasn't going to miss this.

We caravanned in three cars. Charlie and I were armed with photos of our bomber, an armload of confidence, and an espresso shot of adrenaline. We needed a little surprise to capture this guy. We had to assume the bomber had other devices and was prepared to use them, so we needed to enter his lair without arousing suspicion. This had to be delicate.

Royal Janitorial sat in a nondescript warehouse off Frank Sinatra Avenue, surrounded by a kitchen cabinet factory and a plumbing supplies wholesaler. Luckily, both had few patrons, easily sent out of harm's way. Charlie and I waited to go inside. We had to appear non-threatening. That part was easy. As a pair, we looked like attendees of a father-daughter dance. He stood two feet taller than me, and my appearance masked my age. He was black and I was white, but what difference did that make? We looked ordinary.

I checked my pistol—I had a round in the chamber and the safety was on. My gun was ready, although I wasn't sure I was. My heart thudded and sweat trickled down my back. I had never used my service weapon in the line of duty. I practiced, fifty rounds per week without fail, but there was an enormous difference between shooting a paper target and shooting a real person, especially one holding a bomb.

One car guarded the side entrance. The other guarded the back exit. We had to be prepared if the bomber ran. His first instinct might be to set off another explosion.

When chasing a shooter, watch their hands. We have trained for this scenario hundreds of times. But a bomber? He might blow us up, or himself, or the building with a slight gesture, by stepping on a remote, touching a button. We had to watch for anything. Charlie was perfect for this job. He noticed every detail.

Sweat beaded on his forehead. "We can do this," I assured him. Now I needed someone to assure me. My phone vibrated. Who could be calling me now? It was Mom. Did this mean Robin . . . Fearing the worst, and knowing I couldn't focus until I knew, I held up a finger for Charlie to wait a second. "Hello?"

"Donna, my baby. Dear, did I wake you?"

"No, Mom. Already up."

"Robin's doctor said he hasn't gotten any worse, which is something worth celebrating."

That was the first good news I'd heard in a while. "That's great, Mom, but I really don't have time right now to—"

"You don't have time for your only mother?"

Freak. "Yes—I mean, no. I mean . . . I can't talk right now."

"You know, your father and I hate that you have this dangerous job." Had she read my mind? Had she sensed my fear from across town? Or was it just a mother's intuition?

"Mom, I'm okay. My job is not really dangerous." That was a bold lie, since I held my service weapon, ready to use it. "Seriously, I'm okay. But I can't talk right now."

Charlie overheard my conversation and fidgeted with his gun, likewise on his phone.

"Mom. Mom. Mom, I'm fine. I'll see you at dinner." Then I hung up. Yes, I hung up on my mother. I would pay for that.

Charlie was engaged in a similar phone conversation. "Yes, I'm being careful."

He nodded to me. He smiled, so he must have been talking to his wife or girlfriend. He never, ever talked about his family, so I had no idea of her name. Or if they were married or not.

"I love you too, Luke." Charlie ended the call.

I didn't know what to say. Finally, I found my voice. "Luke?"

"My husband."

"You never talk about your . . ."

Charlie nodded. "I'm a gay, black cop. I keep my private life private. I don't hide it, but I don't announce it. Not everyone is accepting."

"I accept you." We bumped fists. "Now, let's make sure we are both breathing an hour from now." I inserted the two-way earpiece so I could hear the rest of the team and they could hear me. "Test, test."

"Heads up everyone," Charlie said, turning on his earpiece. "Our bomber may run once he's cornered. If he gets by us and reaches for any kind of device, take him down. Everyone ready? We're going inside."

CHAPTER THIRTEEN

Wednesday 8:25 a.m.

A MAN HAD OBVIOUSLY DECORATED the janitorial
business, which meant it wasn't decorated at all. It had the
warmth of an alley. The only wall coverings were a few faded
positive thinking posters taped to the wall. The closest one read
"Excellence" and showed an eagle soaring. I had no idea how
an eagle applied to janitorial work, but I wasn't able to give it
my full attention. The building was one giant room with two
small offices to the right. In the back, uniformed janitors loaded
and unloaded several vans. Charlie and I moved to the first
office.

"Wait. Wait, Donna." came the captain's voice in my ear.

"Wait for what?" I whispered. "In the middle of it now."

"The bomber might know your face. He probably saw you
on TV."

Freak. The captain was right. I was so eager to participate I
forgot I gave up the element of surprise by being here. The
bomber might not recognize Charlie, but he would remember

me, the butt injury girl. I screwed this up. "It's too late now. Already inside," I whispered. "Surprise blown. Everyone be ready to take him down."

The manager didn't look up when we stepped into his office. He was a solid man with a flattop haircut and a cigarette in his mouth. He stared at spreadsheets on his desk. He glanced up. If he was surprised, he didn't show it. "If you're here to apply for a job, applications are on the table." He pointed to a small table in the corner. "Fill it out and bring it back anytime were open. Be ready to take a piss test."

Charlie flashed his badge at the manager. "Sorry, not here to apply for a job. We're looking for one of your employees."

"Which one this time?" The manager obviously had several employees with police problems.

"Actually, we don't have a name. We just have his picture." Charlie unfolded the black-and-white image from the bank video.

"You sure he works for me?" the manager asked, studying the photo.

"He recently cleaned the Second United branch downtown," I said.

The flattop started his elevator pitch. "We're one of only five fully bonded janitorial services in the valley. We work for a lot of banks, casinos, anywhere you need someone you can trust."

"Do you recognize this man?" I asked.

"No, but I have over a hundred and fifty employees. Let me get the supervisor for the Second United team." He pressed the intercom switch. "Hal, question about one of your workers."

Hal arrived and was equally unimpressed with our badges. Police visits seemed common in this industry. He stared at the grainy photo. "Oh, him." Hal explained this worker, Jason

Oliver, was a recent hire. He had worked for the company only a couple of months.

"Do you have a background check on Mr. Oliver?" I asked.

Hal and the manager stared at each other. "No," the manager finally said.

"But I thought your employees were bonded?" Charlie asked.

The flattop hung his head. "Bonded employees are more expensive. When the bank is closed, we use some . . . uh . . . cheaper employees."

Hal continued, "Oliver has a drinking problem. We didn't want him listed on our bond or our health insurance."

Charlie was stunned. "You mean you lie about all your employees being bonded?"

Hal frowned. "Hey, just trying to make a living."

"So where is Mr. Oliver?" I asked.

Hal shook his head. "Didn't show up yesterday or for his shift today."

"Stand down," I announced into my earpiece. "The suspect is not here." The manager handed me Mr. Oliver's job application.

"If Mr. Oliver shows up," Charlie said, "call us immediately, and don't tell him we're looking for him."

I texted Mr. Oliver's job application details to Ben at headquarters as Charlie drove. We arrived twenty minutes later, and the investigation into Mr. Oliver was impressive. This was our best lead. Freak, this was our *only* lead, but now we had a name. The biggest surprise was no surprise. Oliver's information was legit—name, social security number, even his address, everything checked out. The photo from his driver's license matched the video. We had the right guy. Ben learned Oliver had lived at the same place for four years and had been employed in home building and repairs until the housing crash.

Now, he scrambled for odd jobs. This janitor position was short-term.

"Any ties to Second United?" I asked.

"No accounts," Ben said.

"Any links to domestic terrorism or drug cartels?" the captain asked.

Ben shook his head. "Nothing on the extremist chat rooms. No real online profile."

"Maybe that makes him smart," Helen said.

"Or maybe we're looking at the wrong person," I said.

CHAPTER FOURTEEN

Wednesday, 9:02 a.m.

"WHAT ABOUT A CRIMINAL RECORD?" I asked.

The only blemish on Oliver's record was a couple of DUIs. No criminal ties, never married, no kids, and no family. We could write his biography now, and he didn't seem like a career criminal or a terrorist. He seemed ordinary. We had no motive. Once I caught him, I would ask.

We planned a raid to capture Oliver at his home. I could have used a nap, or better yet a three-egg Denver omelet and some cinnamon rolls, but I was too invigorated. My hands trembled.

Charlie held a map of Oliver's neighborhood and marked Oliver's house with a red X.

Captain Creek pointed with his cigarette. "Six units. Three at the front door, three covering the back. And four additional units covering the neighborhood from all directions in case he tries to escape." The captain rattled off the names of each team. I wasn't mentioned. Holy crap. Did Captain Creek think I would sit this one out? Was he insane? This jerk planted the bomb that . . .

"Donna?" the captain asked. "You can watch."

I nodded.

The captain continued. "Capture him alive, if possible, dead if necessary. If he touches anything, take him down. He doesn't get to hurt anyone else. And remember our two goals—"

"Catch the bad guy," we said in unison.

"And . . ."

"Don't scare the damn tourists."

A mile from Oliver's home we gathered in a Vons grocery store parking lot. We rechecked the map and ensured every person knew their role in the pending operation. Charlie and I did a quick drive-by of the house. No activity, so we returned to the Vons parking lot. Everyone departed to their pre-assigned stations. While we waited, I pondered Oliver's motive in bombing the bank. Why this bank? Why any bank? Why a bomb? No clues yet of his rationale. My rump still ached.

Everyone was deployed into position. The backdoor crew approached first as they had the most cover. We got the signal to approach. Without a word, the eight well-armed officers crept toward Oliver's front door. I was about twenty steps behind the SWAT team, since I still needed my cane. We wore Kevlar vests and helmets, although none of us were confident the bullet-resistant fabric would protect us from an explosion. No one walked the street, but people in this neighborhood had seen plenty of police raids before and knew to stay inside and keep quiet. We were near the front porch when a loud engine roared overhead. Dust blasted my exposed face like sandpaper. I stared up at a hovering News Channel 5 helicopter.

"Who the freak called the TV station?" I asked.

We had lost the element of surprise. We stood in the bomber's front yard, and unless he was deaf and blind, he knew something was about to happen. The first officer rammed into the front door with enough force to jerk it off the hinges. Officers charged inside the home, guns raised, screaming, "Police! Don't move!"

Silence was the only reply. They darted in and out of each room. The modest house was empty. Once secure, I examined the scene. Oliver's house was decorated in alcoholic bachelor-salvage theme, cheap mismatched furniture but an expensive television, a dated and stained table, a pile of bills, all unopened. Empty beer cans stood on every counter. The refrigerator was empty except for three cans of beer, mustard, and strawberry jelly. The trash can overflowed with empties and stunk up the house. Mr. Oliver was at the end of his rope. He had no bomb-making supplies, or even the most basic tools. His garage contained two screwdrivers and a hammer. He wasn't our bomber. He was just a delivery person, desperate for a little cash for an errand, no questions asked. This was one giant dead-end.

I hobbled to the curb and dropped my helmet. This raid had been a huge waste of time. My cell phone rang. "Now isn't a good time."

"You're the short officer who saved the little girl at the bank and injured your butt, right?"

Someone called to torment me with short jokes. Freak. "I'm Detective Wyznecki." Silence from the other end. Was this a reporter—or worse yet a practical joke? "Who is this?"

"I'm sorry, Little Donna. No names yet."

"Don't call me 'Little Donna.' I hate short jokes."

"As you wish. What would you prefer I call you?"

"Detective Wyznecki will do fine."

"I prefer Little Donna. And this is not a joke."

This conversation was going nowhere. "Who is this?"

"My name is not important."

"Why are you calling me?"

"I want you to understand me."

Understand him? I understood that he was wasting my time and that was enough. "I'm going to hang up now."

"Please don't. I made the bomb."

CHAPTER FIFTEEN

Wednesday 10:06 a.m.

THE WORDS TOOK a moment to sink in, and even then I wondered if he said what I thought he said. This guy made the bomb? That seemed unlikely. But if he had . . . *Freak*. The idea took my breath away. I had to play this cool. "What bomb?"

"What bomb? Really? Were you blown up by more than one bomb yesterday? The bomb in the bank."

"And you're calling to confess? Why?"

"Good question. I don't want anyone else to take credit for my work."

"The story has been all over the news. You could be anyone. How do I know you really made it and you're not just some nut looking for attention?"

"Do you know any of the details of my bomb?"

"A few."

"I didn't use any shrapnel."

Freak. We hadn't released that detail to the public. "Why not?" My heart pounded.

"I don't want to kill anyone. Yet."

"Yet?" I asked. What else did he have planned? My body went cold from fear. I had to keep him talking. "My butt hurts, all the time, you jerk. And my brother is still in the hospital—"

"That was inadvertent. I did not know you would be there."

"What about that kid, that young boy? He never hurt anyone."

"In war, some innocents are always lost, Little Donna. It's an unpleasant fact."

"War? Why are you reaching out to me?" My brain churned ideas a mile a minute as I checked my surroundings, wondering if he was in sight. What would I do if he was?

"I saw your press conference. Sad and humorous."

"Don't remind me." I changed the subject. Maybe I could learn something if I confronted him. "Are you Ivan . . . Ivan something. I can't remember the last name?"

"Sorry, Little Donna. My name is not Ivan."

"Are you part of a group?"

He ignored my question. "A utility company explosion? Really? What a ridiculous explanation."

"I didn't think that story was convincing either."

"I was insulted."

"Why were you insulted?" I had to keep him talking. The more he talked the more details I could gather. Maybe this guy was legitimate. Maybe crazy. Maybe both. "Why did you do this? Was this related to terrorism?"

"Oh, please. Terrorism? I don't care about politics."

"Then what was it? Why did you do this?"

"This is personal. This is about respect."

Respect? Like Aretha Franklin? "I don't understand."

"You don't understand? You look like a junior high boy. You know what it's like to be disrespected."

"I have a metabolism—" I stopped. He had tried to rattle me. I needed to keep him talking. "Have you been disrespected?"

"Of course. But this isn't about me. I'm just a messenger."

"Who? Who is it about?"

"I'm afraid that would be too much of a clue, for now."

"For now? So, I'll be hearing from you later, Messenger?"

"Yes, and I'll be watching you. All the time."

"Are we finished, Mr. Messenger?" I asked.

"No, we're just getting started. One other thing, Little Donna. Tell your officers to get out of Mr. Oliver's house."

I dropped the phone and wobbled towards the front door, screaming, "Get out, get out! Bomb in the house. Get out! Bomb—" Officers dashed out of every door and jumped out the windows.

The explosion knocked me flat onto my sore rump. The front door flew within inches of my face and landed in the street. I struggled to inhale, as if someone stood on my chest. The smell of burnt plastic filled my nostrils. Tattered remnants of the house rained down in the yard and street. Several of my team crawled through the remains, bloody and battered, but they all moved—a positive sign. I instinctively got up to aid my fellow officers. The blast had messed up my hearing and balance, and I fell after two steps. I checked myself for injuries. I could feel blood seeping from my rump wound. I had some new cuts and scrapes, but I was lucky.

I looked around the scene that had been so tranquil only moments before. The house was little more than a frame. Only one wall remained untouched. The messy contents of the home had been scattered across the yard. Another bomb and more injuries. I *had* to catch this guy. A plume of smoke rose from behind a neighbor's house. Did The Messenger bomb another house? Wait. Where did the helicopter go?

I limped around the neighbor's house, following a first responder to see the helicopter on its side, ablaze. The home's walls served as shrapnel and must have downed it. The two occupants were ejected. They were both bloody and mangled, but moaning, so at least they were alive. The results could have been much worse, but the day wasn't over. Another explosion and a burning helicopter would definitely scare the tourists. *Freak.*

CHAPTER SIXTEEN

Wednesday 11:03 a.m.

AT THE PRECINCT, the mood had gone from excited to disappointed. We were confident we would have a suspect in our grasp, only to find we had nothing, and three more officers were injured. I still coughed up dust from the helicopter. How in the world did this Messenger guy know about our raid ahead of time? If I didn't know better, I would swear someone on the inside was helping him. Did Vegas PD have a traitor?

In the fishbowl, five conversations competed for an audience. I waived and cleared my throat but was still invisible. I attempted to politely get their attention to no avail. I tried to climb onto a chair, but my sore tush protested. Finally, I threw a coffee cup on the floor, where it shattered with an electrifying sound. "Dammit. Everybody, listen. I talked to the bomber."

The captain's large belly heaved as he took a breath. "We're getting plenty of calls from those claiming credit. Twenty-three at last count."

"Twenty-four," Sandy said in her typical upbeat voice.

"Twenty-four," Captain Creek repeated. "All are being investigated. Most just want to hear their name on the news. They are crazy, and all of them are lying."

Steve Shale from the mayor's office was here, which meant politicians were getting worried complaints from casino and hotel managers. Rule two: Don't scare the damn tourists.

"Then how did he know to contact me?" I asked.

"Probably from your press conference," Steve Shale said.

Freak, that did make sense. Still, I stood my ground. "No. This 'Messenger' guy is the real bomber."

"How can you be so confident?" Shale asked.

"He knew about the lack of shrapnel. No one released that detail to the press."

Shale pondered. "That's interesting, but not conclusive. Perhaps he has an inside source."

"No, I'm confident this guy, The Messenger, he's the bomber."

"The Messenger?" Shale asked. "Hmmm. Can you identify him? His name?"

I shook my head.

"Nationality? An accent perhaps?"

"No."

"Anything about him?"

My self-confidence plummeted. I'd felt so certain just a few moments ago.

"Before we run off on a wild goose chase, can you guarantee this caller wasn't some kid with a sick sense of humor?'

Shale's question made sense. Was I being scammed by some teenager with too much time on his hands? I hoped my doubts didn't show.

"Did the caller claim any allegiance to any specific group?" the captain asked.

"He wasn't fueled by terrorism."

The captain looked relieved. "Then what was his motive, Donna?"

"Respect."

"Come again?" Shale said.

"He blew up the bank because he was disrespected." Now that I heard it from my own lips, respect didn't sound like a real motive.

Charlie came to my defense again. "We should take this seriously. Investigate it at least."

Shale shook his head. "People don't detonate bombs because of disrespect, Donna."

"This one does."

UNTIL I COULD CONVINCE them I'd spoken with the real bomber, I had to focus on the three suspects we had. I reviewed the files on them. All were easy to hate. Gar Vickers, the career criminal, really was only interested in making a profit. He was more a salesman, offering his deadly wares to anyone with ready cash. I doubted he would have planted the bomb, but I was confident he could have supplied the explosives. Ivan Kutner, Ivan the Terrible, was a disgusting excuse for a man, but he seemed more likely to rob the bank than attack it with dynamite. Still, I couldn't rule him out. I concentrated on Raymond Soames as the most likely of the three. Was this from my following the clues or an expected reaction to a possessive, violent, jerk ex-boyfriend? Jilted boyfriends have done crazy things, but bomb his obsession's place of work? Soames was in the hospital. I needed to check his phone log. I had to admit that as a woman, his piggish behavior moved him to the top of any list.

One of the fishbowl's big screens flashed "Breaking News."

Three local channels reported a house in the city had exploded and a helicopter crashed. Tourists did not seem to care. The house was nowhere near the Strip and tourists ignored local news anyway. But Vegas residents watched. They were alarmed and complaining loudly. The mayor's office had called the captain three times this morning. I was so glad I was not in the captain's smoke infused shoes.

Charlie stood in front of a giant screen, another breaking news update, a regular occurrence. He turned up the volume.

"We at News 3 can confirm that someone in the Las Vegas Police Department has been talking to the person claiming responsibility for the explosions at Second United Bank, and in the North Las Vegas suburb. In addition, we have reports that the officer . . ."

I felt dread engulf me.

". . . Donna Summer Wyznecki . . ."

My photo with my unmanageable hair appeared. I was on every local station. Freak. My mind spun but I registered words like "blame" and "responsible." Charlie hit mute on the remote.

I shook my head. 'Great. Now everyone hates me."

"Who leaked this story to the press?" Sandy asked.

"How did they get the story so fast?" Ben asked.

We always had informants in the department, always would, but on this investigation, we were tight-lipped, no details to the public. None. We were a family, a team, working together. Someone had betrayed that trust.

Helen waved from across the room. When I got close, she whispered, "You have a visitor downstairs. He wouldn't leave his name."

I raised an eyebrow. "No name?"

"He's cute."

Hot damn. "How do I look?" I stood at attention.

Helen winked. "Leave the cane here."

I put on my emergency date heels that I kept in a desk drawer for such occasions. The heels made my butt hurt, but they were so worth it to add a couple of inches to my height. If I took short, delicate steps, I could minimize the trauma to my rear end. I trekked slowly to the lobby. I ignored the activity around me, as I had a gentleman caller. I was about twenty tiny steps from the lobby when I was hit hard by the shoulder of a uniformed officer and nearly lost my balance.

"Sorry," was all he said as he stood beside me. He looked vaguely familiar.

I said, "Excuse me," and moved sideways to go around him. He countered, blocking my way.

"Excuse me," I said again, and tried another lateral move, careful to take small steps to protect my rump. Who was this guy? I stared at his face. I was sure I knew him from somewhere, but where? I glanced at his name badge below his shield. "Officer Soames."

"Raymond is my brother," he said, inching closer to me. "You should be very careful making accusations about my family." The threat was implied, barely.

He gave me another hard shoulder and walked past me. A family of charmers, I thought. *Raymond Soames has three protective orders for violence against women, and a brother on the force?* Anger toward females seemed to run in his family. This brief encounter really zapped me of the positive outlook I had just moments ago. I continued my tiny steps to the lobby, heels clicking.

In the lobby, a trim, handsome young man stood up.

"I'm Detective Wyznecki."

"Donna Wyz-check-nov-skiny?"

Why can't people pronounce my name? Ever heard of phonics? "It's pronounced Wizz-neck-ee."

"Donna Summer Wizz-neck-ee?"

I flashed him my best smile. "How can I help you?" Was this a potential admirer?

He pushed some folded forms to my chest. "There, you've been served."

What? Served? Oh, freak no. A process server? I scowled. Helen dropped her tarot cards and shooed him away. I unfolded the papers The top page read, "Clark County District Court, Petition, Alexander F. Higgins versus Donna Summer Wyznecki, Las Vegas Police Department, and the City of Las Vegas . . ." Blah blah blah. *Who the freak is Alexander F. Higgins?* I read further. "Plaintiff was injured by the excessive force of Officer Donna Summer Wyznecki—" *What?* I was being sued for excessive force? *Oh, bite me.*

I found the nearest computer terminal and searched for Alexander F. Higgins. Two speeding tickets. That couldn't be it. Then his driver's license photo popped up. He was an older white guy, no smile, no hair, but looked familiar. Who was this guy?

I looked at his photo again. Then it hit me. Higgins was the Toupee Man. Mister Toupee was suing me. For excessive force? I never touched him. *Good luck, jerk. I have six hundred and eighty-one dollars in my savings account, so try and get it.* Mister Toupee wasn't suing only me but also the police department and the City of Las Vegas. Freak.

I called Lynn Parsons, my union rep, my best friend, and now my personal defense lawyer. She answered on the first ring. "Relax, Donna, I just got served as well."

"How did this lawyer move so fast?" I asked.

"Personal injury lawyers move fast so another lawyer can't take the case. We need to meet and discuss this."

"Excessive force? He slipped on my latte. I never tripped him. He fell. I don't have time to worry about crap like this. I must find this bomber."

"We'll talk about it at lunch. Don't say a word to anybody about this, and I mean no one. Meet you in thirty minutes, Blueberry Hill Diner on Decatur."

Great. Comfort food. I needed it. I spent the next thirty minutes worrying and fretting. How could this jerk sue me? Really? He slipped on my latte, which he knocked from my hands. It was his own fault. Excessive force? Bite me.

CHAPTER SEVENTEEN

Wednesday 12:25 p.m.

I WANTED to take Robin's fancy car, but my still-aching backside discouraged me. Taxis were cutting deeply into my donut funds. The Blueberry Hill Diner's familiar baby blue sign and matching awning greeted me. Twenty-four-hour comfort food. I loved it. I arrived first, so I got a booth. This was my second breakfast, or first lunch, but who's counting? I ordered a chorizo skillet with extra bacon, a side of biscuits and gravy, and a Belgian waffle for myself and Lynn's usual, straw-berry crepes, which she would only eat half of. A full tummy would help. I was recuperating from a grievous wound.

Lynn, radiant as always, sauntered in and turned every male head in the room. She hugged me and introduced her father, George.

I shook his hand. "If I had known we would have a hand-some gentleman joining us, I would have dressed up."

George smiled. "I wanted to meet you and buy you lunch. My way of thanking you for protecting our bank."

"You work at Second United?"

George nodded.

"I don't think I deserve it, but I'm too hungry to stop you." I smiled.

The server brought my biscuits and gravy, and George ordered a chicken fried steak. I knew George and I would be good friends. That heart healthy menu stuff is garbage.

Lynn peppered me with questions before she took a bite. "Do you even remember this guy?"

"Yeah."

"Does he have any excessive force claim against you?"

"No. I never touched him."

Lynn furrowed her brow.

"Remember the explosion at the bank? Well, before the explosion, I kind of had an . . . incident . . . with this guy."

"Listen," Lynn said, grabbing a dainty bite of her crepe. "You need to hide from the captain. LVPD policy is to take your gun and badge until this excessive force claim has been investigated by Internal Affairs."

Internal Affairs never made any friends. My father served in IA for fifteen years before retirement, which explained why he was always given the cold shoulder at the precinct and was never, ever invited to any police social functions.

"I can't believe this guy is claiming I pushed him!"

"Well, I have to ask as your lawyer. Did you?" Lynn asked.

"I wanted to kick him, but he slipped and fell in my latte puddle before I had a chance."

Lynn chuckled. "Nuisance claim. Don't worry about it. I have some surprises in store for these personal injury lawyers. This isn't my first rodeo."

I nodded, still not relieved.

"These lawsuits happen all the time," Lynn assured me. After a second nibble of strawberry crepe, she continued. "This guy won't win, and even if he did, any money would be paid by the city, not you." My heart rate dropped twenty beats a minute. I might survive this.

George smiled like a proud papa. "Doesn't she have the appetite of a bird?"

So did I—the appetite of a pterodactyl.

Lynn beamed, passed me a magazine, popped it open, and pointed. "What do you think?"

I stared down at an ad for Preparation H. "I don't really need that."

"No, silly, the dress." Lynn turned the page. I stared at some ostentatious bridesmaid dress that looked great on a curvy model but would look ridiculous on me.

"Look at these gorgeous dresses." Lynn's smile lit up the room. I feigned excitement, knowing what a skinny girl like me would look like in one of these dresses, more flower girl than bridesmaid.

"What do you think about these colors?"

Oh, please, not pink. The last time I wore pink someone asked if my troop would sell cookies again this year.

Lynn smiled. "I think I found you a date for the wedding."

I was so caught up in the bridesmaid dress humiliation I had forgotten about the *plus one* trauma. No way this would be good news.

George gave me a fatherly smile. "You haven't found Mr. Right yet?"

"I'd be happy with Mister Mediocre at this point."

Lynn giggled. "You'll have a great time. His name is Andy . . ."

It wouldn't be Jeffrey Dahmer, too obvious.

". . . and he's handsome . . ."

That meant he was broke.

". . . He's got a good job . . ."

Oh, then he lived in his mother's basement.

". . . and he is really smart . . ."

And probably a serial killer.

". . . and I think you guys would really have a great time."

"Lynn, I . . ." I could find a date for a wedding, right? I ran down my list of usual suspects. None seemed viable.

Lynn gave me her 150-watt smile.

"Okay, I'll meet him. No promises."

Lynn's smile erupted into joy.

I feigned excitement. "What's his phone number?" Great, now I had to call this guy. It just reeked of desperation.

"I gave him yours. He'll contact you soon."

He's calling me? He must be a predator. How could I get out of this?

Lynn smiled. "I think you'll have a great time together."

How many times had she said, "great time together"? She really oversold this. Was this guy in prison? Anyway, he was my best option from the last few weeks. Lynn closed her eyes and sniffed. "I think love is in the air."

No, that was the smell of my Belgian waffle. Crap. A blind date for a wedding. Wait, this guy might really be blind. What had Lynn gotten me into?

CHAPTER EIGHTEEN

Wednesday 2:14 p.m.

I BROKE down and drove Robin's fancy car, still emblazored with the price sticker which both surprised me and made me jealous. I rolled through town with disco music from the Bee Gees blaring. I had almost learned to use the stick shift. Back at the precinct, I parked safely away from other cars to avoid a scratch on Robin's pricey toy.

I trotted past the eagle eyes of Helen. "Hey, Disco Diva." She put down her tarot cards. She only called me a "Disco Diva" when our women's detective group needed to meet. I moved closer. She whispered, "Sandy needs us."

I grimaced. "Is it her stupid boyfriend again?" I had been so wrapped up in this case I had overlooked Sandy's worries.

Helen nodded. "Sandy discovered a small velvet box. She got her hopes up."

"And . . ."

"Earrings." Helen hung her head.

I sighed. "She's been waiting on a ring for two years."

"Three," Helen corrected.

"Set the place and time and I'll be there."

The Disco Divas worked together to commiserate. Sometimes the Divas needed a little wine and a lot of dancing. Sometimes, a lot of wine and a little dancing. Sometimes, margaritas and no dancing. This sounded like a tequila problem. Men were usually a tequila problem.

We called our group "The Disco Divas" because on one ill-fated night we went dancing during a disco revival. After far too many margaritas, we entered the group dance contest—and won. We got a small trophy, which sat in a huge trophy case. Amongst lots of large and small police league trophies from basketball, flag football, volleyball, and—the most prized—an enormous trophy for the three-state regional champions of the police slow pitch softball league, sat our little golden cup. Most men bragged when they showed the trophy case to new recruits. In an overlooked shelf, half-hidden, our small trophy commemorated our prized achievement. I was proud to be a Disco Diva.

I shuffled past the trophy case to Ben's workstation. I wanted to see if we had made any progress on finding my caller, The Messenger. Ben slowed his battering of computer keys. "Phone call came from a burner phone, of course. Location of call from pinging cell phone towers—the Strip, in between Bellagio and Paris."

Captain Creek wheezed. "So, we're looking for a man on the Vegas Strip? That narrows it down."

It seemed hopeless.

Sandy looked intently at me. "Are you okay, Donna? Looking a little pale."

"I need a donut." I followed Sandy to the donuts and coffee table. Sandy pulled a donut from a white box and handed it to me. I bypassed her hand and took the box. "This will help." I leaned closer and whispered, "Helen told me about your boyfriend. Do you want me to kill him?"

Sandy shook her head. "No. I want him to suffer." She smiled. Changing the subject, she said, "I'll never understand how you stay so thin."

"Hot yoga," I replied.

"Really?"

"No. It's my metabolism."

"What do you do for exercise?"

"I guess . . . being on top." We smiled and bumped fists. It had been a while, but I heard it was just like a bicycle . . .

Ben waived. "I've made some progress. Your Messenger call was from the same batch of phones as the one from the bank bombing. Serial numbers are two digits off. No coincidence. Must have been bought at the same place."

Now that was a real clue.

"Do we know where they were purchased?" Sandy asked.

The click of Ben's rapid-fire keystrokes filled the air. Two minutes and a caramel iced long john later he paused. The silence got everyone's attention. "Tracing the phone purchases back through the transaction codes. I don't know who bought them, but I know they were purchased at Quickie Foods, north of downtown."

Quickie Foods was managed by one of my dear friends. "I can help," I said.

I called up my buddy Vijay, who ran Quickie Foods—great convenience stores with small delis inside. Around lunch time, they made yaki man doo—homemade Korean dumplings, which should be their own food group. Trust me, I knew food, and Vijay made great food.

I let him know he was on speaker phone and that I was calling on official business.

"Always glad to help my favorite customer," Vijay said,

when I explained what we needed. "But I sell many disposable phones. Do you have a day and time?" Ben conveyed the information down to the minute. "I'll check my records. Give me a moment."

I looked at John-Boy. "Remind me to not keep any secrets from Ben."

"Ditto for me. He knows everyone's secrets. You can't trust anyone." John-Boy wore his regular cologne, which I adored. And he never wore too much, like most men. Damn John-Boy for being delicious. My mind wandered where it shouldn't.

Vijay's voice snapped me back to the issue at hand. "One of my regulars, a straw man, bought five phones that day." I cringed. This was a dead end.

"What's a straw man?" Ben asked.

"He buys things for a price," Vijay continued. "Kids want beer, they approach him, give him money, he buys beer, and they give him five dollars for his efforts."

"You sell beer to kids?" Ben asked.

"No," Vijay replied. "I sell beer to legal adults, who then sell to kids. Happens all the time, at every minimart on earth."

"Weren't you ever a teenager?" I asked.

"We're not concerned with the beer," the captain stated. "Just the phones."

Vijay continued. "Some people want phones anonymously, so they have Slow Denny buy the phone. Voilà. Cell phone with no record."

"Who wants these phones?" the captain asked.

"Not as obvious," Vijay said. "Sometimes kids whose parents don't approve. Straying husbands, maybe. But I would bet most are the purveyors of illicit substances."

"What's his real name?" I asked.

"Not sure. We call him 'Slow Denny.' He's slow."

"Slow, like retarded?" I asked.

"We don't say 'retarded' anymore, Detective Wyznecki," the captain chastised me.

"Is his real name Denny?" I asked.

"Not sure," Vijay said. I feared we had reached yet another dead end. I could imagine Shale complaining about time wasted on my idea. "Perhaps if I sent you his photo?" Vijay offered.

Ben perked up. "Great. If you have a clear shot of his face, I can use that."

Vijay emailed the picture of our phone purchaser—and he wasn't Gar Vickers, Raymond Soames, or Ivan the Terrible. That would have been too easy. Through the magic of face recognition technology, in eight minutes we had an answer.

The captain gathered the investigation crew. "Our lead, our only lead, is Dennison 'Slow Denny' Doogan." Charlie taped a color print of Denny's most recent arrest beside the grainy picture of him purchasing the phones.

Ben explained his findings. "Denny's a low-level criminal—panhandling, trespassing and nuisance claims, in jail six times, mental health issues. He's obviously not the brains of the operation."

"Do we think he's the bomber?" Helen asked.

"No," I said. "The guy on the phone wasn't retar— I mean special. I know that much."

"He's not the bomber," John-Boy said. "No way a special guy could make a bomb like this. It required great skill."

"Well," the captain said, "he's our only suspect now, so let's find him fast and see what he knows."

Ben tapped a few more keys. "He lives in a dumpy neighborhood in North Las Vegas."

Charlie adjusted his reading glasses to view the printout before him. "He has a brother, Kevin Doogan, at the same address, with a long history of theft offenses as well."

The captain called to me from across the fishbowl. Crap, I was supposed to lie low and avoid him.

With my sore rump, I really couldn't outrun him, so I waited.

"Donna, did you know you're being sued for excessive force?"

I nodded. "Yes."

"I need your gun and badge until you are cleared by Internal Affairs. You shouldn't even be here."

THE MESSENGER SOLDERED *a fuse under a magnifying glass. He tested the timer on and off. It worked flawlessly. He smiled at his latest creation and the twenty identical bombs in a row. He was preparing for his big day. "This will be epic," he announced to no one. "The selfish will be punished."*

CHAPTER NINETEEN

Wednesday 4:29 p.m.

CHARLIE AND JOHN-BOY were dispatched to Slow Denny's home to question him. Having been excluded from the investigation, I waited in the parking lot. *If you can't get permission, don't ask for it.*

Amazingly, we bumped into each other. "Just headed home," I said.

John-Boy asked me to ride along. Historically, I had difficulty telling him no. John-Boy was a take-charge kind of guy. I liked that about him. Charlie rode shotgun. With his long legs, he needed the space. He also outranked me, but he never mentioned it. I rode in the back, which was more than spacious for me. I noticed the lingering smell of nervous sweat, common to the back seat of all police cars.

Ten minutes later we arrived at Slow Denny's home address in a seedy North Las Vegas neighborhood. Charlie and I walked to Slow Denny's front door. John-Boy went around to the rear, to catch anyone trying to leave.

The mobile home resembled the after photos from a hurricane. Weeds in the front yard hid trash lying about. A plain screen door with large holes covered the paint-deprived entrance. Charlie knocked on the door.

A voice from inside the home muttered, "Come in." Not the typical welcome when we visited a suspect's home.

I was cautious. The last suspect's home I visited was Oliver's—and it exploded.

We entered the small living room. By comparison, the front yard was pristine. Fast food wrappers and empty beer bottles littered every surface. The floor had not been vacuumed in years. I could have used a place to rest my sore rump, but I wasn't going to sit anywhere in this pig pen. We flashed our badges. I recognized the man at the Formica table from his mug shot, Slow Denny's brother, Kevin. His shirt was covered in mystery stains, his eyes were bloodshot, and he reeked of body odor and spilled beer.

Charlie started the conversation. "We are worried about your brother, Denny. Do you know where he is? We need to ask him some questions."

Kevin reached into the ashtray and inhaled from his cigarette. He puffed out a large cloud of smoke.

"That's not tobacco," I said. From the smell, brother Kevin had some potent skunkweed.

"Yeah, I got my card. This is *medical* marijuana. Hurt my back at work. Can hardly walk straight without pain."

"Sorry to hear that." Charlie picked up his cane and placed it back on the stained table.

John-Boy came back into the living room. "I found marijuana growing in the back bedroom. It seems Kevin here is quite an entrepreneur."

"Hey, you got a warrant? The law says you got to have a warrant."

Charlie shook his head. "Part of your probation rules say you consent to a search anytime one is requested."

"I got a grower's permit, too."

Charlie examined Kevin's medical marijuana cards. "When was the last time you spoke to your brother?"

"When was the last time you kissed my ass?"

This wasn't productive.

"My brother is slow," Kevin said. "People always taking advantage of him, talking him into doing things because he can't think so good. He ain't no criminal. He's just slow."

"Can you tell us where your brother is?" Charlie asked. "We would like to talk to him."

"You guys are so stupid. He's in the damn morgue. Garbage man found him. Damn drugs got him. Why don't you do something about that?"

"I'm sorry," Charlie said. "We didn't know." Charlie pulled out photos of our three suspects. "Do you—"

"Now get out of my house." Cooperation had stopped and everyone knew it. We filed back through the broken screen door and onto the weedy lawn. "Go on, get out."

"Don't call the police," John-Boy said. "We're already here."

Charlie called the morgue. Kevin had told the truth. His brother had died from an overdose, on the seedy side of Las Vegas, far from the glitz and lights. The coroner's office promised to send a report, but what good would it do? Our suspect or lead or potential witness, whatever he was, was dead.

CHAPTER TWENTY

Wednesday 5:03 p.m.

SANDY and I entered the interview room. "Thank you for coming in," Sandy stated.

Audra Barclay sat on the opposite side of the table. She seemed like the girl next door, the kind of girl I would be friends with.

Audra fidgeted with her hands. "Why am I here?"

I smiled. "We're investigating the bank explosion."

"I was there," she replied. "The police already questioned me twice."

Sandy gently reached for her hand. "I know this is an imposition, but this is a profoundly serious case. We don't want to miss a single detail."

Audra recalled for a third time her description of events, which aligned with the other witnesses. A normal day, then boom. Panic and confusion, but nothing that stood out as unusual. Ben's video had revealed similar findings. Nothing seemed out of the ordinary until the blast.

"We are also interested in Raymond Soames. Did you see him at the bank?" I asked.

Audra sighed. "What has he done now?"

Audra described to us a very brief relationship, if you wanted to call it that. From her perspective, there were no sparks, and she was ready to move on. Raymond was not. He followed her, always from a distance, called her multiple times, but she never answered. Audra summarized, "He was creepy, but not in a violent way. He was just clingy. Annoyingly clingy."

As women, we both knew what she meant. Raymond didn't rise to the level of being a stalker, and there was no indication of him being violent or a bomber. This was another cold trail for our investigation.

Sandy and I stood to escort her out of the police station when Audra paused.

"Raymond would never harm anyone. But his brother's a jerk with a temper."

Maybe we were looking at the wrong Soames brother. I had only interacted with him for twenty seconds and already had a strong dislike.

Sandy walked her out as I wobbled into the fishbowl in dire need of a snack.

Charlie smiled as he stood to greet me. "Gar Vickers is no longer a suspect. Vickers is in FBI custody as a cooperative witness. That's why he wasn't in the database as being in custody."

I was excited to eliminate him as a suspect, but I would be happier if we'd made progress on a legit suspect who was in custody.

"I have good news," Charlie announced. "The FBI is sharing information." Once Charlie had everyone's attention, he continued. "Our newest suspect, and frankly where most of the FBI's resources are spent, is Phillip St. Gregory, whom the FBI calls 'The Professor.' He is facing charges for setting off explosives in Oregon, Washington, and Idaho."

Ben posted photos of our newest suspect on the big screens around the room. Phillip St. Gregory looked like a typical professor in a shirt and tie, with a closely cropped beard and glasses. I envisioned him carrying a stack of books through a library. The screen changed, showing two photos side by side. On one side, St. Gregory looked normal but in the second, he had wide eyes, messy hair, and a straggly beard. It was definitely the same person.

"St. Gregory had some kind of mental breakdown," Charlie explained. "He went from college professor to a doomsday believer who thinks it's his mission to warn the world. Think of the Unabomber with a double scoop of crazy. He hides among the homeless community to live completely off the grid. He was being monitored by local police in California but disappeared three weeks ago. He believes Las Vegas is home to a global financial cabal, manipulating the world's economy."

Captain Creek assigned an all-male task force to search for St. Gregory. Typical.

The cold stare of this crazy man made my pulse race. I was afraid, very afraid. I needed to get out of there. Fast. The Disco Divas had plans.

CHAPTER TWENTY-ONE

Wednesday 6:45 p.m.

HELEN, Sandy, and I carpooled to the Big Sky Casino, a giant mega resort on the south end of The Strip. We strutted through the immense lobby and made our way to the entrance for the Hideaway, their classy club. We got a booth, courtesy of security who happened to be an off-duty LVPD officer.

The Hideaway offered trendy drinks and outrageous appetizers, which on the weekend would cost a small fortune. Wednesday nights were a little slower and much more affordable for public servants.

Sandy, Helen, and I exchanged quick fist bumps as we slid into the booth. *Mothers, hide your single sons. The Disco Divas are on the prowl.*

Lynn, with her bright, movie-star smile joined us two minutes later. Her curves made me feel inadequate, again.

"Everyone knows Lynn, right?" I asked. Sandy nodded.

Helen asked, "Counselor, how's our union rep doing?"

Our server came by. "Got an order here for the Disco Divas." She placed the portable table down as she steadied the heavy tray of food. Did they pre-order without me? *No bueno.*

Lynn smiled. "I ordered everyone a salad with low-fat dressing on the side and some lemonade."

The server looked confused as she lowered the giant platter of their Kitchen Sink nachos, two orders of Southwest egg rolls —my favorite—and a pitcher of margaritas with salt-rimmed glasses for everyone.

"Yes, that's mine," Lynn said with a wink.

A second server appeared with a smaller tray with tequila shots for everyone. When we started with tequila, we had a problem.

Lynn distributed the shot glasses and lifted her own. "For Sandy and her next boyfriend."

"For Sandy," we repeated in unison.

The Patron Silver burned a little all the way down. I needed food. When tequila hit the bottom of my empty stomach, I was not responsible for my actions.

The rest of the Divas had a similar thought as we devoured the Kitchen Sink nachos and ate most of the Southwest eggrolls.

Sandy didn't eat anything. "Sorry, I'm on a new diet." She shrugged her shoulders, her broad smile still shining. She finally agreed to eat half an eggroll. That left more for me, so I didn't complain. We laughed and eyed the dance floor like a lioness scans the Serengeti plains.

The public address speaker sparked to life. "We have a special musical request for the Disco Divas." The speaker blared The Bee Gee's "You Should Be Dancing", and we strutted our stuff. We got a few cheers and someone in the crowd whistled. It was probably intended for Lynn, but I counted it. My sore rump limited my motion but not my enthusiasm.

We laughed a lot, blushed a little, and retook our seats, very gently. I really needed stress-free time with friends. This was perfect. I noticed two wolves approaching. I winked to alert my Divas for the inevitable come on. We quieted as they approached.

The first one to speak approached Lynn. So typical I thought her enormous engagement ring might deter him, but no. I hoped the other would chat up Sandy, as she could use the confidence espresso. The second guy spoke to me. That was a surprise. I usually attracted the runt of the litter when a group of males approached.

We exchanged small talk, and Lynn let her suitor down gently through a great deal of practice. I was smiling and considering a dance. Could my rump take the pain of shaking it on the dance floor a second time? I was about to accept his invitation when I spied a television behind the bar with local breaking news. Of course, it was about the bank bombing, and the house explosion, and the helicopter crash. Locals were transfixed. Tourists were unconcerned. These events happened three miles off the Strip. To our tourists, the explosions could have been on another planet.

The tenor of the Disco Divas changed from party central to working the front lines. Time to be serious again. "Should we head back to the fishbowl?" Helen asked.

Then my phone buzzed.

"Hello, Little Donna."

The Messenger was tormenting me again, but I was ready to push back. "Are you insane or just wanting some attention?"

"I assure you, I'm not insane."

"Are you a terrorist? Is this religious or political?"

"No, no, no. This is not terrorism. Terrorists are crazy. I am perfectly rational."

"What are your motives?"

"My motives will be revealed soon enough, but I hoped you would figure them out first, Little Donna."

"Is your name Gar Vickers?"

"I have no idea who that is."

"So, why destroy Oliver's house? We never found his body."

"There was not a body to find."

"Then why blow up the house?"

"If you're as smart as you think you are—"

"Are you Phillip St. Gregory?"

The Messenger laughed for a good thirty seconds. Finally, he caught his breath and spoke. "Of course I am, but I prefer to be called 'Professor.' I thought you would never guess." He giggled some more. "But I'm not crazy."

"And your motive is . . .? Tell me."

"A smart detective could figure that out. Are you a smart detective, Little Donna?"

"I am quite smart."

The Messenger laughed. "You don't know what's going on around you, Little Donna. You're the one who is lost. And I told you to call me Professor."

"Who is your target?" I asked.

"A bank."

"Why a bank? Why Second United?"

"You'll uncover my motives in time."

"How? Professor, if you really are the Professor, how do I know you're the one responsible? Give me some proof."

"She— I suppose a psychiatrist would say that all actions are motivated by power, either the use of it or the lack of it."

"She? Who is she? I don't suppose you could explain that."

"Sorry, Little Donna, no more time to talk. I have much to do. They owe us."

"Wait. Don't hang up. Who are they? Who is us? Messenger? What do you have to do?"

"The selfish will be punished."

"What? St. Gregory, we practically have you in custody."

He laughed. "I doubt that. I have always known what you're about to do. I have help. Enjoy your Southwest eggrolls. They're delicious." He ended the call.

The line went dead. Such a jerk. Wait. Southwest eggrolls? He knows I'm here? The Messenger was watching me? He had to be.

I limped to the six-lane loading zone at the front of the casino complex with the Disco Divas on my heels. Nothing suspicious. Busy, but no Professor. I wobbled into The Strip. Traffic honked at me. I needed to see this crazy man, Phillip St. Gregory. The cars were too dark to see faces.

In despair, I shouted, "Damn you, St. Gregory! I will catch you!"

"Donna, what's wrong?" Sandy asked.

"That was The Messenger. He admitted he's St. Gregory." Now we can catch this jerk. I made a quick call to the captain. All our efforts would be spent on St. Gregory. He issued an APB for St. Gregory through all law enforcement in Nevada and a BOLO on his last known automobile. But the captain warned me I was too close to this case. I was still on restricted duty because of my injury—and my excessive force lawsuit didn't help.

The captain informed me that Vegas Police would put a photo of St. Gregory in the hands of every shelter, every soup kitchen, and every charity that worked with the homeless. If he was hiding in the homeless community, they would catch him.

My services were not needed until I was cleared by the department psychiatrist and Internal Affairs.

We moved back to the Hideaway but didn't dance. Instead, we planned the investigation, each Disco Diva with an assigned task. We needed to find out everything we could about St. Gregory—his friends, family, co-workers, anything from his background that could hint why he held a grudge against a bank. This was a big task, but both Helen and Sandy would dig into St. Gregory's life. Lynn could look into the court files of known associates with criminal records. We also knew that St. Gregory liked to hide among the homeless community. That was my specialty. I had the perfect informant.

The Disco Divas would solve this case. We could do this.

From the entryway, I overheard, "You can't come in here." The staff held back Ronnie, my personal investigator. Raincoat Ronnie, a long-time member of the Vegas homeless scene, earned his nickname because rain or shine he always wore a raincoat. Considering Las Vegas's sweltering heat, wearing a raincoat year-round required tremendous dedication or severe mental illness. I was confident he had both.

Ronnie had served as an informant for me during my uniform days. Strange that I described them that way since my uniform days had ended less than a week ago. Ronnie was the perfect informant—always present, always watching, and invisible. He wasn't really invisible, not even my Ronnie believed that. But since he was homeless, no one noticed him. He blended into the background with Las Vegas's other less fortunate residents. And he moved like a ninja.

I darted over to the manager and explained that Ronnie was with me. Most businesses discouraged the homeless from making camp in their lobby, but I vouched for him. I had some clout. When I announced I needed to place a large order to go for Ronnie, they were completely cooperative.

Ronnie reported for duty. I handed him a photo of Phillip St. Gregory. "Ronnie, can you find this guy for me?" He nodded.

I finally felt like we were making some progress on this case. Time to place that order for Ronnie. And maybe add a little something for myself.

CHAPTER TWENTY-TWO

Wednesday 8:05 p.m.

I PICKED up another iPhone charger on the way to the hospital. I needed something to keep my attention while I sat with Robin and Elaine. Besides, I had several ideas that needed more investigative attention. I handed the key to Robin's fancy new car to the hospital's valet. "Guard this with your life," I warned.

"I will," the kid said, holding Robin's key fob like it was the Hope diamond. Males and their cars . . .

Gloria was in the room already. Elaine had fallen asleep with the TV volume on low, and Gloria signaled me to be quiet. I sank into a plastic chair and leafed through Lynn's bridal magazine. Lots of pictures of happy, shapely bridesmaids wearing a variety of soft-toned shades in several styles, some traditional, some off-the-shoulder, some strapless, all of which would look ridiculous on boy-figured me.

I googled "bridesmaid dresses for petite girls." What did I find? More pictures of super models wearing the same dresses.

Really? They couldn't find one picture of a tiny girl? I scanned through several online bridal magazines. All proclaimed their dresses looked good on any sized girl, but never showed a girl smaller than a C cup, and always one of them wore a pink dress. Pink? Freak. I should just put my hair in pigtails and carry a giant lollypop.

"Oh, Lynn. Damn. You've got me doing it too. Now I'm wasting my time looking at bridesmaid dresses."

"What?" Gloria asked.

"Just talking to myself," I assured her. Talking to myself was never a good sign. I alternated my reading, shuffling between the bombing suspects and bridal magazines, killers and sequined dresses.

Was I psychotic?

I searched for terrorism in America. My stomach dropped. We had plenty of home-grown crazies, some based on religion, some on politics, some plain crazy. America had enemies, ranging from small and silly to large and super-violent. The Oklahoma City bombing showed that terrorists don't need an army. Two sickos with high school chemistry created a disaster with fertilizer. What could a zealot do with six hundred sticks of dynamite in Las Vegas? My stomach clenched into knots.

My phone rang and I answered it without checking the caller ID. No one called besides work and Mom anyway. "Wyznecki here."

"Donna Wyz-chur-neck-ski?"

Close enough, I thought. "Yes."

"Lynn said I should call you. She said we would have a great time together."

Great time together? Crap. My blind date. How could I gently ask if he really was blind? "She told me you would call," I said with no commitment. I moved to the hallway so I wouldn't disturb Robin or Elaine—and so Gloria couldn't eavesdrop and report back to Mom that I was talking to a guy.

"Yeah, blind dates aren't my favorite either. So awkward."

Could I politely say I wasn't interested?

He took the lead. "Listen, blind dates are always terrible. How about we just get it over with so that Lynn will stop bugging both of us?"

He had a nice voice. Did I hear jail sounds in the background? Should I give this guy a chance? Where did he want to eat? That would predict the future of our relationship. If he picked fast food, I'd be out.

"Do you like Mexican food?" he asked.

"Of course. Who doesn't?" Did I hear wedding bells playing?

"How about tomorrow night at Lindo Michoacan restaurant?"

I was about to give him the brush off, but Lindo Michoacan? Their Taquitos Dorados and Queso Fundido were magnificent. I salivated thinking about their Carnitas a la Coca-Cola and Tacos Frito Chorizo. I think I'm in love. Should we start looking at engagement rings?

"Their Queso Fundido is wonderful," he added.

Was he reading my mind? Wow. Three. Yes, three. We will have three kids, maybe with "J" names.

"Let me buy you dinner," he said. "You can see if I'm as awful as you imagine."

"I don't know how any girl could turn down an offer like that."

"What time should I pick you up?"

"Why don't we just meet there?" Mother always warned me not to tell strange men where I lived. I guessed that should apply, even to my newly found soul mate.

"Great. Meet you tomorrow at Lindo Michoacan, seven thirty?"

"See you then." I hung up smiling broadly. Tomorrow night, I have a date. I have a date! I have a date at Lindo Michoacan Restaurant for some delicious Mexican food with . . . uh . . . what was his name? I checked my notepad. All I had written was seven thirty and Lindo Michoacan. *Freak, I didn't write down his name. Ugh. Wait.* Lynn said I would like him. I tried to recall the conversation with Lynn. He would be calling. His name . . . Adam? Adrian? Andy? Alex? Allen? One of the A names. I might have to admit defeat and call Lynn. No, I would wing it. If I could interrogate criminals, I could learn a date's name without blowing my cover. His name was tomorrow's crisis.

Back to reality. I looked back at the image of St. Gregory. He had committed grizzly crimes in the past, including a string of bombings. Had he acted alone? I thought terrorists usually worked in teams, like the 9/11 terrorists. Who was on St. Gregory's team? Could St. Gregory and Ivan the Terrible be working together? Freak, I hoped not. Or with Vickers? Ugh. How could we stop them if they were working as a team?

My phone buzzed again. Lynn was calling. Hallelujah. "Donna, did I catch you at a bad time?" Lynn's voice was bright and bubbly, and I knew she was smiling.

"No, perfect timing. What's going on?"

"I was working late and wanted to tell you I got a deposition set for tomorrow."

"Deposition?" My thoughts were a million miles away, still wondering about my blind date's name.

"Donna, you know, the guy that you kicked . . ."

"I didn't kick him. He slipped on my latte and fell. And I'm glad."

"Well, he's suing you for excessive force. Remember?"

"How could I forget Mister Toupee?" Ugh. And just like that, my world went to crap.

I called Ben, who always worked late. I don't think he ever sleeps. He might be a robot. "Sick of searching facial recognition for our suspects?" I asked.

He groaned. "Don't remind me. I see these faces in my nightmares."

"I didn't think you ever slept."

"I don't. It's a figure of speech."

"I need help with a computer search."

"No problem. What do you need? Investigate a boyfriend?"

"Wait. You do that? Another issue for another day, my friend." Another day, indeed. I explained what I needed. "Enemies of Second United Bank. Then cross-search for any ties to Phillip St. Gregory. On second thought, you better also search for Vickers and Raymond Soames too."

"Do you think these suspects might be working together?" Ben asked.

"I just don't know. Listen, if we can figure out this tie to the bank, we might be able to predict his next move. Maybe this is silly, but it's the only thing we can do besides wait for this next attack. Where should we look for enemies of a bank? Facebook?" I was out of my element.

"Chat rooms on the dark web might discuss unflattering views of the bank."

Dark web? I was lost.

"How soon you need this?" he asked.

"Yesterday would be fine." I liked this secretive stuff. I was Agent 007 and Ben was my Q. He owed me a car with machine gun headlights and a ray gun. I would settle for boyfriend screenings. I filed that detail away for later. "How could St. Gregory know where I was last night?"

"Too easy," Ben said. "If he hacked your phone, he could

track you with GPS. Did you change your phone's password after you bought it?"

"My phone has a password? I use that face thing."

"Bring it by and I can fix it."

"This guy knows everything in advance. He must have help from the inside. Any ideas, Ben?"

"The insider could be anyone, someone right in front of you and you wouldn't know it."

"The Messenger mentioned a 'she.' Any ideas who 'she' might be?"

"You know women hold up half the sky. Fifty percent of the people on earth are a 'she.' Sorry, St. Gregory has no family. Could be a friend, significant other, no clue."

My mind went in a thousand directions. In St. Gregory's his mind, a female was involved. But who was she? Did she really exist?

I saw Elaine stir. "Ben, I have to go. Let me know if you find out anything." I hurried back inside the room. "Has Robin woken up yet?" I asked.

Gloria shook her head. "Not yet."

"But we're hopeful," Elaine said, stretching and yawning. "He has not gotten any worse. The doctors said that was an encouraging sign." Her voice broke. I held her, wishing I could fix this somehow, but even the doctors had no suggestions.

"Gloria, you can go," I said. "I'm going to stay tonight, and I know you need a break."

"I can do this," Elaine objected. "I'm fine alone."

"No," I replied. "We're family and we're in this together."

"I'll take you up on that. I got a hot date tonight," Gloria said.

"Tonight?" I checked my watch. "Kind of late."

Gloria smiled. "The really good clubs don't get going until midnight."

I just didn't have the endurance to be single anymore. A hot date? Freak. I tried hard not to be jealous, but I was.

Gloria went into the bathroom and stared into the mirror. "Do I have time to change clothes and curl my hair?"

Seriously? She looked like a runway model already. Envy was my downfall.

A mother always worried about her babies. Even with the concerns about Robin, Elaine fretted about hers. I reassured Elaine the kids were fine and being spoiled with all the attention from the family. That gave her a little peace. She drifted off back to sleep a brief time later. Elaine had a well-stocked hospital room, complete with several magazines and two novels, a new thriller by Harlan Coben and a romance by Nora Roberts. I wasn't in the right mood for a novel.

I reviewed the timeline from the police records, determined to figure out how The Messenger was always a step ahead. Someone had to be helping him, someone with inside information. But who? I finally had a short nap in the chair.

Robin's doctor came into the room before six in the morning. He checked the charts and monitors. Elaine didn't stir. I took this opportunity to ask questions without her hearing.

"How is Robin?" I asked. "I'm his sister, Donna."

"No changes," Dr. Pike said.

"When will he regain consciousness?"

"Hopefully soon."

"When will you stop the induced coma stuff?" That didn't sound terribly intelligent, but I didn't know the fancy medical terms.

Dr. Pike said, "He's no longer in a medically induced coma."

That revelation shocked me. My heart stopped. "So, what's wrong? When can he wake up?"

"He should have already. He's in a vegetative state, with no sign of improvement."

My head spun. Vegetative state? That sounded hopeless. This was too much to absorb. "Is this normal?"

"No. He should be showing some signs of recovery."

"What's next?"

"We'll remove the life support and see if he can breathe on his own."

"And if not?"

Dr. Pike stared at me without comment. I understood too quickly. *Freak.* The temperature in the room dropped thirty degrees. My eyes filled with tears, but I didn't want to wake Elaine. "Does his wife know?" I asked.

"No. I will tell her later this morning, unless you want to tell her."

Freak. Don't put this on me. "I think you should tell her. She'll have plenty of questions. I know I would."

CHAPTER TWENTY-THREE

Thursday 8:01 a.m.

IN THE MORNING, I limped to Raymond Soames' hospital room. I needed to interrogate him, but the sign on his room said, "No Visitors." Maybe I should pretend to be a nurse. Instead, I did the honest thing. I stood in his room and waited for him to stir.

"I'm Detective Wyznecki with the Las Vegas Police." He nodded. "Were you at Second United during the bombing? Can you describe what you saw before the explosion?"

"I already told this to the other officers . . ."

I smiled. "I know. We are reinterviewing everyone. Any little detail could help."

Raymond told me about coming to the bank, a typical day. Nothing was unusual until the explosion. He didn't really convey any details.

"Why were you at the bank?"

"I was just going to see my girlfriend, Audra . . . Audra Barclay. Do you know if she is alright?"

"I will check. Is your relationship serious?"

"Yes, I plan to propose soon." He grinned ear to ear. He really seemed sincere.

"Do you remember anyone in particular before the blast occurred?"

Raymond described Shale's wife number five and Penny.

"Did you see anyone put an item in a trash can in the lobby?"

He shook his head. I showed him a photo of Oliver. "Does this man look familiar?"

"Sorry."

"Do you work at the bank?" I already knew the answer, but I wanted to see if he would be honest with me.

"I used to. I was an auditor." He didn't expand any further.

"What made you leave the bank?"

He sighed. "Problem with management. Personality clash."

That sounded sufficiently vague. "So where are you working now?"

"Valley-Ho Limos."

"Doing their accounting?"

"No. I'm a driver."

Bank auditor to limo driver seemed like a step down, but I kept my thoughts to myself.

"Did you have any problems in the past with Audra?"

"I think our relationship is perfect."

"Didn't she file a protective order against you?"

"That was a misunderstanding. It's in the past." He dismissed it too easily.

"Didn't Audra file three protective orders against you?"

"Those were . . . mistakes. We are in a relationship. We are in love."

"Did you have any problems with the bank?"

"No. I told you already. A personality clash."

"Are you angry with the bank for being fired?"

"What? Are you accusing me of something? Am I a . . . a suspect?"

I was struck by his strong resemblance to his brother, the jerk that shouldered me in the precinct hallway. I looked to my left and saw the brother two feet away. He had snuck up on me while I was talking to Raymond.

The jerk spoke. "Are you interrogating my brother?"

"I wouldn't say interrogating. Just asking a few questions between friends. It's lonely here in the hospital." I smiled, but the brother scowled.

He moved closer, into my personal space until our noses almost touched. "You stay away from my brother. You can leave now."

"I have just a few more questions."

"No. You are done. Get out of my brother's room." With that, he gave me a little shove, which made me fall back against the hospital bed.

"You like hurting women. Is that a character trait that runs in your family?"

I could see the vein in his forehead throb. "Get out of here before I do something rash."

This guy would hit me. I could sense it. I turned to Raymond. "I'll visit you later, sir." When I turned back to his pushy brother, I smiled and pointed to his mouth. "You should drop a mint into that dumpster."

I left the room, never taking my eyes off the jerk.

Audra was right. Raymond was clingy and obsessed with her, but he was harmless. Raymond's brother was something else. He had a short temper and a poor view of women.

CHAPTER TWENTY-FOUR

Thursday 9:15 a.m.

ROBIN WASN'T the only Wyznecki with medical issues—I had an appointment to be checked by a doctor. Having someone look at my embarrassing rump injury was a crappy way to start my day. To compensate I had two packages of Hostess cupcakes with my extra-large mocha cappuccino. I blared "More Than a Woman" by the Bee Gees to drown out my off-key singing. At the stoplight, the driver next to me, a nice-looking man, glanced my way. Then I realized he was staring at the window sticker for Robin's new car. He gave an approving nod. Oh, well.

The healthcare bureaucracy gave me a headache. I had the city's insurance which meant a different teenage doctor on every visit. They needed to check my stitches and make sure they weren't getting infected. Today's doctor, Dr. Ross or Cross or Toss or something, seemed nice. I didn't pay attention since the next visit the doctor would be someone less experienced. I took off my slacks. He had me stand while he examined my sore rump. Every touch made me flinch.

"Wow," he said. "How did this happen?"

"The explosion at Second United."

"Yeah, that was terrible. People still in the hospital. Water line or something, right?"

"Right." I forgot that Charlie had created the utility company story, and the public assumed it was true. I wasn't interested in small talk. Every time I recalled the explosion, I envisioned Robin still in a coma.

I stood as he examined my tender backside. "No signs of infection. That's good. A little while longer before we can remove the stitches. Taking your antibiotics?"

I nodded.

"Got enough pain medicine?"

"I don't need any."

"You sure? You know, a beautiful young woman like you might want to take a chemical holiday." He caressed my non-injured butt cheek. What was going on here? "I can get you a six-month supply of oxy, Vicodin, anything you want."

Didn't he know I was a detective? He must not. He massaged my rump. *Freak.* What was happening? Had this guy had a stroke? Had I? "What do you mean?" I asked.

He locked the door. "I find you extremely attractive. Maybe we could have some fun?" He approached me, his face inches from my own. The bulge in his pants communicated loud and clear what he had in mind.

"Intimate fun?" I asked.

"Exactly. You get a large script for oxy, and we both have fun. We both win. Get it?" He loosened his belt and his trousers fell to the floor.

I smiled and gently, over his tighty-whities, cupped his testicles. He sighed with pleasure. Then I squeezed with all my might. I had a surprisingly good grip, and I used all my force. His eyes bulged. His face reddened and his whole body went rigid, like he had been electrocuted. I squeezed even harder and saw tears leak from the corners of his eyes.

"Stop," he mouthed, sweating.

"You want me to stop?" I asked.

"Stop. Please. Stop." His face darkened.

"All right," I said, keeping my grip. "But first we have to agree on something."

"Anything," he whispered.

"Don't try this piggish behavior on any other female, ever. Do you hear me?" He nodded. "I'm serious. If I ever hear you did this to another woman—"

"Never, never," he whispered, and I released my grip. He took in great big breaths. Color returned to his face.

"Oh, I forgot one thing." He recoiled but didn't speak. "Am I ready to return to active duty?" I tossed him the folded form I had in my pants pocket. Sweat rolled down his face. He nodded. "Say it out loud, please."

"Yes, you're cleared for active duty." His voice was an octave higher than when my exam began. He scribbled his signature on the form and handed it back.

"Damn right, I am." I tossed him my cuffs. "Put those on."

"Why?" He blinked in surprise. "Just some harmless flirting—"

I glared at him and simulated squeezing his *brains*. His eyes widened as he snapped the handcuffs into place. My first arrest as a detective. Jerk.

CHAPTER TWENTY-FIVE

Thursday 10:06 a.m.

ON THE DRIVE back to the precinct, my arrestee became quite talkative. "I'm a respected member of the medical community—"

"I doubt that."

"This could be a career mistake," Doctor Loss or Hoss or whatever said.

Really? He had the nerve to threaten my job? I stomped on the brake and his head hit the back of my seat. "Sorry," I said. "I'm still learning how to use the stick shift." That kept him quiet for a while. "I've got to run a quick errand."

"Welcome to Sonic. Can I take your order?"

"What?" Doctor Grabby Hands said. "You're stopping for food?"

"I'm hungry." It was too early for popcorn chicken, so I ordered a small snack to keep me going: a bacon breakfast toaster, a sausage breakfast burrito, and a giant coffee.

"You didn't get me anything?" The doctor complained as I drove to the window.

"You want some cheese with that whine?" I replied. He started again with his tirade about being respected and how my career would suffer, blah, blah, blah.

I picked up my food, and Doctor Happy Hands spoke to the attendant. "Can you believe she won't get me anything?"

The attendant, Suzy, looked at me. I held up my badge. "Taking him to jail."

Suzy shook her head. "He still should get food. This is America." She reached for a bacon, egg, and cheese breakfast burrito for the doctor. "What did he do?"

"Sexual battery of a police officer."

Suzy paused, holding the warm, tasty burrito in midair, then took it back. "Not how you should treat women, jerk."

Doctor Grab Ass attempted to defend himself. "You don't know—"

"Hey," I interrupted. "You have the right to remain silent, so shut up." I threatened him with "the grip" again and he quieted down. I finished my snack as I drove him to jail.

I dropped Doctor Handsy at jail intake. I winked at the supervisor and whispered, "Just put him in a cell for a while then release him." I didn't have time to waste on this low life. I think I scared him enough to put an end to his antics. Charging him would take time—time I needed to find St. Gregory and get justice for Robin.

CHAPTER TWENTY-SIX

Thursday 11:45 a.m.

I MET Lynn in the precinct lot to carpool to today's big event. We exchanged compliments as we always did, but I felt invisible next to her. Her lips were glossy and flawless. Her skin seemed to glow.

Could today get worse? It could. Just add sleazy, ambulance-chasing lawyers. Check.

"Why are we doing this now?" I asked.

Lynn looked at me. "I like to do depositions before the other side is ready, catch them unprepared. Besides, the captain insisted I take you away from the precinct."

We stopped, awe-struck at the immense building in front of us. I really didn't need this today.

Lynn sighed. "Another day, another snake pit."

"This is quite a snake pit," I said. "Impressive." The snake pit in question was a three-story, southern-style mansion the size of a hotel. Lynn and I entered the law firm's lobby. It didn't have typical scenic paintings. Instead, it was decorated with framed newspaper clippings of legal victories, success always measured by dollar amount. Everything looked new and overpriced.

Raymond's aggressive brother, Officer Soames, stood at the reception desk. The sight of him made me tense every muscle. I wasn't going to be shoved again by him.

He turned and scanned Lynn head to toe, like a lion eyeing a gazelle. "So wonderful to see you, Lynn. I was just here delivering subpoenas."

That was scut work. He must be facing discipline for one of his many bad decisions.

"Looking very sexy today, Lynn." He smiled like a devil. "I think you've earned a date with me. Should we skip dinner and go right to a hotel?"

Lynn was not impressed. "Hard pass. You're a predator."

Rebuffed, his expression changed. "Nice to see you, counselor."

He stood beside me. If he shoved me again, I was going to kick him somewhere quite intimate.

Looking to me, he said, "Later, dwarf."

I was disappointed we didn't have a physical exchange. I was ready this time. I looked at Lynn. "How do you know him?"

"He's had so many harassment complaints that he has his own file cabinet at my office. He's also asked me out like thirty times. He doesn't seem to take the hint. He's a knuckle dragger."

The receptionist held a flute of champagne. "We're celebrating an eight-figure settlement today." I was reaching for a crystal stem when Lynn declined for both of us. Probably for the best. Champagne was my kryptonite. I did the math in my head. An eight-figure case was over ten million dollars. I didn't want to change my profession, but I wondered about the social justice of the pay differential. Maybe I was a little jealous. Okay, a lot jealous. It is a trend of mine.

After two minutes we were ushered into an over-the-top conference room, designed by someone with an unlimited budget. The immense table could seat two dozen personal injury lawyers or two dozen people, whichever was appropriate.

The battle lines had been drawn. The enemies, Mister Toupee's legal team, were seated on the other side, a lot of lawyers for a deposition. They glared at us like we were a mutt that crapped on their manicured lawn. Silent disdain.

A man stood to greet us. I recognized him from the framed photos in the lobby, the leader of this litigating cabal. Why were ambulance chasers always men? He wore an expensive double-breasted suit with a custom shirt, a shiny silk tie, and a flashy pocket square. He passed out his business cards, a personal injury lawyer's instinct. Why would I want one? It looked expensive, embossed letters on fancy card stock. He had a name, but I would think of him as "Ambulance Chaser" until the end of time. I envisioned his television commercial: *Were your kids born ugly? It's someone else's fault. Call me at 1-800-SuperDuperLawyer!*

Toupee Man sat between four of Ambulance Chaser's robot-like assistants. The three men and one woman wore matching blue suits and matching blank expressions. Four helpers? Ever heard of freaking overkill? Toupee Man wore a neck brace. A neck brace? Was he blind too? Did he have a red and white cane? My mouth might get me into more trouble. This would be a long day. I hoped Lynn had some Tylenol.

Lynn and Ambulance Chaser greeted each other, polite, but not welcoming. She introduced herself to the four assistants. The men were immune to Lynn's charms. Maybe they were robots? "Are we ready to begin?" she asked.

"Mr. Higgins will need to rest and take some medication later."

Please. Lynn tapped me on the leg to make sure I said nothing loud and tacky, which was my normal behavior. I straightened my shoulders as the reporter administered the oath. Ambulance Chaser shuffled his notes into a single pile.

"What is your full name and occupation?"

"Donna Summer Wyznecki." He raised an eyebrow. "You know, after the disco diva?" Lynn and I broke into the chorus of "Bad Girls." The snake rolled his eyes and his female assistant smirked.

"I'm a detective with the Las Vegas Police Department."

"Miss Wyznecki, do you recall the events of March fifth at Second United bank?"

I nodded.

"You have to answer out loud," Lynn chided me.

"Yes, and I didn't trip him."

The ambulance chaser smiled. "Thank you. Were you on duty?"

"No." Lynn tapped me several times on the leg. "I mean yes."

"Which is it?"

"I was there for personal and professional reasons."

"Please explain your reasons for bludgeoning my client."

I couldn't hold back. "Bludgeoning? Are you serious?" Lynn's hand rapped my leg.

"Can we do without the theatrics, Counselor?" Lynn asked.

"Fine." Ambulance Chaser adjusted his tie. "Did you touch my client?"

"No. *He* pushed *me*."

"I see. How did my client end up on the floor?"

"He slipped." Lynn constantly tapped my leg.

"Are you claiming you didn't push him back?"

"I wanted to, but I didn't. I'm a professional."

"I see. You wanted to push him."

"Yes." Lynn's expression told me I shouldn't have mentioned that.

"So how did my client slip and fall?"

"He pushed me, and I dropped my coffee."

"Coffee?"

"It was a caramel mocha latte." It sounded silly when it left my lips. The female assistant giggled. "And I ripped my slacks." I didn't mention those were my favorite black slacks. I doubted if they cared.

"Where did your pants rip? The hem?"

"Object to the relevance," Lynn stated.

Ambulance chaser was trying to embarrass me. Too late. "The seat." I offered.

"Didn't you rip your slacks when you kicked my client?"

"No, I didn't kick him. He slipped."

"And you never touched him?"

"No. He shoved me."

"But my client's the one who ended up injured on the floor."

"You know what they say about karma." I smiled.

"I see." Ambulance Chaser moved to a new page of notes. "What police training did you receive in hand-to-hand combat?"

I let Lynn answer this question. "We will stipulate that Detective Wyznecki had the standard police academy training." Lynn gave me a stern look, silently urging me to allow her to answer more questions.

"That is acceptable for now," Ambulance Chaser replied. He placed his notes into a folder, and a wave of relief passed over me. "One more thing . . ." He looked at me eye to eye. "Do you have any martial arts training?"

"I took a few lessons." I didn't like where this was going.

"A few lessons? Don't be so modest." A male assistant handed him a printout. "Didn't you have *seven years* of Tae Kwon Do lessons?"

Crap. Lynn looked surprised. We had never discussed this before. "Yes, but it was mostly social."

"Social?" Ambulance Chaser asked. "Didn't you achieve the rank of black belt in Tae Kwon Do? Excuse me, third-degree black belt?"

"Okay, yes, I am a third-degree black belt." How did he know so much about me?

"That doesn't sound very social, Detective." He was trying to provoke me, and doing an excellent job of it, but I couldn't think of anything else to say. "One other matter we should get out of the way while we're being candid." Ambulance Chaser stared at me intensely. "How many times have you been subjected to police discipline?"

I knew not to answer that one. Lynn spoke up. "We object to those questions. Violations of police protocols or record keeping are not relevant to this matter."

Ambulance Chaser nodded. "We quite agree, Counselor. Let's ignore any discipline over timecards or uniform irregularities. How many times were you subject to discipline for physical harm to a member of the public?"

Lynn nodded. I mentally counted. Dealing with crazy stupid people led me into bad behaviors. I scratched down several names on my note paper. Five times? Maybe. No, six. I remembered six times. I didn't want to answer aloud until I was sure.

"Detective Wyznecki, would you agree that the number is

seven?" Ambulance Chaser listed the seven names. I had forgotten one.

I nodded. "That sounds correct."

Lynn interjected, "Again, we object to this line of questioning as irrelevant to the incident in this case."

"Noted, Counselor. Lastly, Officer Wyznecki, did you have a physical altercation with three other suspects that you apprehended?" He rattled off three more familiar names.

Lynn tapped my leg again vigorously.

"Yes, but none of those resulted in discipline."

"So, you have incidents involving violent behavior that are not reflected in your disciplinary file?"

"Don't answer that," Lynn said.

"I guess we don't need an answer." Ambulance Chaser smiled.

How did they know about those? He must have someone on the inside helping them out, searching unofficial police records, someone with computer access. Who? Soames's brother? He was just here, but did he have computer access? The opposition's team stood in unison for dramatic effect. That must have been rehearsed.

I was freaking mad. He accused me of trying to hurt this creep. Super pissed. Now I was thinking of kicking Toupee Man and that damn Ambulance Chaser.

"We'll take a brief break before Mr. Higgins's deposition." Ambulance Chaser gestured to a side room. "Please enjoy some French pressed coffee, juices, bottled water, and treats from Saint Honoré."

Saint Honoré? Freak, yes. Their beignets were a work of art. I hoped this thing would go into overtime, whatever that was for depositions. The caterer described each sweet treat and placed them on a crystal plate with silver tongs. She also described their signature flatbread pizzas, but I had a craving for sweets. I snagged a Candied Hazelnut and Nutella and a Maple with Pearls. Being an ambulance chaser must pay well. They could depose me any time.

The opposition gathered in another room, probably to worship the devil or something. I floated the idea of letting me remain in the room with the caterer. An hour, maybe two, trapped in a room with Saint Honoré sweets? I was in heaven. Lynn was not swayed. She wanted me to monitor Toupee Man's answers. I had just enough time for a Powdered Raspberry. Lucky me.

Their coffee was magnificent. I filled my cup to the rim and grabbed a beignet for nourishment during Toupee Man's deposition. Lord, help me not say anything tacky.

Lynn had a call to make, so I phoned Charlie.

"Donna, aren't you in court?"

"Deposition, and we're on break. Can you check out Officer Soames? Any history of excessive force complaints?"

"I don't have to check. He's had complaints since his first week on the force. He's been sidelined for about a month now, on subpoenas and admin duties."

That meant Soames had computer access.

Lynn was still on the phone, so I took the time to approach our donut concierge. I asked her for a box to go and tried to slip her a twenty-dollar bill. She refused to take my money. "Please, it will be my pleasure. I enjoy seeing people loving my sweet creations." She smiled and lowered her voice. "Besides, I'm already double billing this law firm."

CHAPTER TWENTY-SEVEN

Thursday 12:58 p.m.

DURING THE BREAK, the legal robotoids had clearly adjusted Higgins's toupee, and now the part in his hair was on the other side of his head. Was I the only one who noticed this? Freaky. Two assistants made an elaborate production of rolling Toupee Man's wheelchair to the head of the table, a little over the top. If he had a service dog, I would scream. He didn't. They adjusted the microphone and camera to capture Mr. Higgins's well-rehearsed testimony. I wondered if he could cry on command.

"What is your name?" Lynn asked.

"Alexander F. Higgins."

Lynn had been clear. I wasn't to speak, not a single word unless the building was on fire. When I thought I was about to lose it, I should stare at his toupee. That should keep me out of trouble. Lynn continued to ask Toupee Man basic questions, like his age, address, and job. Mister Toupee's lawsuit claimed lost wages, but those had to be verified.

Ambulance Chaser slid a folder to Lynn, who opened it where I could view it. "These are Mr. Higgins's current pay records."

I stared at a plain paycheck stub. It showed Mr. Higgins was on track to make $54,000 this year. Not bad. I made more at LVPD, but I actually worked.

"Fifty-four thousand dollars per annum," Lynn stated.

"Doing what?" I asked.

"Objection," Ambulance Chaser stated. "She can't ask questions. She's a witness."

Lynn tapped me on the leg for the hundredth time today. "I will ask. Doing what, Mr. Higgins?"

Ambulance Chaser spoke up. "I'll address that. Mr. Higgins's professional services are unique and proprietary."

"So, what does he do?" Lynn repeated.

"For this lawsuit it's sufficient that he has wages that are verified and that he's not able to work as a result of your client's egregious attack."

I looked at the paystub again and pointed out a key detail to Lynn. Her smile faded. "This business has the same address as your law firm. Do you work for this law firm?"

Ambulance Chaser shook his head. "My client works for an independent company located in this building. That business has offices upstairs, but the company is completely an independent legal entity."

Lynn's face burned bright red, and her lips pressed together so hard I thought they might burst. She was as angry as I had ever seen her, but she held it together. "This job sounds like a sham, Counselor."

"I resent that comment. Do you want to continue with this deposition or not?"

"Tell us about your health, Mr. Higgins," Lynn said.

"Prior to this tragic event?"

Tragic event? Freak. Did they have a drama writer on staff?

"Yes, before the incident at the bank," Lynn said with a smile.

"Perfect. I was in perfect health."

"Perfect? Perfect health? Really?" Lynn pressed him.

"Yes, perfect. Couldn't be better. Maybe could stand to lose a few pounds, but otherwise as healthy as I was in my twenties."

"Did you have any other injuries in the two years preceding the bank incident?"

"No. Nothing. Perfect health, until your client kicked me."

"I thought you were tripped?" Lynn retorted.

"No. Your client kicked my leg out from under me."

"I see."

"She kicked me and now I'm confined to this wheelchair."

I struggled to keep silent. Lynn was practically breaking my thigh with her tapping.

"Mr. Higgins, have you ever given a deposition before?"

Ambulance Chaser spoke up. "Object to that question. Mr. Higgins has given depositions before and is aware that this testimony is given under oath just as though he was a witness at trial."

"So, Mr. Higgins, you're aware that your testimony is under oath?"

"I am telling the truth."

The fish had a hook in his mouth. It was time to reel him in.

"Mr. Higgins, were you involved in any lawsuits in the two years prior to this incident?"

Ambulance Chaser sneered at Lynn. "Mr. Higgins's other legal matters, if any, are not relevant to the substantial injuries caused by your client."

"Good," Lynn said. "Have your client answer the question so we can move on."

Toupee Man stared at Lynn. "None."

"No lawsuits in the two years preceding the bank incident?" Lynn repeated.

"No lawsuits in the two years preceding the bank incident," Toupee Man confirmed.

"Absolutely sure?" Lynn asked.

"Absolutely sure," Toupee Man parroted.

Boom. Mister Toupee had struck out, but Ambulance Chaser didn't know it yet. Lynn reached into her Coach messenger bag and removed a file folder about an inch thick. I could feel the tension in Toupee Man and Ambulance Chaser rise, and I loved every second of it. Lynn passed three pages to Mister Toupee and his legal counsel. "The record should reflect that I am handing Mr. Higgins and his counsel a copy of what I have marked as 'Exhibit A,' a list of Mr. Higgins's lawsuits in the previous two years. Mr. Higgins, can you confirm this list as accurate?"

Ambulance Chaser's face grew red. "I've never seen this list before. None of this is relevant to the violent attack by your client."

Lynn smiled. "Mr. Higgins, this list indicates you have filed three personal injury lawsuits in California within the past two years. One indicates you were injured in a car wreck in Thousand Oaks, the second alleges you were injured as a pedestrian walking in Beverly Hills, and the third alleges you were injured at the Newport city library parking lot. Are these correct?"

Toupee Man and his legal counsel whispered in a heated exchange. Toupee Man's expression soured. Ambulance Chaser took the helm. "My client will have to review the details of these cases before making any statements on the record."

Lynn smiled. "Perfectly acceptable. Are you sure my client kicked you?" Lynn paused for dramatic effect. "We'll come back to that. We can schedule a continuation of this deposition for further questions on the California lawsuits." She reached in her bag and distributed some more papers. "Exhibit B lists two personal injury cases in Arizona from the last two years with you listed as plaintiff. In the first case, you were allegedly struck by a car as a pedestrian again, this time in Scottsdale. In the second case, you sued a driver for an auto accident occurring in Tempe. Are these correct, Mr. Higgins?"

Ambulance Chaser's smile was gone. "Again, my client will have to review the details of these cases before making any statements on the record."

"Are you sure Detective Wyznecki kicked you?"

Toupee Man grimaced.

Lynn smiled and turned her attention to the Ambulance Chaser. "Should we schedule the continuation of this deposition?" She was so confident but remained cool.

Ambulance Chaser regained his composure without his typical arrogance. "It might take a while to review all these matters."

Lynn stood. "We'll wait. Perhaps you could point us to the ladies' room."

I followed Lynn out of the conference room. I wanted to scream, "Suck it, Toupee Man! You just got your ass handed to you," but I remained silent until we got to the ladies' room.

Lynn hugged me. "I don't think we'll be hearing from Mr. Higgins or his lawyer. We have a word for him."

"Just one word?" I could think of several.

"Mr. Higgins is *vexatious*."

"A what?" I asked. Lynn liked to use Latin, to make herself sound intelligent, which it did, and to confuse me, which it also did.

"He constantly sues people, businesses, whoever, as his primary source of income. People do have accidents, but no one on earth has bad luck like Mr. Higgins. It's a scam." Lynn explained that Mister Toupee wouldn't confess he made up the story. That only happened on *Perry Mason*, *Law & Order*, or maybe *Matlock*. Let Mister Toupee spin his lies and get caught in his own web. "Higgins's credibility is trash. His pain and suffering, just bad acting. The wheelchair, just drama. He'll ditch it before he leaves this office."

"Do his lawyers know?"

"Of course they know. Only the sleaziest lawyers would touch him as a client."

I had an idea. *Play piñata*. Tie Higgins to a tree and hit him with a stick until candy came out. Lynn smiled at my suggestion. We returned to the conference room, where several animated discussions were taking place. We must have unsettled the legal eagles. Maybe Higgins's toupee was spinning on its own.

"Are we ready to continue?" Lynn asked.

"Perhaps," Ambulance Chaser stated, "we should focus our attention on the explosion."

Lynn looked perturbed. "That incident is not relevant to this lawsuit."

"Not that explosion."

Lynn's eyes narrowed. "Then what?"

"The explosion today."

Ambulance Chaser gestured to a large flat screen that showed Breaking News on Channel 3-KSNV where a grave-looking announcer said, "We have preliminary reports that another bomb has gone off in Las Vegas . . ."

CHAPTER TWENTY-EIGHT

Thursday 2:19 p.m.

I FELT like all the air had been sucked out of the room. I turned on my phone. I hadn't wanted it going off during the deposition. I'd missed eight calls and twenty-five text messages, including a Priority One Alert from the precinct. A Priority One Alert indicated all officers should report for duty immediately. We have had only two before, on 9/11 and the 2017 mass shooting at the country music festival. Today was the third.

Lynn and I darted from the snake pit to the precinct. The direct path took us across the Strip. On both sides of the Strip, locals were in the street and concerned. In contrast, tourists on The Strip strolled by, oblivious to the rest of the world.

Back at the fishbowl, I bumped into my least favorite officer.

"What are you doing here, Detective?" Officer Soames scowled at me. "Shouldn't you be checking some parking meters?"

"Shouldn't you be eating a Tide pod?" I replied.

Captain Creek interrupted. "Let's work the problem, people."

Everyone moved with fevered intensity. The event we dreaded had happened, before we were prepared, but could anyone have been ready for this? The fishbowl's walls flashed as all the TV stations focused on the same story. Breaking news interrupted every program.

Media reports varied. Some knew what had happened, some knew nothing, some were just frightened, but all got their fifteen seconds of fame. Officers near the scene reported by cell phone. Each fact was jotted on whiteboards around the room. Phone lines lit up. Sandy and I, along with two other officers, scribbled notes feverishly. Dozens of voices overlapped with television audio, like the stock market scene from *Trading Places*, except here we dealt with bombing details, not frozen, concentrated orange juice.

Multiple views came from downtown, one showing flames, one just with black smoke, and another with crowds running away. My heart sank. After twenty minutes of panic, things settled down. Our whiteboards were covered with notes, many duplications and many that couldn't be true. The local stations had video of a car, or the remains of one, burning on Main Street in front of the bus station. We viewed the ruins from several perspectives. Two other cars were destroyed. The fire department struggled to put out the smoldering remnants. Emergency workers treated multiple people on the sidewalks, while ambulance lights flashed red and blue.

Reporters dealt with verified facts, as limited as they were. One car had exploded. Witnesses believed one person was inside the car, dead. Who was the driver? Was the driver The Messenger? Was he St. Gregory? Was the driver the target? Was the driver a he? We had grainy traffic cam video showing the car. Only one person was visible in the car, but someone could have crouched in the back seat, or in the trunk. We couldn't get a good view of the driver. He was a white man but we couldn't tell much more than that.

Was the bus station the target? Maybe this was unrelated to the bank. Maybe the car was a mobile meth lab. Those things catch fire and explode all the time. The car was also near the Fremont Street Experience, the tourist mecca, always crowded. Was Fremont the intended target? We had lots of questions but no answers.

Shale tapped his chin. "What do the bank, Oliver's home, and the bus station have in common?" Officers, anxious for Shale's attention, threw out ideas, none of which gained his approval.

Captain Creek broke the silence. "Are you assuming the bus station was the target?"

"Do you have a better target in mind?" Shale asked.

Sandy nodded. "The target could have been the Fremont Experience."

The captain exhaled his smokey breath. "Maybe the driver was the target."

"Was this bombing by another person?" I asked. "A copycat?"

Captain Creek tapped my arm. "Donna, go downtown and tell me what you see."

I retrieved my personal gun from the storage cabinet. I might be uninvited and unpaid, but I was not going to be unarmed. I detoured to the coffee desk, beautifully restocked with jelly doughnuts and full carafes. I poured myself a to-go cup with a lid, always with a lid, and put two jelly doughnuts on a paper plate. I had moved two steps when my paper plate gave way and my heavenly jelly doughnuts stuck face down on the floor. *If that doesn't describe my life . . .*

John-Boy walked by, and I attracted his attention. I always did. "By any chance, did Soames apply to the bomb squad?"

"Soames?" John-Boy moved closer to whisper. "Repeatedly, but he always washed out. Never could pass the psychiatric screening. Too impatient. That with explosives training is a bad combination. You didn't hear that from me."

I winked. "Hear what?"

John-Boy touched my waist in a familiar move.

"Whoa, cowboy. That wasn't an invitation."

On my way out, I spotted a white pastry box on the front desk. A crown logo signified Saint Honoré. My stomach did the happy dance.

Helen looked up from her tarot cards. "Hey girl, someone dropped off this box for you. Smells heavenly."

I flipped open the lid and grabbed a Strawberry Sprinkled. Helen looked at me with sad, puppy dog eyes. "Okay, you can have one." She grabbed a Cocoa Nib. "Guard this box with your life. I'll be back to claim it later."

CHAPTER TWENTY-NINE

Thursday 3:38 p.m.

ARCHIE, the bomb tech, rode with me. He was overly impressed with Robin's new car, peppering me with questions about special racing features, none of which I could answer. Finally, I said, "It's my brother's car."

Archie raised his eyes. "And he's letting you drive it? It still has the price sticker. Wow, you are lucky."

I didn't feel lucky. My rump was tender, and my brother was in a coma.

Archie was John-Boy's best friend in the force. They talked about nerdy techno-science stuff, and I understood only every third word. Archie was a silver-haired African American man who always wore too much Old Spice cologne. Way too much. I had to roll down the window so I wouldn't gag. Seriously, did he buy that stuff by the gallon?

I flipped on the car radio. Every local radio station talked nonstop about the explosion downtown. Most reports had no facts but repeated every conceivable rumor. A few things were certain. A car had exploded in front of the Las Vegas bus station, near the well-attended Fremont Experience. The driver of the car was killed. Anything else was speculation.

Scared tourists didn't spend money. Shale's office would go ballistic. Radio reports of the bombing were reminiscent of 9/11. Traffic was at a dead stop. Unsure of where to go next, some drivers simply stopped on the road. We finally made it to the scene.

While the bus station and the Fremont Experience were geographically close, culturally they were a million miles apart. The Fremont Experience catered to carefree tourists with pockets full of disposable income. The bus station attracted only Vegas locals down on their luck. Bob Dylan should describe the irony of two places so different being so near, like the White House next to a homeless shelter.

Archie asked me to drop him off near the explosion site. He wanted to see it before time and too many hands contaminated what remained. He said he would get a ride back.

The burnt car was an empty shell. "Someone is not getting back their security deposit," I said. My cell phone rang, and I answered it without checking caller ID. Big mistake.

"Baby, baby, oh my baby. Please, please, please tell me you're safe." Mother's desperation zapped me.

"Mom, I'm safe. I wasn't anywhere near the explosion." A bigtime lie. "Everything is fine." She didn't seem to hear me because she repeated herself several times before pausing. "Mom, I'm fine. I'm okay, safe at the police station." I lied to my mother, but it wasn't the first time.

"You should come home, so I can keep you safe . . ."

"Mom, I'm safe."

"I'm worried about my baby."

"Sorry, Mom, I have to go. I'll be safe."

I pulled up to a casino valet and wobbled over to Pizza

Rock Pizza Kitchen. My stomach guided me, lured by the aroma of the hot crust and gooey cheese merged with the pepperoni. I ordered a slice of New Yorker with extra pepperoni. I loved this pizza, even if it wasn't on my diet, or anyone's diet really. Okay, I got three slices, but I needed to recover from my wounds, and the many healing powers of pepperoni could only help. Hospitals should recommend Pizza Rock instead of pain medicine. No kidding.

Savoring each bite, I walked toward the crime scene. I directed several potential customers toward Pizza Rock. I should get a commission. If this detective job doesn't work out, I have a fallback profession. At Carson and Main Street, I finished the first slice. Complete chaos. About a hundred gawking tourists circled the crime scene, snapping selfies. Four ambulances, two fire trucks, and a fleet of police vehicles crowded the street. Archie stood inches from the car. The burnt remnants still smoldered. A yellow tarp covered the driver's remains.

I needed to find my informant, Raincoat Ronnie again. If anyone knew of a person like St. Gregory drifting in and out of the homeless camps, it would be my Ronnie. He was suddenly the most valuable investigator in Vegas. I retrieved Robin's car, and the valet turned down my tip, saying driving this new car was tip enough. Did all men have car envy?

I drove around the side streets of downtown, almost running over a couple of intoxicated tourists stumbling between casinos. I wanted to yell at them, but I kept my diplomacy in check and simply gave a friendly wave.

I found an empty parking spot, which was rare so close to the casinos. By the time I had turned off the ignition, Raincoat Ronnie stood next to my car.

"Ronnie likes how you smell."

I bit back a scream. Ronnie had snuck up next to me. He

had ninja powers. I was already jumpy after being blown up this week.

"Ronnie, what's going on?"

He smiled. "Explosion. Ronnie saw a big explosion. A bomb. Must have been a bomb."

Ronnie also spoke about himself in the third person, which I found entertaining and endearing. "Did you see it?" I asked.

"No. Ronnie busy checking cans on Fremont. Checking Ronnie's cans."

Ronnie searched garbage cans for food or other discarded trinkets. Once he gathered enough trinkets, he became an entrepreneur and tried to sell them to tourists around Fremont. He was motivated, if not successful.

"Ronnie, how are you doing?" I noticed he had something sticky all over his face. I was curious but afraid to ask. Some things were best left a mystery.

"Great, great. Ronnie is great."

"Need to check in with my investigator. Have you heard about the explosion and who was involved?"

"Ronnie did not learn anything. Ronnie sorry."

I was disappointed, but it was not his fault. Ronnie was a great asset and I cared about him. "Do you need any money? Do you have enough food?"

"Ronnie got doughnuts. Lots of doughnuts. Good doughnuts."

Ronnie fished food out of trash cans, and I guessed he had located a doughnut shop that threw away more than its share.

"Where's your doughnut shop?"

"No shop. Ronnie gets them from the office. The bank always orders doughnuts, and the ladies never eat them. So, they put them out for Ronnie."

"Bank?" There were no banks downtown, at least not one

that gave away doughnuts. They would be overrun with hungry tourists. "Where's the bank, Ronnie?"

"No bank, just an office, upstairs." Ronnie pointed up the block to an old casino that had closed, now converted into commercial space. "Bank offices. Bank offices with lots of doughnuts. Doughnuts for Ronnie."

A bank office downtown? We were close to the bus station, where the explosion took place. "Do you know what bank it is, Ronnie?"

Ronnie reached into another pocket and pulled out a crumpled slip of paper. It read, "Loan Origination Office, Second United Bank of Nevada," and detailed the location on the third floor of the old hotel building. Maybe The Messenger wasn't trying to attack the bus station or Fremont Street. Perhaps he had planned to attack another bank branch when the bomb went off prematurely. That was a logical conclusion, but not the only one.

"Ronnie saw you on TV. Did they pay you money to be on TV? They pay you money to be on TV. Lots of money. Money to be on TV."

"Sorry, Ronnie. They didn't pay me." Ronnie sighed in disappointment. I redirected our conversation. "What about the explosion? How many people were hurt?"

"One guy killed, Ronnie knows. One guy killed. Yes, sure. One guy killed."

"You know who it was, the guy who got killed?"

"Ronnie heard a policeman talking. The driver."

"Did anyone mention his name?"

"No. He's gone. Not much left of him. Gone."

I handed Ronnie photos of our two suspects. I was confident it was Soames or St. Gregory, but we might have a copycat too. Ronnie sniffed my pizza but said nothing. "Do these men look familiar?" I flashed him photos of both.

Ronnie shook his head. "Ronnie likes your car."

I didn't expect this from Ronnie, but he was a male. "It's my brother's car."

Ronnie spied the back seat. "Big back seat. Plenty of room to sleep."

I realized not everyone thought of cars as transportation. My heart ached in sympathy.

"Can you watch the scene for me? You know, observe and report? Can you take notes of what happens, see if anyone else got hurt, all that kind of stuff?"

"Sure. Sure. Yes, Ronnie can do that." He nodded furiously.

I handed him a pocket-sized spiral notebook and pen and held up my bag with two delicious slices of Pizza Rock pizza. "Ronnie, are you sure you can do this for me?"

He nodded, although at that point he would have given me his kidneys in exchange for the pizza. I gave him my two remaining slices. This counted as my good deed for the day. I turned to walk away. *What will Ronnie eat tomorrow?* I dug in my pocket. I had fourteen dollars and handed them to Ronnie. "Be sure and take good notes for me, Ronnie."

"Ronnie will. Ronnie promise."

He would. He never failed.

Before I drove back, I restocked my inventory of Pizza Rock pepperoni, for medicinal reasons. Luckily, they took my shiny, new replacement debit card. On the way back to the precinct, I listened to "Staying Alive" from the Bee Gees, which always lifted my spirits. I needed it. Another explosion, another fatality.

THE MESSENGER SCANNED *the scene at the bus station. The bare frame of the burnt automobile was all that was left. That and a yellow tarp over his incompetent delivery man. What a waste of one of his creations. He worked so hard on each bomb, and this one was a complete failure, missed the target entirely. He knew what he had to do. He would have to deliver every one of his special packages. It would take more time, but he could do it.*

A tourist approached him, asking a question. He ignored the words and pointed towards Fremont Street. The tourist smiled and walked in that direction.

The Messenger's police uniform was a perfect disguise. He was seen, but not seen. The tourist would not recall anything about him other than his police uniform. An ideal way to hide in plain sight.

His day was not yet complete. The selfish must be punished.

CHAPTER THIRTY

Thursday 4:01 p.m.

WE WERE STILL LOOKING for Oliver, our missing delivery man. He hadn't surfaced after we raided his house. If he was the mastermind, he would be somewhere making more bombs. I didn't think so. His home didn't say mastermind or bomber or even organized. He was a hot mess, a loner with a long-term alcohol problem. If Oliver was just a courier, he would have been paid for his efforts. Where would an alcoholic flush with cash be spending his time?

Oliver would be at a bar. Vegas had dozens of pricey places to catch the latest innovative cocktail and gourmet appetizer. That wouldn't suit him. He wouldn't go to an upscale, trendy bar. Too expensive. He wouldn't go to a tourist area. He wouldn't be comfortable there, so the casinos were out. Oliver would go somewhere he felt relaxed, a dive bar for locals. Vegas had more than its share of seedy bars to grab a stiff drink at a low price. Oliver would be at one of those, a place where he felt comfortable. A place he felt at home. With a sudden pocketful of cash, he would be buying drinks two at a time and treating his fellow barstool tenants to drinks with his newly acquired wealth. Several of these establishments were nearby. Since I was already downtown, after dropping off Archie, I decided to do a quick search.

Two steps inside the first bar I regretted my decision. Filthy did not begin to describe it. Sticky floors sucked at the soles of my shoes. The stench of cigarettes and body odor, spilled beer, and what I believed to be dead rodents combined into a powerful stench. I needed a body condom.

I received several inappropriate sexual offers, which didn't really count, did they? As handsy as the inebriated clients were, I was glad I had my pistol. I didn't find Oliver, so I left. After examining the second bar, I needed a shower. I debated throwing away my clothes and doubted my shoes could be salvaged.

At the third bar, simply named the Downtown Bar, I struck gold. As I predicted, Oliver was talking loudly, slurring his words, swaying as he spoke, buying drinks for his newfound chums. To capture the suspect, I lied. I told him that he had an outstanding warrant but didn't mention any details, since I didn't have any. He was not surprised, so my bluff might have been accurate. When I put the cuffs on him, I got some complaints from the inebriated customers, but they stopped their protests when the bartender announced Oliver had already paid for the next round. So much for loyalty among drunks.

Unsteady on his feet, and occasionally stepping on mine, Oliver wobbled towards the door. "You're a . . . a cutie. Wanna go . . . ah go dancing?"

Was he hitting on me? I wouldn't count that either. But it was nice in a queasy way.

When I got him into the car, I realized the stink was not

just the bar. It was Oliver. His body was a chemical weapon. His hands shook. His eyes were fire engine red, and he stunk. I longed for a blast of Archie's Old Spice. Robin would be pissed. I'd have to get his car detailed before I returned it.

At the precinct, I let the uniforms take possession of my arrestee. They recoiled from the smell. "Bring him to interrogation first."

Helen and Sandy high-fived me for finding Oliver. Captain Creek and Charlie gave me a thumbs up. The captain told Charlie and John-Boy to conduct his interrogation.

"I caught him," I stated. "I should be part of the interrogation."

"Any incident bringing him in?" Captain Creek asked.

"None. He didn't even resist. He did ask me for a dance."

Charlie bowed out. "He's all yours. I can smell him through the glass."

A confined space and poor ventilation in the interrogation room really magnified the smell.

Sandy brought in two Styrofoam cups of coffee and caught her breath from Oliver's strong scent.

"Got any bourbon?" Oliver asked.

"Let's try this for now," I said. We chitchatted, like a boring job interview. We asked for his full name, which he knew despite his intoxication. He also remembered he worked for Royal Janitorial Services. He could even recite his address, although that took two attempts.

We knew this, of course, but we wanted to get him in the habit of answering our questions.

John-Boy leaned in. "You were flashing a lot of cash. Where did you get all this money? Surely Royal doesn't pay you that much."

Oliver smiled. "Delivery services."

"What did you deliver?"

"This and that. I don't look. I just take the money and go."

"Some of them were bombs," John-Boy said.

"Maybe. I don't look."

"Do you have any more packages to deliver?" I asked.

"I don't think so."

"We conducted a raid at your house," John-Boy injected.

"A raid . . . at my house? Why?" Oliver finished his first coffee and started his second.

"Were you downtown, near the bus station?" I asked.

"Bus station? What for? I don't take the bus."

"Were you responsible for what happened today at the bus station?"

Oliver looked genuinely confused. "What . . . bus station . . . what?

Oliver didn't know about the bus station bomb.

"No, no bus station . . . not today . . . but big plans."

"What's the big plan?"

"Don't know."

"When is this big plan supposed to happen?"

"Tonight at eight p.m."

John-Boy and I exchanged glances. This wasn't good news.

I had lots of questions. Was the bus station a copycat or an unrelated crime? Was the bus station bomb supposed to be at eight but went off early? Was Vegas being targeted by another bomber? Freak. I tried to keep my composure.

Oliver giggled.

"Did I say something funny?" I asked.

Oliver giggled some more.

"What's so funny?" John-Boy asked.

"Why you asking me? Cops already know. Boss has someone helping him on the inside."

"Inside?" I asked.

"Like on the police payroll?" John-Boy asked.

Oliver nodded.

"Who's your boss?" I demanded.

"Not sure."

"What's his name?"

"Don't know. Calls himself The Messenger."

John-Boy and I looked at each other. This had to be legitimate.

"What does The Messenger look like?" I asked.

"Never met him face to face."

"Where does he live?" John-Boy asked.

"Don't know, never met."

"Then how did you do this?" I asked.

"All by cell phone." Oliver sipped his second coffee. "A little whisky could make me remember better."

"We'll see," I said.

John-Boy leaned in. "Tell me how this would work."

"He would call with instructions and leave cash. A little up front, more after I delivered."

"Where did he leave the cash?" I asked.

"Different place each time."

"This Messenger is good," I said.

"Messenger said he had inside help."

"Inside of what?" I asked.

"Inside the police."

"Really?" John-Boy said.

"Messenger warned me to not talk. Said if I kept quiet, I might live. So, I'm done talking."

John-Boy shot around the steel table and grabbed Oliver by the collar. "Who's helping him? Who's the traitor, dammit!"

Captain Creek and Sandy rushed in to get John-Boy off Oliver.

John-Boy looked at me. "I'm supposed to protect you. We could have lost you."

We hugged. John-Boy does care about me.

Sandy and Helen marched Oliver to booking. I had to play my hunch. I came up behind the trio and shoved Oliver. "Where is this supposed to happen—tonight at eight p.m.? Where? At the bank?"

Oliver was stunned and not completely sturdy on his feet. He fell against the wall, and I grabbed him by the neck. "Where?" I demanded.

"Not a bank . . . The mall . . . That's all I'm going to say."

CHAPTER THIRTY-ONE

Thursday 5:05 p.m.

VEGAS POLICE ACCEPTED help from anyone, even if the effort was not practical. Sandy told me about twins who worked as a tandem team of psychics and who swore these explosions were the first steps of an alien invasion, but not from Mars. That was too trite. This time, the invasion was from Jupiter. Sandy took down the details for the report without ever laughing. She was more diplomatic than me. Who wasn't?

In the fishbowl, a more terrestrial theory came from Mayor Shale. "I'd like to introduce our psychiatric consultant, a professor from UNLV, who will make a brief report. Dr. Torrance?"

Dr. Torrance stood. He was more comfortable in a college classroom than at a police station. He sported the long, messy hairstyle of Albert Einstein, although Einstein did it better. "We're obviously dealing with a person or persons with an agenda against Las Vegas. More than likely terrorists . . ."

That was a real gut punch. From the hushed response, no

one expected that word: terrorists. Everyone in Vegas law enforcement feared that word more than any other, except the phrase, "The buffet is closed."

Dr. Torrance continued. "We were afraid this would happen, especially with the bombings being linked."

"The explosions were linked?" the captain asked.

"We, my peers and I, are confident they are linked, part of a terrorism campaign aimed at Las Vegas. The one thing we know about bombers . . . they always escalate."

"Escalate?" Helen asked.

"Bigger explosions. More injuries. More casualties."

I felt my pulse quicken.

"When do they stop?" Sandy asked.

"Only when they are caught or killed."

"Why Vegas?" I asked.

The psychiatrist sighed. "New York? Already attacked. Boston? Already attacked. Oklahoma City? Already attacked. Eventually, this had to happen here. Tourist locations are always a target, and Las Vegas is the tourist capital of the world."

Detectives scribbled notes as fast as the doctor spoke. "Bombers have a strong ideology. Think Timothy McVeigh and gun control, Ted Kaczynski and industrialization—even the Boston Marathon bombing was motivated by Afghanistan military action. They are motivated by ideology even if that ideology doesn't match reality."

The one thing I learned: bombers are crazy.

Dr. Torrance continued his analysis, which left lots of holes. The man driving the car died in the blast. Hopefully, his remains could be identified. Other than that, speculation. Only a professor could know so little and still sound so confident. Maybe it was the Einstein hair?

A voice from the back jumped into the discussion. "We

can't let this terrorism threat go public," Shale said. "We're concerned about tourists leaving the area. The shooting in 2017 cost the city a billion dollars in revenue. Everyone depends on tourists. Our economy, all our jobs depend on visitors. A terrorist threat would be catastrophic."

Everyone took a deep breath after the terrorism announcement.

Dr. Torrance continued. "I need to talk to the officer communicating with our suspect."

I held up my hand.

Captain Creek pointed with his unlit cigarette. "Everyone else, let's work the case."

The Disco Divas moved to one side of the fishbowl, trying to avoid the background noise.

The psychiatrist adjusted his Einstein hairstyle to keep it out of his eyes and removed his tweed jacket. This must have been a mandatory part of his wardrobe because tweed and Vegas weather didn't go together. Dr. Torrance asked a variety of questions about The Messenger, especially about the phone conversations I had. I recalled the language of The Messenger to the best of my memory. Dr. Torrance took meticulous notes in a moleskin.

"Why the bank?" Sandy asked.

"Or any bank?" I countered.

Dr. Torrance pondered this for a second. "It could be a real or imagined cabal of evil intent. Maybe the locations represent authority, which The Messenger hates. It could be a personal slight, some insult that this Messenger raised to an epic battle. He could rationalize anything as justification, real or imagined. Don't look for rational thought, you won't find it here."

Then I described my contacts with The Messenger. After my narrative, I stared at him, hoping for a revelation like Sherlock Holmes, Nancy Drew, or maybe Jessica Fletcher. Instead,

I got something different. Einstein held a long pause and sighed. "I think we can bring him to the surface, bring him out in the open, and hopefully he'll make a mistake."

"What's your idea?" the captain asked.

"This Messenger, St. Gregory or whoever, wants to be in control, be in charge, be in power." Dr Torrance paced as he spoke. "If we, I mean *you*." Dr. Torrance pointed to me. "If *you* were to taunt him, challenge his power, challenge his control, his masculinity, I think he would go off of his script."

"What would he do then?" Charlie asked.

"I don't know," Dr. Torrance stated.

Not the answer I hoped for. Freak.

"How would that help?" Helen asked.

"This Messenger has everything planned, every detail in advance. That's why you're having trouble catching him. If we push him to go off his planned schedule, we have a better chance of him making a mistake. That allows us to catch him. Maybe, at least."

Captain Creek wheezed. "So, how do we push him off his planned schedule?"

"We can't." Dr. Torrance pointed to me. "Only she can. She has a relationship with him. She has direct contact. She's the only one who can accomplish this."

Freak. The only thing worse than no solution was a solution that depended one hundred percent on me and me alone.

I met with Dr. Torrance. We detailed a plan of attack. A few suggestions made perfect sense. Some sounded silly, but when Dr. Torrance explained the psychology behind them, the ideas seemed plausible.

"Messing with a person's head is a strange process," Dr. Torrance said. I had to agree. "And the *coup de grace* will be getting him to contact you. If you can put him on the defensive, responding to you rather than you responding to him, the balance of power will change."

"So, how do I do that?" I asked.

"Do you know someone in the media?"

"It just so happens . . ."

I called Zack, the handsome but ethically challenged reporter who pretended to be my nurse and told him that I had a story for him. When I said he had an exclusive, I could hear him salivate through the phone. He agreed to meet at a restaurant of my choosing for an early dinner. Was it a date? Obviously, it was a date, but was it a date-date? I counted it. I picked the Golden Steer Steakhouse, an old-world restaurant that was a favorite of the Rat Pack and other celebrities. I got a last-minute reservation. The local restaurants loved me. My stomach did the happy dance. Zack would pay and pay dearly.

CHAPTER THIRTY-TWO

Thursday 5:45 p.m.

"HELP ME GET READY," I told Sandy and Helen. We made a quick dash to the locker room. I had a few changes of clothes stashed there for wardrobe emergencies. I hoped that something would work for my first-date-meeting/interview/meeting-date, whatever it was with Zack.

Pickings were slim, as I only have three changes of clothes and nothing that screamed "first date." I let Sandy pick my top as Helen started on my hair. Sandy joined in, as my mess of locks was a two-person job.

"What does he look like?" Sandy asked.

I described him as best I could, worried that my memory of him was influenced by the blast of medicine the hospital gave me. "He was tall, trim, with a bright smile and a halo of bright light around him. That last bit might have been the pain meds."

I put on my reserve date heels I kept for such emergencies. "They pinch," I moaned as I squeezed my feet into them. "But so worth it."

"Yes, so worth it," Helen and Sandy echoed.

In front of the full-length mirror, I squirted my neck with my good perfume.

"How do I look?" I asked.

Sandy and Helen gushed with compliments, which helped boost my self-esteem.

I stopped by the fishbowl and got a whistle from Ben. I needed that. I did a slow twirl and got a couple more compliments. Then I overheard something crazy.

"We need to evacuate the Fashion Show Mall," Mayor Shale said.

Charlie said what I was thinking. "Are you crazy?"

"No, I'm your boss."

Charlie shook his head. "No. Captain Creek is my boss."

"Maybe so, but I'm the mayor, so I'm everyone's boss. And I say we evacuate the mall."

"How?" Captain Creek asked.

Shale thought for a second. "We have to do this without making a scene."

I had to jump into this conversation. "How will that work?"

John-Boy sighed audibly. "This idea is based on Oliver's statement. We can't trust him. He's a drunk. He's still drunk."

Shale ignored their comments. "First, we should search the mall for explosives."

"How many square feet is the mall?" John-Boy asked.

Ben tapped a few keys. "Almost two million square feet."

John-Boy grimaced. "An army couldn't do it with a week. We have a couple of hours."

The Fashion Show Mall? Really? Shale wanted to evacuate the big mall on the Strip? This was madness.

Shale stood. "We will evacuate the mall before eight. How many at the mall?"

Ben looked at his laptop. "Estimates are five to ten thousand."

The captain asked, "How are you going to evacuate ten thousand people? Uber?"

"We will commandeer the school buses." Shale had an answer for everything. "No one uses them in the evening."

"Can you get enough buses and drivers to evacuate ten thousand people?" I asked rhetorically.

Shale smiled. "I'm in charge of this city. I can do anything."

"Where do you plan to take them?" Sandy asked.

"Downtown. We'll drop them off at the Fremont Street Experience. Maybe UNLV or the damn airport."

"How will you convince them to go without causing a panic?" Charlie asked.

Shale smiled. "This is Vegas. Tourists believe anything, like they can gamble five dollars and get wealthy. We'll think of some story."

I had a bad feeling about this. Evacuate the entire mall . . . school buses . . . ? Sounded like desperation, not a real plan. I needed to leave before I shared my pessimism aloud. Besides, I had a date—well, mostly-date—to attend.

CHAPTER THIRTY-THREE

Thursday 6:08 p.m.

I ARRIVED at my pseudo date or work-date, whatever it was, by taxi to Golden Steer Steakhouse. If I had wine—and why not since Zack was buying—I didn't want to drive under the influence. Confidentially, I couldn't taste the difference between the fancy wines and the cheap ones. My palate preferred doughnuts and tacos, but on Zack's dime, I would gladly experiment.

Zack arrived, and he was so handsome he took my breath away. Tall and trim, with a bright smile. Wow. The pain medicine hadn't morphed my memory of him. Okay, he didn't have a golden halo, but every other detail was accurate. He complimented me as he sat down. Points for Zack.

He wanted to get right into the story. *Not so fast, handsome.* The only thing better than the food was eating it while he waited for me to talk. What did they say about anticipation? I ordered their Escargots de Bourgogne as an appetizer, their house specialty, and for dinner, the Longhorn, an extra-thick

New York cut served Oscar style with toppings of lump crab, asparagus, and hollandaise sauce. Heavenly. I also ordered sides of sauteed mushrooms, garlic parmesan broccoli, and grilled asparagus. I let Zack order the wine since he was paying. We made idle chit-chat while I ate my escargot. I liked making him work for it, like a dating ritual. Was this a date? I counted it.

When dinner arrived, the aroma made me grin from ear to ear. My steak sizzled on the plate, butter dripping off the edges, and a giant lump of crab meat fell off the steak and onto the plate. I had to fight the instinct to grab the tender morsel and pop it into my mouth. The sauteed mushrooms were so plump and tender, and the light garlic sauce on the broccoli made me do a giant inhale.

I gave teasing details between bites. He was so captivated by my comments, he forgot to eat his steak. I considered taking his to go. I was in carnivore heaven. I explained that while we didn't know the bomber's identity, we did know The Messenger's bomb-making skills were amateurish, little more than a junior high science project.

"Wow, this stuff is great," Zack said. I agreed, as I savored a tender bite of the aged beef, then I realized he was talking about The Messenger story. He was on his second page of notes when I started with the ideas from Dr. Torrance. I mentioned that people who carry out these actions were closeted pedophiles and may have impotence issues. Zack nearly spat wine through his nose. While I finished the last bite, Zack reviewed his notes. He held them like he had the golden ticket to Willie Wonka's factory.

"So, when do you plan on running the story?" I asked without making eye contact, as though I didn't care.

"Tomorrow, of course. Page one."

Hook, line, and sinker. Dr. Torrance was correct, manipulating a reporter was too easy. I hoped St. Gregory or Soames fell for this taunting and went off-script.

Zack popped a bite of steak in his mouth. "Wow, this is wonderful."

"The best steaks anywhere. I hate to rush things, but I'm needed back at the precinct."

Zack got his dinner in a to-go box. Hopefully he took time to savor each bite as I had, but he would learn. He nearly wet his pants when he saw the final tab. Priceless.

CHAPTER THIRTY-FOUR

Thursday 7:14 p.m.

I RUSHED BACK to the fishbowl to hear Shale's sermon. "I wanted to update you on the investigation thus far. After discussions with the governor, we decided not to evacuate the mall."

"I bet that was interesting," I whispered.

"I could hear the governor screaming through the phone." Sandy giggled.

Shale continued, "We'll be posted at the mall to look for suspicious behavior, because we think the threat is credible, but we won't evacuate."

Freak. If it ever came out that we knew about the threat but didn't evacuate, many people would lose their jobs.

Our ranks were already depleted. Captain Creek had doubled the detail at the Fremont Experience after the bus station explosion. Now, a small army of state and federal agents planned to invade the mall. The FBI wanted our assistance to locate the mall, the exits, and the big gathering areas. We were no more than tour guides. Captain Creek assigned the task to me, Sandy, and Helen, three females. *The mall job was all female? So sexist.* Then I learned our captain had never been inside the Fashion Show Mall. Really? He lived here and had never been to the mall? And I thought I was bad at shopping.

Wait. My date. "I have a date tonight," I announced.

"Didn't you just have a date?" Helen asked.

"Yes, but that was a work-date. This one is a real date-date."

Sandy smiled. "Good for you. Who's the lucky guy?"

I knew his name started with A, but I didn't think that was much of an answer. "Blind date. I'll give you the details later. I will have to postpone him, but I don't want him to get away."

I went to the hallway to call my mystery man. I had the number saved on my cell phone. I wouldn't call him by name, since I didn't know it. I hoped he would not ask me. My love life was such a mess.

"Hello," I said.

"Hello, is this Donna?"

"Yes. I'm afraid I have some bad news."

"Go ahead."

"Lynn told you I was a detective, right? Well, I'm a little overwhelmed today by the explosion. I could use a raincheck." I hoped this wouldn't scare him away.

"How about tomorrow?" my nameless admirer asked.

He was interested too. Hmmm. Between Zack and my unnamed admirer, I practically had a cult following. Wait. I would be missing out on Mexican food. I had visions of a bath-tub-sized bowl of chips and queso. Could I squeeze in a late dinner? No, no, no. I should concentrate on The Messenger. Why do these things always happen to me?

We made a date for tomorrow evening. Just me and my unnamed admirer.

Walking by the fishbowl, I attracted John-Boy's attention. "Wow. You're wearing perfume. Your fancy date perfume."

"I had a date, an early dinner." John-Boy was jealous, and I loved it.

Back on task, Sandy, Helen, and I escorted the all-male FBI contingent to the mall and gave them a brief tour. We passed by See's Candy Shop, not an accident. Today, their sample tray consisted of their dark salted caramels and their milk chocolate strawberry creams. Everyone took a nibble. I shared, sort of. I think it is morally wrong to leave chocolates uneaten. I bought a two-pound box of their milk chocolates with soft centers, which was only polite since I ate half the sample tray. I also grabbed a box of their peanut brittle, in my effort to stimulate the local economy. Helen pointed to a framed picture of me on the counter, describing me as the Customer of the Month. I should list that on my resume.

The FBI men departed to their assigned posts. Sandy, Helen, and I went to the food court. If any place in the mall was always crowded, it was the food court. Besides, I could use a snack. Maybe Chinese food. I had a craving for egg rolls.

Helen and Sandy scoffed when I ordered a platter of egg rolls, but they wanted some when I sat down. Typical. We kept an eye out for anyone acting suspicious with no real idea who we should be targeting. I supposed a villain in a black cape twisting his moustache would have been too obvious. Nothing seemed out of the ordinary.

Helen stared into her paper cup. "My tea leaves are giving me a warning."

Sandy turned pale.

"What's the danger?" I asked.

"I'm out of tea. A little clairvoyant humor." Helen smiled and went to get a refill. Halfway to the counter she froze and dropped her cup. She put her hands to her mouth, and I swore she was about to cry.

"What's wrong?" I asked, as Sandy and I guided her back to her seat.

Helen looked pale, like she was about to faint. Her eyes were locked on something in the distance. Something I couldn't see. Finally, she made eye contact with us.

"Helen, what is it?" Sandy asked.

Helen inhaled deeply. "I had a vision. A psychic vision."

"I didn't think you believed in that stuff," I said.

"I don't. That's why this is so scary."

"Tell us about it," I said.

Helen looked off into the distance again. "It was hazy, but I swear I could see the Second United bank building and everything was painted in polka dots."

"The outside of the building?" I asked.

"No. The inside. The lobby. The vision was the bank lobby, and everything was covered in polka dots."

The bank lobby painted in polka dots? That sounded like HGTV gone wrong.

"I don't know why," Helen continued, "but the polka dots were frightening."

Frightening polka dots? That made even less sense. "Helen, are you supposed to be taking any medicine?" I asked.

"It's not related to medicine. This was a psychic vision."

Sandy got Helen a tea refill and she slowly took a few sips. She had no further visions from beyond.

I thought all that psychic stuff was fake, and I was surprised to have Helen admit as much. But she saw something. She had some kind of experience that involved the bank lobby and polka dots. It didn't make any sense.

Color returned to Helen's cheeks, and she made a mild joke about her experience, but I knew her well enough to know she was rattled. Was this a vision of the future? Would the bank paint their lobby in polka dots?

We looked around the food court. No one stood out. Only normal shoppers and hungry tourists. At 7:59, we got tense, even too tense for egg rolls. Should we run outside? Would that start a panic? The next sixty seconds slowly ticked by. Then?

Nothing. Not a damn thing.

After all this fanfare, it was disappointing. By 8:03, still nothing. The deadline had come and gone. No explosion, just like I had predicted. We munched the last of the egg rolls, and by "we" I mean "just me."

Nothing to report.

"Ladies, I guess it's time to leave," I said. Sandy and Helen stood.

"What about the FBI agents?" Helen asked.

I shook my head. "This is Vegas. Let them take a taxi." That was not the collegial FBI and local police partnership thing to do, but it felt right. I needed new black slacks, but I didn't consider clothes shopping to be a team sport, especially since I usually shopped in the boys' department. I would save that humiliation for another day.

All our phones buzzed in unison, multiple times. The text messages were coming in too fast to read each one completely, but the pattern was clear. The phrases that repeated were "Forum Shoppes" and "explosion."

Caesar's Forum Shoppes was another mall on the Strip.

Freak. We protected the wrong mall.

CHAPTER THIRTY-FIVE

Thursday 8:15 p.m.

ALL OFFICERS WERE ORDERED to report immediately to the Forum Shoppes at Caesar's Palace, the glamorous shopping promenade on the Strip. The Shoppes were always packed. An explosion there could be catastrophic to numerous restaurants I loved. Those eateries had to be protected at all costs. The tourists were important too, I supposed.

We dashed to our LVPD minivan, but it was hopeless, hemmed in by traffic. We didn't have the luxury of waiting. We had to get to the Forum Shoppes.

A limousine pulled up in front of us, idling in traffic. Three young women posed out of the sunroof, each with a champagne flute in hand, the middle one wearing a banner proclaiming "Bride-to-Be." Music blared and the girls sang along with the Go-Go's "We Got the Beat." The bachelorette party was going strong, and this was not their first glass.

I went around to the driver and flashed my badge. "Police

emergency. Can you take us to the Caesar's Forum Shoppes?" The driver nodded.

I tried to get in the front seat, but the passenger's side was overflowing with shopping packages, all the way to the roof. These girls had hit the mall hard. Good for them.

Helen, Sandy, and I got in the back with the girls, now singing along with Beyonce, "If you liked it then you should have put a ring on it."

Two empty champagne bottles sat on the floor.

"Drinking a lot," Sandy commented.

"Yes, but they're not driving," Helen added.

The girls now popped into the seats, giving us their full attention.

"Oh wow, you're, like, real police?"

Helen nodded.

"Do you have a gun? Can I see it?"

"Maybe later," Sandy said.

I looked around the interior, illuminated like a crowded disco floor—lots of champagne, lots of cleavage, and little food. Ugh. It reminded me of my bridesmaid trauma to come.

"At least take a sip of champagne," the bride-to-be offered.

We relented during the mile-long trek in the limo. As we jumped out, the bride-to-be insisted that we take a selfie with her and her entourage. It seemed like a small sacrifice for the ride. If it wasn't for them, we would still be stuck in traffic.

The Forum entrance looked like a police convention. Fifty squad cars with lights flashing blocked the exits. We darted through the casino entrance. Sandy, Helen, and I ran through the rows of slot machines and into the Shoppes.

Slowly, panic spread through the crowd like a contagion as each person checked their phone and discovered they were at the scene of a police emergency.

Detectives had cordoned off the shopping area and

screened anyone leaving. Uniformed officers swarmed the area. We would have the bomber in custody soon. As I moved farther into the Forum Shoppes, I sniffed the air—and coughed. Was that the smell of gunpowder? Helen and Sandy noticed it too. It was impossible to ignore. We went left at the big fountain.

We went deeper into the shopping area. Tensions were relaxed. Officers and agents exited past us with disgruntled comments about wasting time. Did this mean The Messenger had been caught? Please let this nightmare be over.

We finally arrived at the large aquarium near the Cheese-cake Factory. I detected the wonderful curry and coconut scent of their Bang-Bang Chicken and Shrimp. My stomach leaped into action. Did I have time to place a to-go order?

About a hundred officers stood in a large circle. I needed to see The Messenger in custody. I used my shortness to my advantage and burrowed into the crowd until it opened like the eye of a hurricane. Four men were prone on the floor. Upon closer examination, they weren't men, just high school boys. Two wore hoodies, one wore a letterman's jacket, and all were from Las Vegas High School. The Messenger was a group of highs school kids? That couldn't be right. Mall security stood over the four teens. I spotted Captain Creek and approached him for an explanation.

"Are these boys The Messenger?" I asked.

The captain shook his head. "Just boys carrying out a stupid prank. They set off fireworks in four trash cans at the same time. Created a hell of a panic. Then the alerts went out. Mall security caught them. By the time we arrived, the situation was over."

Fireworks. That explained the smell. "So, they aren't The Messenger?" I was confused.

"No, just teenage boys acting stupid."

I wanted to punch each of them in the nose. Did they have

any idea the panic they had just created? "What's next, Captain? How are we going to explain a hundred officers at the Forum Shoppes?"

"Charlie told reporters this was a training exercise. That should slow the hysteria. I told the officers to act like they were surveying the scene and writing reports."

I hoped this deception worked. We didn't need more panic in Vegas. Officers moved the four boys in handcuffs, jackets pulled over their heads to hide their identities, which indicated to me they were juveniles by age, not just by action. I wanted to kick each of them.

Dammit, Oliver gave us a false lead.

A Cheesecake Factory server walked into the mass of bodies, holding a large plastic tote. "I have a to-go order for Donna Wizz . . . no . . . check . . ."

"That's me." I motioned to the server. The smell was delicious.

My phone vibrated. Mom, again.

"Donna, dear," Mom panted. "Get to the hospital. Now."

CHAPTER THIRTY-SIX

Thursday 8:55 p.m.

MOM DIDN'T KNOW about the incident at either mall and had no idea what I was dealing with. "What's wrong?" I asked her.

"Robin . . ." She sobbed. "Something is wrong with Robin. He won't stop shaking."

I handed Sandy my Cheesecake Factory order. "Please put this in the office fridge."

Sandy and Helen gave me a quick hug. Sandy winked at me. "Go, we got this."

I took a taxi to the hospital in a fog of panic. I stumbled to the elevator. I had spent too much time in this damn hospital. Robin was two floors up.

I darted to his room on the heels of two nurses. Two nurses? That wasn't a good sign. Robin was convulsing. His eyes were closed, and his body jumped off the hospital bed in one violent spasm after another. One nurse fought to hold him down as a second struggled to draw medicine from a small vial. His body seemed possessed. He hadn't moved in days. Now he couldn't stop. Watching someone you love thrash about is unsettling. I fought back tears without success. Elaine held Mom as they sobbed.

I had no idea what to do. Help hold Robin down? Hold Mom? Elaine? Just stay the hell out of the way? I should do all those things, but what first?

"Push Diazepam, stat," Dr. Pike ordered.

"Going in now, Doctor," the nurse said.

Robin's body shook. The change was drastic and immediate. He convulsed four more times, but each shudder was half as strong as the one before it. Finally, he flopped on the bed one last time and then lay motionless.

The room fell silent, except for an annoying, constant beep, one long dull tone. I had seen enough episodes of *Grey's Anatomy* to know that sound. Flat line. Robin was dead. My legs felt like lead. I could not move.

The nurses stepped back, realizing their work was done. Mom and Elaine huddled next to the bed. The last nurse to retreat silenced the beep of the monitor. Mom and Elaine, still holding each other, collapsed to the floor in slow motion.

Tears leaked, blurring my vision. I moved in close and put my arms around Mom and Elaine. I wished I had another arm to hold Robin's hand. I blinked away the tears. My brother was dead. Dammit, this was not supposed to happen.

What a nightmare. I stared at Robin's still body. I remembered so many events from our childhood. We took piano lessons together. He had so much musical talent. We climbed trees and rode bikes together. I was his little almost-a-boy sidekick. When we were older, I had crushes on all his friends, and later he warned me about which boys to avoid. So many shared memories, and now he was gone. As my heart shattered into a thousand pieces, I silently vowed to rip out The Messenger's heart so he could feel the same pain.

I looked at Dr. Pike. He checked the time. He never said out loud, "Time of death is . . ." but I was confident he had noted it.

I focused on Robin. He was deathly quiet. I inched forward. He was so still, after thrashing around so much just seconds ago.

Then it happened.

His mask fogged up. He was breathing. Shallow, but breathing. "Look," was all I could say before my voice cracked.

Dr. Pike's stethoscope plopped onto Robin's chest. "He's still with us. Check all leads." The nurses scooted us out of the way. They checked his IV lines and his oxygen, then a nurse uncovered the culprit. A wire from his heart monitor had become disconnected during the seizures. Once reattached, the slow but faint beat of Robin's heart filled the silent room.

"Praise God," Mom exclaimed. We joined in a group hug again, this time with joy. Tears flowed and finally my heart pumped again.

I smiled at the doctor. He shook his head.

"What?" I asked. "He's fine, breathing, his heart is beating, just a loose wire."

"These are spontaneous physical reactions. He could be brain dead. We should consider taking him off life support."

"What? But he's better. He's breathing!"

Dr. Pike continued to shake his head. "Not better. The convulsions just stopped, for now. The next outbreak will be worse, and the one after that worse still. We're just prolonging an inevitable outcome and his suffering."

This couldn't happen, not after losing him just seconds ago. We got Robin back, a miracle to be celebrated, not a sign of doom. "Please give him more time."

"He is suffering needlessly. It won't help him."

"Then it won't hurt him either." My tone was a little sharper than I intended, but the doctor took it in stride, and mulled it over.

Finally, he nodded. "Okay, we will try his breathing tomorrow." Then he touched my arm. "Don't be optimistic. Tomorrow will be bad. Your family should be prepared."

CHAPTER THIRTY-SEVEN

Friday 8:15 a.m.

I FELT numb after a long night with little sleep. Visions of Robin convulsing haunted me. Today could be his last day on earth. I was also worried about The Messenger's reactions. Would Dr. Torrance's idea work? The world rested on my shoulders, and I felt the weight.

When my brother Barry relieved me, I took a taxi to the precinct. I sipped my second cup of coffee with my third donut. Sandy and Helen tried to console me, but it did not work. Hugs were more effective. Sandy tried to change the subject. "Was your lawsuit thing yesterday? How did that go?"

I'd forgotten about that personal hell, my deposition for excessive force from that bald jerk, ugh. My Disco Divas followed me into the fishbowl with no further comment.

Notes and photographs were plastered to the wall of the fishbowl, updated information on our quest to catch The Messenger. We knew everything about him except his real name, maybe St. Gregory or Soames, but my instincts said it was Soames. I favored Soames because I disliked his disgusting brother.

We waited for The Messenger to react. I had followed Dr. Torrance's suggestions and described the taunting images to my personal newspaper reporter and maybe-boyfriend, Zack. I was confident Zack would report my every word, but it was calming to read the story posted online moments ago. He didn't miss a single point about how The Messenger's bombs were amateurish and made the innuendo that making the bombs indicated some kind of sexual failing. That would get a reaction from any man.

I had lit a fuse and now waited. The fishbowl monitored every local news station, and each had repeated the breaking news about my comments to Zack. The Messenger might not subscribe to Zack's tabloid, but no way he could miss this. The internet was an echo chamber for insults and this one was a gem, psychiatrist approved.

We didn't know how The Messenger would react, only that he would. Hopefully, his impromptu actions would be sloppy, and give a clue about his identity, his location, or his next target, or hit a trifecta and get all three.

How would he react? Where? What would he say or do? I didn't know. Dr. Torrance looked like I supposed he always did, confident or detached, with messy hair and a tweed jacket, although today a new one in grey tones. How many tweed jackets did he have?

Officers gathered around the fishbowl's video wall. Channel 5 Action News flashed the still image of Phillip St. Gregory. The reporter stated "sources close to the investigation" believed this was the bomber. Freak. Did Charlie also leak that Soames was a suspect? That might ruffle some feathers because of his brother. Whoever he was, The Messenger had to be seeing this.

The story was repeated by every news station, since those insults were too good to miss. Newscasters snickered with references to sexual dysfunction. At the station, the reaction was outright laughter. All we could do was wait and wonder how long it would take The Messenger to react. Then, we had an answer.

Action 13 News's female anchor stood behind a plain background. "We have just received an email message from the person claiming responsibility for the bombings."

This is it, the big reaction by The Messenger.

The screen switched to scrolling text, like the opening for Star Wars. "I am acting today because of the slanderous statements of detective Donna Wyznecki. I warned her of the previous bombings, and she failed to take me seriously. She is responsible. Donna Wyznecki is responsible for the deaths from these explosions. I avenge the actions of Detective Donna Wyznecki and I will take my wrath out upon Las Vegas . . ."

Channel Four stuck my official photo from the LVPD website on the screen, beside a stock image of Zack he used in every article. I wanted to hide but my legs wouldn't move. My body was numb. The Messenger was at war with me and my handsome fake nurse, almost boyfriend, Zack.

Another local reporter, a young woman with bright red hair spoke from the Vegas Police media room, three stories below me. Captain Creek was the next person on screen.

"Ben, turn up the volume," I called. The room fell silent.

"Detective Wyznecki has been working diligently on this case," his booming voice said. "Despite The Messenger's comments, Detective Wyznecki is not to blame for the explosions. The Messenger is to blame, one hundred percent. He has wrongfully implicated Detective Wyznecki and reporter Zack Garrett to deflect attention. We understand the concern and worries of the people of Las Vegas, but don't blame Detective Wyznecki or Mr. Garrett for these events."

"Second, the media reports of our suspect, Phillip St. Gregory, are correct." The captain held up a photo of the crazy professor. "We are actively searching for this man. His name is Phillip St. Gregory. If you see him, please call Vegas Police immediately."

Wow. The captain just put his neck out for me. Way out. I dropped my donut. It was my second donut of the day. Okay, it was my sixth. The calories didn't count if they didn't have sprinkles, right?

Dr. Torrance was certain this would get him to act, we just didn't know the result. After thirty minutes of nervous donut eating, we had an answer.

"Breaking News: Vegas Bomber Strikes Again," flashed along the bottom of the screen.

"This is it," Captain Creek announced. "Quiet everyone."

The reporter stood in front of the Golden Nugget sign as crowds rushed by. "We at NBC News 3 have reports that a bomb threat was called into the Golden Nugget Resort downtown less than ten minutes ago. The casino and hotel are being evacuated at this moment." A crowd surge pushed the reporter out of camera shot. Utter mayhem.

Screens across the fishbowl flashed similar events at the Four Queens, Binion's, Fremont Hotel, the Golden Gate, and the California. All the downtown hotels had received bomb threats. Crowds rushed out of the Fremont Experience holding suitcases or handfuls of poker chips. Even the nearby strip clubs evacuated, but the dancers and their patrons split apart once in the light of day. The media only added to the panic. One newscast showed a frozen margarita machine slowly spewing out its contents, the bartender having fled in mid-drink. *What a terrible waste of a margarita. Great, now I'm hungry for some chips and queso.*

The downtown pedestrian area, usually quiet during the morning hours, looked like a beehive. People scrambled in every direction, bumping into one another. No one felt safe but everyone was unsure where to find safety.

Las Vegas hadn't seen this much panic since the 2017 shooting. Rumors ran wild. In just ten minutes, the world changed. Emergency calls flooded in. Tourists and locals were worried. Every officer was called in for duty until further notice. The situation got worse by the minute.

Shale would burst. We had to protect the tourists and the local businesses, owned by so many registered voters.

Time passed and the frantic actions had slowed but not stopped. We monitored every television station; every officer was reporting in real time. All the local hospitals were put on alert for incoming. Fire and ambulances were dispatched to all downtown hotels. We waited. Nothing happened. No explosions. That was good. Lots of rumors, but no bombs. That gave us a little relief.

When the evacuations were not followed by explosions, the crowd shifted from fear to anger, duped into hysteria over a false alarm. Police and hotel security tried to hold back the immense crowds, but they were outnumbered by the angry mob. The monsoon of tourists pushed back into the hotels and started feeding the slot machines and crowding the buffets like nothing had happened.

The Disco Divas and I watched this event repeated at casino after casino. After the false alarm, no one would react the next time there was a bomb threat, and that scared me silly. We all knew it. This had to be part of The Messenger's plan. If the public wouldn't react to warnings, we would have a disaster.

CHAPTER THIRTY-EIGHT

Friday 10:45 a.m.

WHAT WAS ST. Gregory's—The Messenger's— next step? Within seconds we had an answer. Officers monitoring the Strip casinos announced the unwelcome news.

"I have a bomb threat called in to Caesar's Palace."

"A bomb threat at New York, New York."

Then the officers overlapped with each other.

". . . Mandalay Bay."

". . . Circus Circus."

". . . bomb threat at Harrah's."

"The Wynn is being evacuated."

". . . threat at Paris."

"Luxor is being evacuated."

". . . Cromwell."

". . . bomb threat at MGM."

"Aria is being evacuated."

Freak. Every casino on the Strip reported a bomb threat. Each Strip casino was a city unto itself, with thousands of hotel rooms and dozens of restaurants, bars, and shops, each with its own army of employees. The Messenger could not have a bomb in every casino, but we had to treat the threats as real. The psychiatrist's suggestion was a disaster. The Messenger was off his script, but this was much worse. Panicked people flooded out of every casino.

If this had happened on a Tuesday, Vegas would only have about a third of the crowd that was present today. On Friday, Vegas was bursting at the seams, and we had a bomber loose.

Three officers were posted at each hotel on the strip. That seemed like a small contingent, but we had the full strength of Vegas Police guarding the downtown hotels, the Fremont Experience, all the shopping malls, and now all the casinos on the Strip. We were spread thin.

Panic, just like that from downtown, occurred, a tidal wave of reaction. Also, just like downtown, the threats were not followed by any explosions. That was positive. Minor injuries due to the panic, people getting trampled, but no fatalities. The Vegas economy would not fare as well.

After panic downtown and on the Strip, Las Vegas was in exodus mode. We patched into the security feed at McCarren Airport. Imagine Black Friday at Walmart with everyone dragging luggage. Complete madness. Officers at the airport reported that tourists offered a thousand dollars in cash to get on a flight today. Every rental car in Vegas was taken. Local taxi drivers made a fortune hauling carloads of panicked visitors to Los Angeles. Tourists even overran the bus station, making an interesting mix of local poor and visiting wealthy riding the same Greyhound out of Vegas. Elvis Costello should write a song about it.

I accidentally but on purpose overheard Shale on a call. "Governor, I assure you we are taking every precaution . . . Yes, Governor, I suppose that is necessary . . . Yes, please deploy the

National Guard to help with crowd control." Shale ended the call. He was overwhelmed, sweat beaded on his upper lip. I felt sympathy for him for a second, then I remembered he was a politician and a womanizing creep.

I stood behind Ben as he worked his techie magic. "Any clues from the post?" I had no confidence The Messenger had left a hint, but I had to ask. Should I check out witness protection on the international space station? No one on the space station hated me. Yet.

Ben shook his head. "Digital footprint is zero. Nothing. Forwarded multiple times, anonymous servers. No way of knowing anything. He could be in this building, and we wouldn't know it."

My head ached. "How did he make all these threats?"

"The bomb threats were pre-recorded and sent all at once through a robo-calling program."

"Are those programs rare?" I asked.

"As rare as Facebook pages."

Freak. I was frustrated to the boiling point but felt completely helpless. I wasn't allowed to go because the sight of me would have caused a riot. I was the face of "false alarms." Zack was too, but I didn't really care about him. I busied myself examining the computer maps that allowed me to avoid eye contact with the few remaining in the fishbowl.

CHAPTER THIRTY-NINE

Friday 12:25 p.m.

WE NEEDED to interview Jason Oliver again. His mall prediction was a bust. A night without alcohol and the fear of spending a long time in jail could help refresh his memory.

John-Boy and I sat across from him in the interrogation room. His hair dripped from a recent shower, thankfully. His pores still exuded leftover remnants of whisky. I suspected his liver looked like an old tire.

John-Boy got things started. "Mr. Oliver, Detective Wyznecki and I are with Las Vegas Police."

"I remember you."

His short answer didn't indicate a great deal of commitment to this process.

"I'm afraid some of your details were off."

"I had a lot to drink."

Sandy appeared with two more cups of coffee.

"Would you like to revise your statement?" I asked.

Oliver resigned. "I thought yesterday was Friday."

"So, what does that mean?" John-Boy asked.

He was so drunk he didn't know what day it was. Wow, that was bad.

"The eight p.m. deadline?" John-Boy asked.

Oliver smiled. "It is for tonight."

"Tonight?" I repeated. "Are you sure?"

"Yes, Friday at eight p.m. That much I can tell you."

"What's the target? Is it the mall?" John-Boy asked, his voice sounding more panicked.

Oliver silently smiled.

"Is the target a mall? The bank? A bank in a mall?" I tried to reason with him. "Give us a clue.

"Sorry. I told you everything I know."

John-Boy stiffened his posture. "You know if you keep information from us and people get hurt, that's on you."

"Lots of people are going to get hurt."

"Let us help people get out of harm's way," I pleaded.

Oliver did not say anything further. I decided to approach this from another angle. "The Messenger said he was doing this because of a woman."

"Any idea who the woman is?" John-Boy asked.

He shook his head. "No idea."

"Any idea why the first bomb was at Second United Bank?" I asked.

Oliver shook his head.

John-Boy asked, "Any idea why he's doing this today? Why is today special?"

"No idea. Listen, I'm just a delivery driver."

I held up my phone with a picture of St. Gregory. "Is this him?"

"I told you before, I never met him."

I changed my screen to a picture of Soames and passed it back. "How about him?"

"I recognize this guy."

My heart skipped a beat. We had an identification. I had to go by the book. "How do you know him?"

"He arrested me for DUI. He's a cop. Wait, do you think a cop is involved in the explosions?"

Oliver was our only real person of interest in custody, and he had details that would help us. I had to keep him talking. "Did The Messenger have help making the bombs?"

"I don't know. Maybe."

"Any idea how many bombs he made?" John-Boy asked.

Oliver paused to consider. "Twenty, maybe more."

"Twenty? Where did you put them?" I asked.

"I only delivered a few. He had other delivery guys."

"Who else helped him deliver?" John-Boy asked.

"Don't know. Never met them."

"Any idea of places to look?" I asked.

"I think I'm done talking."

"We can protect you," I said.

"How? How can you keep me safe when someone on the inside is helping him?"

That ended the productive part of our second interview. We asked more questions, but Oliver would not respond. He feared reprisals from The Messenger's insider more than he feared prison.

Back in the fishbowl, frustration was increasing as the deadline approached and we had no concrete idea where to look for at least twenty bombs.

John-Boy shook his head. "He's a drunk. We can't trust anything he says."

"But I think he's trying to help us," I said.

Captain Creek grunted. "I'm not convinced he's helping. He's working for a terrorist."

"The bank was a test of his bombs. A trial run," John-Boy said, which made sense.

"Where would you put a bomb to injure a lot of people?" I asked.

Helen summarized our dilemma. "In Vegas on a Friday night? Anywhere."

CHAPTER FORTY

Friday 1:15 p.m.

WAS I crazy to think the explosions were linked to the first bank? Were Oliver's house, the bus station, and the bank all tied together? If nothing else, I needed to rule out the bank as a target. Who could help me? I needed help from inside Second United. I had two people in mind: Valerie, the bank manager, and Lynn's father, George. I called Lynn. She assured me her father would help. My team expanded.

I didn't have contact information for Valerie, the bank manager whom I met shortly before I was blown up. It sounded strange to say that, blown up. I called the bank and was connected to Valerie.

Lynn arrived twenty minutes later with her father in tow. Of course, she looked radiant. She always did. I supposed she got up before daybreak to look this way.

"I didn't have time to fix myself. I came direct from the gym," she said.

Great. She looked like this after the gym. Well, I give up.

George held a familiar box of heaven, Pinkbox Doughnuts. I tore open the lid like a child unwrapping presents Christmas morning. A giant box of Peeweez, their bite-size doughnut holes in an assortment of flavors. I could eat my weight in Peeweez, and I might do so today.

Valerie arrived five minutes or nine Peeweez later, depending on how you measured time. We tried to identify any potential enemies of the bank. Ben had done an excellent job searching the computer records, but they turned up an unwieldy number of potential suspects. Second United had over four hundred foreclosures and lawsuits in the last eighteen months.

Four hundred was too many to investigate, and our ranks were severely depleted. How could we narrow the focus of the investigation? I guessed that lesser amounts would not be sufficient motivation for bombings. We eliminated loans less than $20,000, and that eliminated a few. We increased the amount to $50,000 and that narrowed the group to a little over one hundred foreclosures. A hundred potential suspects? This seemed hopeless. And we had not even started looking at all the other lawsuits. An investigation like this could take weeks, and we only had a few hours.

George finally asked, "Maybe the bomber is a disgruntled past employee?"

"Do you have a lot of disgruntled ex-employees?" I asked. That seemed like a big reaction to losing a job.

"We have our fair share, and we have a lot of ex-employees."

I'd only reviewed current employees and only found Soames. Maybe if we looked further back, we could find more suspects. At least with ex-employees we had information like names, addresses, everything we needed to locate them. We weren't starting with a blank slate.

"Maybe we should also check out investors," Valerie said. "As a result of the foreclosures and the housing bubble, our investors have taken quite a hit. Nothing makes a rich person angrier than the threat of becoming a poor person."

Freak. Foreclosures, ex-employees with a chip on their shoulder, and bitter investors. We had narrowed it down to someone in Nevada, but we had to start somewhere.

"I will need to check my files," Valerie said.

We carpooled to Second United. I hadn't been there since the day I got blown up. No sign of the massive explosion that hurt Robin and damaged my sweet rump. They had transformed the entire bank lobby. Still a work in progress, but very impressive. Valerie explained that bomb damage was bad for customer morale. It was also bad for my butt. The coffee and bakery corner were repaired too, a giant leap of progress.

John-Boy and Officer Soames arrived. Was he here to rescue me? I wasn't a damn Damsel in distress. Ugh, men. Why was that weasel with him?

"Got to drop off subpoenas. Thanks for the ride, John," Soames said. "Lynn, so sexy. Is that a new blouse? Do you want to take it off for me? I think you do." His eyes raked over her like she was a piece of meat.

Lynn's eyes went cold. "I want to vomit, but I'll report you to HR instead."

"Again?" Soames chuckled. "You're always thinking of me, aren't you?" He dropped a packet of forms off to the bank's receptionist and exited from the main entrance to the benefit of all women in the building. I rejoiced in seeing him leave. I hoped to never see him again.

Valerie went to the records room to locate the files of disgruntled investors while George searched the HR department for vindictive former employees. Lynn, John-Boy, and I remained in the lobby.

My personal investigator, Raincoat Ronnie, guarded the bank from outside, consuming the last of our Peeweez. The bank was hopping, like always. Businesses applied for financing, couples applied for mortgage loans, young people opened a first account, a big shiny vault door protected the safe deposit boxes. This bank looked like any of a thousand banks across America. A nice, neat line of customers waited for service.

Of course, they only had one teller window open. *Just one. Please.*

The aroma of the bank's coffee bar and bakery called out to us. Well, it screamed to me. I still had the gift card from Valerie. John-Boy ordered an exotic coffee while I chatted with Lynn. The drink sounded good, but I thought I would go for plain old black coffee to help counter the effects of the two pounds of sugar I'd already consumed today.

Lynn stopped mid-sentence and her face went pale. "Oh, my God."

"Lynn, what is it?" I asked.

A voice behind me said, "They have great coffee here, Little Donna."

CHAPTER FORTY-ONE

THE MESSENGER LOOKED *across the Second United bank lobby.* I hate this place, *he thought. Marble was so tacky. It displayed selfishness, not confidence. The ceiling looked like marble, but was fake, like everything about this bank. The fake ceiling had absorbed his first blast. The Messenger would not make that same mistake again. He'd distributed his special creations all over town. Now, he returned to the scene of his first.* This one will complete the circle, *he thought. Today, he would get justice for his mother and inflict justice on those who had wronged her, simultaneously.*

The Messenger couldn't rely on others to carry out this task. It was too important. If you want something done right, you must do it yourself. *He needed to leave his creation where it would go undisturbed until the big moment. It looked innocent enough, a plain briefcase, like any of a hundred an office worker would see every day and never notice.*

The Messenger froze in place. He saw her, that nasty little woman cop. She talked with a sexy woman. The Messenger recognized her but couldn't remember her name. She was a lawyer, but too pretty to be a lawyer.

The Messenger wanted to kill his little nemesis now. It would mess up his plan, but he needed to kill her now. This opportunity was too much of a gift to ignore. Little Donna wasn't even looking in his direction, unaware of his presence, unaware her tiny, insignificant life was about to be extinguished.

The Messenger should stick to his plan, drop off his special package. Why not both? Drop off the package and get revenge against Little Donna now? It might spoil the surprise, but his big day would still be historic. Now my dream can come true. Two birds, one stone, or, two targets, one briefcase bomb.

Little Donna and her shapely friend moved to the coffee bar line, oblivious to anything behind them. The coffee was the only thing this bank sold that was legitimate. He hated this place.

The Messenger grabbed his disposable phone. He dialed 277 to activate the bomb. He heard a reassuring beep. No one nearby noticed. He dialed 477 to activate the external trigger. He heard another reassuring beep. A nearby child looked at him.

"Candy Crush, a new level," The Messenger whispered. The child accepted this explanation and turned back to her mother. He then texted "800" which set the timer at eight minutes. A third beep confirmed the timer had started slowly ticking down. The Messenger felt delight like he had never experienced before. This was the crowning moment of all his hard work. Now he would get justice for his mother and so many others.

The Messenger moved to the back of the coffee line, directly behind Little Donna and her beautiful friend. Every second delighted him. He was about to kill her, and she didn't know he was in the building. He could reach out and touch her messy ponytail. So tempting. He could grab her and throw her to the ground. And the most delicious part, she was blind to him. He *savored this moment. Should he wait for her to notice him? No, he wanted to shock her.*

The Messenger sighed with joy.

The beautiful friend turned around and her face went pale. "Oh, my God," she said.

Oh well. It's showtime. *"They have great coffee here, Little Donna."*

CHAPTER FORTY-TWO

Friday 2:10 p.m.

I WAS glad for the short line at the coffee bar. Lynn was still distracted by the ogre, Soames. He was gone, dragging his knuckles to his next subpoena delivery. What a jerk. But the coffee and pastries. How could those heavenly scents not improve her outlook?

Lynn's expression had turned to stone. I had never seen her so frightened.

"They have great coffee here, Little Donna." The voice filled me with dread.

Who was it? I turned. I didn't know who I expected but this was a complete surprise.

"Little Donna, I've been waiting for this for a long time."

I was stunned. Only one person called me Little Donna. Only one. My brain felt disconnected. How could this be? "Wait. What? You— You're The Messenger?"

Lynn stood beside me, holding my shoulder protectively.

Toupee Man spoke slowly and deliberately. "Of course I'm The Messenger."

I was frozen. Lynn too. I wanted to call out to John-Boy for help, but my brain didn't cooperate.

"Please consider this my special gift," Toupee Man said, and thrust his briefcase into my chest. I grabbed it. Toupee Man clamped one end of a handcuff to my left wrist. The other end was attached to the briefcase.

John-Boy realized the danger and stepped toward The Messenger. "What are you doing?"

Toupee Man shuffled back two steps and held out a cell phone. "Come any closer and I push this button, and everybody dies."

The noisy bank lobby went completely silent.

My voice returned. "What do you want? What's in this briefcase?" I knew the answer even before I uttered the question.

"It's very simple. I want you to die. I also want this bank to be rubble. Luckily for me, I can accomplish both."

Color returned to Lynn's face. "You jackass."

"Stay back," he shouted to John-Boy. "You too, prom queen." Lynn took another step back. Toupee Man straightened the briefcase, so it was horizontal with my arms supporting it. Damn thing was heavy, very heavy. Then he clicked a button on his phone and the briefcase beeped. My heart skipped a beat.

Toupee Man tilted the briefcase at an angle, and the case responded with rapid beeps. After leveling it, the beeping stopped. My heart thudded at a lightening pace.

"My little science experiment also has an internal gyroscope. Keep it level and it won't explode." Toupee Man grinned, knowing he had our rapt attention. "Excuse me, I

misspoke. Keep the briefcase level and it won't explode for"—
he looked at his phone— "seven minutes."

"Can you stop this?" I asked. "Will you stop this?"

"No," he responded and turned away.

Freak. I looked at John-Boy. "Please help," I whispered in
disbelief. This wasn't a nightmare. My nightmares were never
this vivid.

"Oh, and one other thing," Toupee Man said. "Don't try to
remove those handcuffs or else . . . boom."

I instinctively wanted to run out of there as fast as I could,
but I was chained to the menace. The briefcase must have
weighed at least forty pounds. My grip loosened, tipping the
case, and a loud, rapid beep assaulted me. I righted the briefcase and the beeping stopped. Lynn helped me steady it.

"Keep it level or everyone dies. If anyone tries to follow me,
I push the button, and boom."

Toupee Man had everyone's attention. The room was
frozen in fear. Toupee Man stared into my eyes. "You have
seven minutes to live, damn you. I hope you agonize for every
second." He backed out the door, slowly and steadily, and once
to the sidewalk, took off running. I guessed his severe injuries
from the lawsuit had miraculously healed.

"I should go after him," John-Boy said. "But I . . . I . . . I
don't know what to do."

Tears streamed down my cheeks.

Lynn was the voice of reason. "Stay here and stop this
bomb."

"I need to put this down. It's heavy." My arms strained
under the weight of the briefcase. How long could I keep it
level? Lynn helped me balance it.

"I need some tools," John-Boy shouted.

People sprang into action. Valerie called out to the bank's
janitor who sprinted to his closet. She stood on a chair.

"Everyone evacuate out the back doors in case he is still watching." The crowd followed Valerie to the exit.

"Call the bomb squad," John-Boy shouted, but in a lower voice said, "No way they can get here in time."

Valerie approached with soft steps. "Should we move to the vault? The vault will shield most people from the blast."

Most people? But what about the others, like me? The vault would do little for me since I was handcuffed to this damn death box. I was scared, frightened to death. My chest thudded and my head pounded. Was this happening? John-Boy, my cheating ex-husband, was my only hope to survive? *Freak.* I never expected to spend the last few minutes of my life with him.

Valerie cleared the way to the bank vault and pushed any furniture from my path. Lynn helped me navigate and keep the briefcase level. If I tripped, well, I wouldn't have to worry about bridesmaid dresses.

The heavy case strained my back, but adrenaline helped. My arms trembled. Inside the vault, we approached a table for safety deposit box visitors. Once I placed the bomb on the table, my arms relaxed. I inhaled deeply as I felt blood rush back to my arms. I wasn't going to touch the handcuffs.

The janitor appeared with a small collection of tools. John-Boy dumped them out on a table. A well-used hammer, pliers, mismatched screwdrivers, a couple of grease-stained wrenches. "These are all too large. Do you have any smaller tools?" The janitor shook his head. Hope drifted away and the world started spinning, like an awful carnival ride I could not get off.

Lynn slid a stool next to me so I could sit while I stayed handcuffed to the bomb. "Should I stay?" Lynn asked. "Maybe I could help—"

"No," John-Boy said, his voice serious. "Leave. Nothing you can do."

Lynn left after a quick hug, careful not to move the brief-case or my shackled wrist.

"Should I shut the vault door?" Valerie asked on her way out.

John-Boy nodded. "At least push it shut."

"To protect most people," I said with no emotion.

Everyone left except for John-Boy and me. I had never felt so isolated. I could hear my pounding heartbeat, the whoosh from the air vent, and nothing else.

"What about the bomb squad?" I asked.

"Standard procedure is to report to the precinct and move as a group to the site. They won't get here in time. We're on our own."

What was the bomb squad joke John-Boy always said? Once the timer starts, how long do you have to disarm a bomb? *The rest of your life.*

CHAPTER FORTY-THREE

Friday 2:15 p.m.

I EYED the harbinger of my doom, an ugly, brown, boxy briefcase, made of rigid plastic supposed to look like leather or something. It looked outdated, like Toupee Man's wardrobe.

"First, let's try to remove you from the bomb," John-Boy said. Wires from the handcuffs went inside the briefcase.

"I have a key," I announced, finally realizing I could add something positive.

"Damnit," John-Boy said in frustration. "The handcuffs are a trigger. Open them and it detonates. We can't risk trying that until we get a look inside."

"Okay, let's look inside." My voice trembled, revealing my panic.

The briefcase had cheap key locks on the right and left side, the kind that used those little bitty keys that were useless on anything else. John-Boy struggled with the latches. Had Toupee Man locked the briefcase? Of course, he did, the jerk. Every second of delay worked to his advantage.

John-Boy darted out of the room without a word. Was he abandoning me? I wanted to scream but I was too stunned to react. I stared at the vault door in total silence. Now I was completely alone. I could not hear anything but the *thump, thump, thump* of my heartbeat. I would die alone.

John-Boy returned with a handful of office supplies and dumped them on the table. I felt a wave of relief when he came back to me. I almost laughed at the irony. I was relieved to see my cheating ex-husband. He bent a paper clip and picked the locks of the briefcase.

My voice returned. "How do you know it won't explode if you pick the locks?"

"I don't."

"Not funny," I said.

He paused and looked at me. "No good choices here. We can sit and wait for the timer or try disarming the bomb."

I offered no more resistance. John-Boy picked the locks and released the latches. If the bomb was set to explode when we opened the briefcase, this would be my last second on earth. I hoped the rest of the bomb was as poorly made as the briefcase locks. I tried to look away, but I couldn't.

John-Boy flipped open the briefcase and we stared at the obstacle before us. Another hope crushed. The bomb looked like something from NASA, crisscrossed wires in an assortment of colors. John-Boy examined the timer. Another sight trans-fixed me, eight sticks of dynamite on each side with a metal box in the middle. Twice as much as the first blast. This was bad.

The digital timer read 6:21 . . . 6:20 . . . . 6:19 . . . My heart sank a little with each second.

"Tell me you can do this," I said.

John-Boy didn't look at me, a bad sign. "With my regular tools and another bomb tech, absolutely. With few tools and no help, maybe."

Maybe? Freak. "Please try. Please, please try." *Freak.* My voice went even higher. I needed some positive reinforcement, a shot of tequila, a hug from Mom or John-Boy, but I didn't want him to stop working.

John-Boy whipped out a special tool he had in his holster, a flat, black pair of pliers with strange-looking notches. "Wire stripper and cutter. Primary tool of a bomb tech." I had never seen him so intense, at least not with his clothes on. He muttered to himself. "Red and white wires, always cut the red . . . White and black wires, always cut the white . . ." I stared at him. "Sorry, chants from training help with the stress."

"Chant all you need." The chants were not helping my stress, but I nodded to go ahead.

"First, we need to disable the phone detonator, so The Messenger can't set it off."

"What about the timer?"

"That's next." John-Boy slowly and expertly traced the wires from the cell phone to the eight sticks of dynamite on the left side.

"The cell phone is only tied to this part of the device," John-Boy announced.

The timer read 5:30 . . . 5:29 . . . 5:28 . . .

"Let's cut the last wire and move the cell phone out of the way." He snipped the wire and the cell phone clattered to the floor, a startling sound in this metal deathtrap.

The timer lowered one minute upon cutting the wire. It now read 4:26 . . . 4:25 . . . 4:24 . . .

"Dammit," John-Boy said. "Okay, he has everything booby-trapped. A wrong move speeds up the timer. This guy is good."

My chest tightened. Was I having a heart attack? Why die from a heart attack four minutes before I would be blown to bits? I looked away from the bomb to lower my blood pressure. I'd never spent much time inside a bank vault before. Rows of safe deposit boxes in perfect lines and right angles, obviously designed by someone with obsessive-compulsive disorder. I tried counting them to slow my breathing, but I could only reach seven before the bomb chained to my wrist distracted me.

"I need your help," John-Boy said.

"I have one hand free. What do you want me to do?"

"Help me remove this cover."

I looked at the cover. It didn't look complicated. In the center of the briefcase was a silver metal box with a lid secured by six screws. *I can use a screwdriver.* I picked up the yellow octagon handle, my hand shaking.

"Relax," John-Boy said. "Deep breath. Just unscrewing a screw, that's all. Focus on the immediate task and nothing else."

The only sound was my breathing and my pounding pulse. Together, they were deafening. I got the first screw out and dropped it to the floor. The second screw was just as easy. I got the third screw loose, but it fell back into the briefcase. "Dammit," I instinctively reached for the screw.

"Don't reach for it." I froze. "You might set it off."

I think my heart stopped. I meant to answer, but my voice failed me.

"Just don't help anymore, please."

"We don't have anyone else. I can do something. My small hands might help."

John-Boy considered this and nodded. I reached through the wires, careful to not touch anything else, and found the screw and dropped it on the floor.

The timer ticked down, 3:42 . . . 3:41 . . . 3:40 . . .

I finally had all six screws out and froze in place. John-Boy removed the cover, and my heart sank again. Inside the silver box were twenty more sticks of dynamite and another timer. No wonder the damn thing was so heavy.

I'm going to die.

CHAPTER FORTY-FOUR

Friday 2:19 p.m.

I LOOKED AT JOHN-BOY. "Another timer? Why?" I didn't understand all this bomb making stuff, but this seemed insane. A second timer?

"Backup," John-Boy explained, "in case the first one is diffused in time. This guy is good."

Good? Not the word I thought of. Scattered among the dynamite were cut pieces of wire. Hundreds of them, maybe thousands. "What's all this?" I asked. "Scraps from making the bomb?" I supposed this wire was to confuse anyone trying to disarm it.

"Cut wire. Highly effective shrapnel."

"Wire can hurt you?"

"It will when it tears through your body at eight hundred miles an hour." Perspiration dripped down the side of his face.

I didn't know much about bombs, and I didn't want to know any more.

The timer continued to count down, 3:10 . . . 3:09 . . . 3:08 . . .

John-Boy glanced at me. "You're about to have an anxiety attack. Look away."

I looked around the bank vault again. A heavy silver cart held boxes of something. Coins. The cart was full of giant, brick-sized boxes of quarters, dimes, nickels, pennies. Hundreds, thousands of dollars' worth of coins must be outrageously heavy. How many nickels did a bank need? Did anyone still use nickels? For what? I tried to remember the last time I spent a nickel. I usually left nickels and pennies in the little change cup at the cash register. I hoped that counted as being generous. I might be meeting my maker soon.

Coins instinctively made me think of vending machines. I knew this seemed like a strange time, but I was starving. I looked around for vending machines or office snacks. Nothing. I guessed I wouldn't be hungry for long.

John-Boy efficiently uncurled the mass of colored wires and cut them in order. I assumed he cut them in order since I was still alive. The multiple wire colors created an interesting piece of abstract art, like a Jackson Pollock painting with a deadly undertone. He disconnected the timer and remembered to leave the final wire attached rather than risk losing another sixty precious seconds.

"That went well," I said, eying the timer at 2:24 . . . 2:23 . . . 2:22 . . .

"The bomber used the typical color coding and it worked."

He pulled out the second timer with a trail of wires behind it. "Shit."

I looked but didn't want to. All the wires from the second timer were black. Every single wire. No color coding. It was like sorting spaghetti noodles. How would he know which one to cut? Still, John-Boy kept up his intensity as my positivity sank.

I would die here, right here, today. I would die in this damn bank vault. I wanted to run away. I wanted John-Boy to hold me in his arms. I wanted to hear my mother's voice. I wanted to strangle the life out of Toupee Man. I wouldn't get the opportunity to do any of those things. I was going to die today. I wanted to focus on positive thoughts, but not a single one would populate my mind. Damn, I was hungry.

John-Boy never slowed his pace. He had found several black wires that weren't connected to anything, just to confuse us. He had removed three wires already, but too many remained.

The timer ticked down, 1:40 . . . 1:39 . . . 1:38 . . .

The vault door swung open as the timer read 1:30. A wave of Old Spice cologne hit me. Archie darted inside, completely focused on the task. "John, where are we?"

"Archie, going to need your help," John-Boy welcomed our new arrival. "I need some more hands."

"Archie, please help," I pleaded. "I don't want to die here." I think that panic attack might have returned.

Archie wore a vest with bulky pockets. "How does the timer look?"

"Under ninety seconds," John-Boy said.

"Please help." My voice sounded an octave too high for normal. What was normal about dying in a big explosion?

John-Boy pointed to a mass of black wires. "Test these wires. See if they're active and run a quick bypass."

"Where's your bypass setup?" Archie asked.

"Don't have one."

"Luckily, I came prepared." Archie removed assorted tools and wires from his vest pockets. "This one is active, so leaving it. This one is dead." Archie snipped the black wire before

John-Boy could warn him, and the timer lowered one minute, now 0:28 . . . 0:27 . . . 0:26 . . .

"Shit," Archie said. "Booby trapped."

Loud, rhythmic beeping emanated from the briefcase when the timer reached 0:20: *beep*, 0:19, *beep*, 0:18, *beep* . . .

"Out of time," John-Boy said, and I knew what that meant.

Archie grabbed more wires. "Let's try the handcuff trigger."

Working in tandem, John-Boy and Archie worked on the handcuff wires.

The timer read 0:10 . . . and started a louder, double beeping rhythm: 0:09 . . . beep beep, 0:08 *beep beep* . . .

"Leave me, get out, and shut the vault door." I had no idea where that bravery came from. It didn't sound like me. In my mind, I was already gone, the bomb had already taken me, but I could save John-Boy and Archie. They didn't move an inch. Three wires left: one, two and three.

"Got to risk it," John-Boy said. "Cut number one—no, no! Cut two, number two."

I closed my eyes. This was it, my last breath.

I heard a snip, and Archie and John-Boy lifted me up as we ran out of the bank vault and dove to the hard, marble floor. John-Boy landed on me, covering me, protecting me.

The timer in my head continued the countdown:

0:03 *beep beep*

0:02 *beep beep*

CHAPTER FORTY-FIVE

Friday 2:23 p.m.

THE BRIEFCASE GAVE three sharp beeps. I didn't remember closing my eyes, but I must have. The blast launched John-Boy away from me.

The room was silent. I guessed I was still alive. My shield was gone. I saw John-Boy. He had protected me. His split-second instinct was to protect me.

I tried to stand and stumbled, like I was on an amusement park ride, violently lurching in different directions. Was this another nightmare? Same damn bank, another explosion? Was I cursed? I was never coming back to this freaking bank, ever.

Maybe this was how death felt. My stomach growled. I doubted that would occur in heaven, so I must be alive. I got up on my knees.

"John-Boy?" I called out. I stumbled into him, and we embraced. He was alive. I was alive. "You saved me," was all I could mutter before tears streamed down my face. We had survived. It seemed like a miracle. His face blurred in front of me. John-Boy groaned, holding his ribs, trying to regain his balance. The rest of the bank was empty—at least empty of people. Valerie had evacuated in time. *Good job, Valerie.*

I was starving. Like divine intervention, a remnant of the coffee bar landed at my feet. A scone rested a foot away. I picked it up and shook off the dust. Blueberry. Maybe chocolate chip. My vision was still a little fuzzy. If I could survive two bomb blasts, a little dust wasn't going to hurt me. I was in no position to be choosy. I took a bite—blueberry, not chocolate chip. It tasted better than anything I had eaten in a long time. I took two more bites then put the rest in my jacket pocket.

Red lights flashed around the bank's interior. The burglar alarm signaled a disturbance, but it was a little late. I eyed the steel cave that had almost been my burial chamber. Red lights also flickered from the interior of the vault, masked by dark smoke.

A second later, water rained down on me from the bank's sprinkler system, and my ears popped, now overwhelmed with the sound of the bank alarm's insistent buzzing. The fire alarm, tied to the sprinkler system, was even more shrill. In combination, the two alarms were impossible to ignore, and I supposed that was the point. I faced the ceiling to remove the grit from my face. The sprinklers were like a bad motel shower: low water pressure, lukewarm, but sufficient to rinse away some of the dust that covered me. With all the grit and the water, I felt like a breaded chicken before being put in the fryer.

John-Boy, battered and bleeding from cuts on his scalp and hands, would survive. He held his ribs. We hugged, gently because of his ribs and my sore rump, relieved to be still alive and breathing. At this moment, his skanky girlfriend was not much of a concern.

"Where's Archie?" he shouted in my ear to be heard over the alarms.

I shook my head. He had to be around here somewhere. I scanned the bank, now damp with dusty water. The room had been penetrated with hundreds or thousands of wire fragments. It looked like it was covered in polka dots. Helen's prediction came true.

Everything glass was shattered. Furnishings, if recognizable, were also polka dotted, and thrown about. Somehow, we had survived this. A miracle. The heavy vault door provided a shield, a wedge of the bank not damaged by the shrapnel. I could see my outline in the dust, and John-Boy's, both safely in the protected wedge.

Archie wasn't in the safe wedge. A pool of bright red blood spread from his body. John-Boy cradled his shoulders, chanting, "No, no, no!"

Wire had penetrated Archie's chest in multiple spots, which might have been fatal alone. He also had been hit in the face, his eyes open and fixed. His facial expression was one of pure terror. Death must have been instant. It was the most grotesque thing I had ever seen. I pulled out the remainder of my blueberry scone and dropped it on the floor. For the first time in my life, I had no appetite.

CHAPTER FORTY-SIX

Friday 2:26 p.m.

A MEDIC SQUATTED BESIDE ME. "Can you wiggle your fingers for me?" I could. I didn't feel good, but I could move my fingers and had feeling in them all. On the positive side, my middle finger still worked, so I could drive in Vegas traffic. I appreciated the sprinklers now. Refreshing. They rinsed off the outer layer of dusty crud. Now if I could only find a bar of soap.

The fire alarm quieted, and the sprinklers stopped seconds later. The flames from inside the vault were extinguished. I wobbled to the vault and peered inside. Was this the same place? The safe deposit boxes which had looked impenetrable were bent, damaged, or torn off from the blast. Charred coins littered the floor. The heavy cart that had held them was reduced to a skeleton. Under my foot, a quarter was bent at a 90-degree angle. How hard did you have to hit a quarter to bend it like that?

The minimal furniture was gone. Devastation was total. The chair where I had sat just moments ago left scorch marks on the floor. That would have been me, gone with only a mark on the floor to indicate where I had been. Back in the lobby, I saw flashing lights through the shattered windows.

Valerie leaned close to my ear and screamed over the burglar alarm. I understood her on the third try. "You have a call on the bank's line four. Captain or something." Valerie guided me to a phone that survived the blast.

I grabbed the receiver. "Wyznecki here." I got a garbled reply. "Captain Creek, can you hear me?" More static and broken syllables. "Captain? Can you hear me now?"

"Sorry about the subterfuge, Little Donna. I am not your captain."

The Messenger's voice made me livid. I gripped the phone like a vise. "You are a jackass. And stop calling me Little Donna."

"I am soooo disappointed to hear your voice, *Donna*."

"It is Detective Wyznecki to you, jerk."

"As you wish, Detective. I wanted to inform you that I shall have my vengeance. Tonight is my grand finale."

"How about a clue?" I asked.

"I suppose you have earned one, Little Do— Detective Wyznecki."

"Who's the target?"

"The bank."

"Which bank? Second United Bank?"

"All banks. The selfish must be punished."

My hopes for productive hints from Toupee Man died.

"Also, Little Donna, I mean Detective Wyznecki, many bank executives live in the Vegas area. I do hope they are safe at home." The implied threat lingered in the air. "The selfish must be punished."

Freak. Toupee Man had a vendetta against all banks in Las Vegas. That was too many targets to count. He was targeting the executives, too. Could be hundreds of potential targets. I would've had more confidence if he had said nothing. If I could learn more about Toupee Man, maybe I could reduce the number of targets.

I stuck by John-Boy for the hospital ride, holding his hand the entire way. John-Boy had broken ribs and internal injuries. But John-Boy was strong. He would make it. Archie was not so lucky.

John-Boy, my cheating ex, saved me. Toupee Man had set out to kill me today, and he almost succeeded. If John-Boy hadn't been there, I would have died.

CHAPTER FORTY-SEVEN

Friday 3:04 p.m.

BACK AT THE PRECINCT, I hobbled to the ladies' room to wash Archie's blood off my hands and blouse. It didn't work. I changed to another top, further depleting my wardrobe inventory. I had to get my head back in the game. We had to find our bomber—The Messenger, dear Mister Toupee—which should be easier now. We had the dirtbag's name, Alexander Higgins, the dirtbag's picture, the dirtbag's address, everything. We had every piece of the puzzle. Mister Toupee's deadly game was over, and he would pay, pay for what he did to Archie and John-Boy and me, pay for what he did to Robin and so many others.

We had to narrow the scope of his targets. Blowing up all the banks in Las Vegas would require an army of helpers and truck loads of explosives. How could one crazy guy accomplish all this?

Rage set my stomach on fire. I saw Toupee Man's picture and wanted to scream. He pretended to be handicapped for the lawsuit, such a worm. Printed above his driver's license photo was "Alexander Fontaine Higgins." So that was what the F stood for. It wasn't my first guess, not even my tenth. Fontaine? Hmmm. Even his name angered me.

We had to catch this monster. Every person left a large digital footprint, even a gutter dweller like Higgins. We had his place of birth, which turned out to be Toledo, Ohio, not hell. As each detective and agent learned a fact, it was scribbled on whiteboards. He wasn't employed. That job at the snake pit was a sham, like his injuries. He had bank accounts across the valley, flush with cash. He could not be worried about money. Why would he do this?

A team staked out Higgins's home. We watched remotely from the fishbowl. No activity, but it was late. Maybe Higgins was asleep? Maybe he was dead? What would he die from? Probably wouldn't be dandruff.

I was so drawn into the investigation I had forgotten about the rest of the world, until Sandy gave me a hug. "I just heard about Robin. How is he?" Hearing Robin's name again brought me back to his bedside, straining, hoping for him to breathe on his own. I broke down. This day had been too much. Sandy hugged me again. She was such a great friend. My Disco Divas gathered in the hallway. My office family was always supportive. I was glad to have them.

This had been a day for the Guinness record books. I had almost gotten blown up, again, Archie was dead, John-Boy was hurt, and the city was under attack. Every bank was a potential target and the executives' homes . . . Freak, I was exhausted.

The fishbowl hummed with activity. Police had raided Higgins's apartment, hoping to catch our killer asleep. Bomb-sniffing dogs cleared the area before the officers went in. He had already proven he would risk someone else's life and property to strike at the police. Would he risk his own? He was too selfish, too greedy. No one was home, which was expected but still disappointing.

His grungy apartment showed no signs of being the bomb factory. Where was it? He needed space to construct his arsenal. It could be anywhere. He could have set up shop in any vacant house or business. He could have rented a storage unit, a barn, or a garage. His lair might not even be in Vegas. The prospects seemed hopeless. He was arrogant but had to have known the tide had turned on him. He was no longer a digitally altered voice. We knew he was Alexander Higgins. Mystery solved. Now we just had to catch him. People reacted strangely to the prospect of losing their freedom, even for a brief time. Higgins was about to lose his forever. That fact had to change his perspective on risk and mortality.

Lynn surprised me with a hug. Lynn was here? Why? She looked radiant as ever. She should be in Hollywood. "I'm here to help."

"Am I being sued again?"

Lynn shook her head. Two officers carried boxes of legal files, and two more fawned over her looks. I had walked by the same men when I entered the station, and they hadn't even looked my way. Ugh.

Lynn had the legal files on Mister Toupee, although now I doubted whether the details he had provided were true. We divided up the pile among the Disco Divas. His home was being monitored. We quickly learned his entire life history was fake. All we really knew was his photo was accurate.

Lynn said what I was thinking. "Why does Higgins hate banks?"

"Maybe," I thought out loud, "Higgins has some kind of twisted logic that banks owe him."

The captain asked across the fishbowl, "How's the dive into Mr. Higgins?"

Ben shook his head. "He does not seem to have a family. One brief mention of growing up in foster care."

I was puzzled. "Foster care and hating banks? I don't see the link."

"I grew up in foster care," Ben said, "and I don't hate all banks."

So, no family. Then who was "she"? The Messenger mentioned being motivated by a "she." Who was this mystery woman? A love interest that worked for a bank. Could any woman really love him? Maybe "she" wasn't a woman. Maybe "she" was a child. How could a child factor into his behavior? Did Higgins have a child? Why would a child make him angry at banks? Nothing made sense.

The selfish must be punished. He repeated that over and over again. What did it mean? Why was he so mad at the banks? Could he be this angry over bank fees? Angry yes, but to dedicate his life to making bombs and killing innocent people? No, not for four dollars a month. It had to be something else, something we had overlooked. But what? What was I missing?

CHAPTER FORTY-EIGHT

Friday 3:15 p.m.

"I'VE GOT SOMETHING," Ben announced. We crowded around his computer screen. "Higgins was in the military."

"What branch?" Charlie asked.

"Army. Oh, boy, the bomb disposal unit."

That answered the question of how Higgins made them. He didn't need help.

John-Boy arrived in a wheelchair and the sight took my breath away. I wanted to scream at him about his skanky mistress who was very much still in the picture, but I stopped. I instinctively gave him a hug but dropped my arms when he groaned. He said walking made his ribs hurt more. Seeing him in that condition was a terrible reality check. We were lucky to be alive. I was lucky to be alive.

"How's the investigation going? Catch this a-hole yet?" John-Boy asked.

I gave John-Boy the five-minute summation of our investigation. "You are the perfect person for this," I told him. "Mister

Toupee was in the military, served in a bomb disposal unit. Your service times overlapped. Maybe you knew him."

"Let me see his photo again," John-Boy asked, scooting his wheelchair closer.

"Recognize him?" Captain Creek asked.

"He used to have hair," I added.

"Sorry," John-Boy said. "We had units deployed around the globe. He doesn't look familiar."

Sandy interjected. "Can you search Army records for him?"

"Yes, but the official way takes forever," John-Boy said with a groan.

"Maybe some of your military buddies could offer insight to our bomber," I said. "We would take any help we could get." It seemed like a long shot, but so far, we had nothing.

John-Boy smiled. "I still have contacts in the Army. Let me see what I can find *unofficially.*"

"Any progress on the foster parents?" Captain Creek asked.

Ben shook his head. "Can't unseal these records. They're guarded better than bank records."

I didn't know if that was good for the Department of Health and Human Services or bad for the banks. Probably both.

"Give me a minute." Shale took his cell phone into the hallway. I accidentally but on purpose overheard his part of the discussion. Shale said a few comments but was cut off in mid-sentence each time. "Sir, I understand, but I need access— We have a bomber on the loose—" "Listen, I need access to those records, now— We must stop this nutjob— This is the only clue we have—" Finally, Shale nodded. "Yes, sir. I will be discreet, sir."

Shale approached Ben. "Mind if I have access to your computer?" Ben pushed his chair back. "If you could all look away, please." Shale tapped out a long string of keys, then stopped.

Ben scooted his chair close again. "We are in the DHHS records now." He announced each major discovery to the room. "Higgins lived his entire childhood as a foster kid . . . In and out of different foster homes . . . Most of the time with one foster mother, Rosa Arenque, right here in Las Vegas, who raised a couple dozen foster kids for years, decades actually. She was like the Mother Teresa of foster mothers."

"We need to contact her. Got a current address?" I asked

"The long-time foster mother died earlier this month." Ben tapped more keys.

"Was she terminally ill?" I asked.

Ben shook his head. "No. Seems that she repeatedly borrowed money to help her foster kids go to college. Second United foreclosed on her home. She owed . . . wow . . . double what the home appraised for."

"Sounds like she deserved a medal, not a foreclosure," Sandy said.

Ben nodded, still scanning the online reports. "DHHS took her foster kids away because of the foreclosure. That was her mission. She took her own life a week later, just before the first explosion."

"Which banks were involved?" I asked.

Ben scanned the spreadsheets. "All loans were from Second United."

"And the selfish must be punished," I announced.

This was a calculated leap of faith, but we had to assume that Toupee Man only had a grievance towards Second United. That was rational. In his mind, Second United killed his foster mother. Would he really have enough anger at all banks to bomb them? Unlikely. Should we concentrate all our efforts on

Second United? That seemed reasonable, but it was a substantial risk if we stopped screening other banks.

Now we knew why Higgins was targeting Second United. He wanted to make them pay. I would be angry too, but blowing up a bank?

Dr. Torrance brushed back his Einstein hair and said, "He could be hiding at his foster Mom's old house. It might rationalize his anger."

"We have a short window to avert this mass killing," the captain said. "We must inspect all places with a Second United affiliation. Every single one. Ignore everything else."

"What about Dr. Torrance's idea?" I asked.

Shale's tight lips uttered, "Yes, send a small team to his old house."

"A small team?" I asked.

"At this point, we're not looking for his assembly space, just trying to stop the bombs."

The captain echoed Shale's idea. "Get every officer in the field searching every Second United building. My injured officers should help coordinate. Everyone who is mobile scatter to every Second United branch, office, or executive home, and start looking for bombs."

We pulled all officers off traffic duties and office work. The workforce was thin, but we couldn't afford to be sloppy. If we overlooked a single bomb, people would die. The total number of branches, offices, and bank executives in the area was overwhelming.

Ben put maps of the city on all the screens. We coordinated the buildings that should be searched. We had a lengthy list of branch offices, including offices that were not open to the public, but Higgins might still know about them. We also had a list of over four hundred employees. We quickly narrowed the list to managers and executives. I doubted Higgins had deadly animosity towards a bank teller or administrative assistant. That narrowed our list to twenty-three current executives and added thirty-one retired executives in the area. Las Vegas was a popular home for current and past bosses of Second United.

We sent two officers to the mother's former house. We dispatched all other units to Second United branches across the valley.

"Any idea why today is the big day?" I asked.

"Oh, shit," Ben said. "Today, is . . . or was . . . the foster Mom's birthday."

CHAPTER FORTY-NINE

Friday 3:45 p.m.

OFFICERS IN PAIRS searched Second United buildings, and we had some success. We diffused six devices, but we didn't know how many were left, so it was too soon to break out the champagne. Dread hung over all of us—so many Second United places to search. If we were wrong about Second United, a lot of people were going to die.

We shifted the search teams to a different location the instant they found a bomb, and then sent in our depleted bomb unit. We got word that an explosion had damaged a Second United branch on the south side of the city. No one was killed, but many were injured, and the story was quickly picked up by the local media. Rumors ran wild. A panicked public complicated our search efforts. Every phone line glowed from the worried locals.

We had no idea what type of surveillance Higgins had for the bombs he'd already hidden, but we had to risk it and assume he wasn't watching. Besides, he couldn't watch them all. He hadn't reacted to our discoveries, so either he had a lot more explosives planted or had given up surveillance.

The media spread rumors like the flu virus. Reporters questioned whether all banks should close, and many did out of fear. The FBI was talking to Captain Creek about federal involvement since the banks were being targeted.

John-Boy suggested we re-sweep the sites where we had found explosives. He explained that bombers often used two devices. The first inflicted minor damage, and the second, a larger bomb set for a later time, would kill the gathering crowd and the first responders. John-Boy's idea made sense in a sick, morbid way, and it sounded like something Toupee Man would do.

Our officers did a second sweep and found four more devices. Excellent call, John-Boy. These sweeps took time and resources, but we were saving lives.

Charlie reported that the mother's home was now occupied by a new family who knew nothing about Mister Toupee. Another dead end and more time wasted. Disappointing.

Sandy announced they found three devices at bank executives' homes.

Helen shouted, "Explosion at former CEO's home in Summerlin South. Home destroyed, not sure if anyone was injured."

I remembered George was an executive at Second United. "Lynn, your father—"

"I had him and Mom move to the Venetian hotel a while ago. Don't worry about their house. It is empty of people. Things can be replaced."

John-Boy announced, "I heard from my army buddies. Higgins was dishonorably discharged, psychiatric issues. He had a persecution complex. That and explosives is a deadly mix."

We needed more officers. We had too many places to search. John-Boy chomped at the bit to help but realized how useless that would have been. He was far too injured to move from site to site. Besides, we needed his help coordinating all the moving parts of this circus. With search teams all over the city, continuous updates came in. I felt like I was listening to a horse race announcer. Keeping track of which sites had been searched and which ones were next, each of us carried on four conversations simultaneously. This must be how FAA flight controllers felt—stressed and overwhelmed. We needed more help, but that would pull another person off the search for more explosives.

How much help did Higgins have? We had Oliver in custody, but Oliver said there were others delivering for Higgins. He must have worked for days delivering all these bombs. Did Higgins deliver any himself? How was he disguised? We finally had a clue. One executive's home had a single visitor, a pool maintenance man, which home security video confirmed as Higgins. He hid the bomb in a toolbox he left by the back door of the spacious home. Hidden in plain sight.

The pool man disguise wouldn't work everywhere, but once it worked, Toupee Man likely used that method at other executive residences. We called every CEO's home to see if a pool man had come by recently and see if he had left anything behind. Those calls yielded four more explosives. The bomb squad dashed to each home to safely remove Higgins's nasty surprises.

I worried. Had I misjudged this? Was it wrong to limit our search to Second United? That tactical decision could result in a lot of deaths if I was wrong.

CHAPTER FIFTY

Friday 4:15 p.m.

WE HAD a moment to pose uncomfortable questions. Could Higgins have another bomb factory? John-Boy suggested he might be making more bombs while we searched. We couldn't worry about that.

John-Boy approached me. "I know we've had our differences ..."

I turned my head. I didn't have time for this discussion, maybe not ever.

". . . but I still care for you. I worry about you." He was visibly upset.

We embraced, gently. I looked into his eyes. "We will discuss this, we will. But later. We have a job to do."

Higgins was somewhere, waiting to remotely detonate all his devices. He needed a location where he could hide without fear of being caught, noticed, or interrupted. Someone could be helping him hide, someone who knew LVPD procedures in general or our current actions.

I looked to Helen to expand our discussion. "Do we have a mole on the force helping The Messenger?" I asked.

"Oliver said as much," John-Boy replied.

"But he has no idea who it is," Helen said.

Our task was as frustrating as it was futile.

Ben nodded. "You can't trust anyone."

We were looking for a bald man with a cell phone somewhere in Vegas. Hopeless. He could be in any hotel room, any bar, any store browsing. He could be sitting in front of any slot machine at any casino. The more we rationalized our predicament, the worse it seemed. We were already stretched thin searching all the banks, offices, and executive residences tied to Second United, and we still had officers at all the hotels.

I stared at the colored dots on the map of Las Vegas: red indicated a bomb found, green indicated searching now, blue indicated search conducted but no bomb found. The bright red map looked like a Valentine's Day card, which made me wonder if I would get one this year.

My phone rang and I absently picked it up. "Yes? State your location."

"Now, Little Donna, should I really tell you?" Toupee Man, torturing me with another call. "I do have another location for you."

"Do share," I said with sarcasm.

"UMC."

"What?" I asked.

"University Medical Center. You know, the big hospital."

Robin was at UMC. "You put a bomb in the hospital?"

"Sorry, Little Donna. Did I forget to mention that earlier?"

"You're despicable, going after sick people."

"Don't lecture me about bad behavior. Second United went after my dear mother and foster kids. They are the guilty ones."

"Why the hospital?" I asked.

"They could have saved her. They didn't do anything. Pronounced her dead after a ten-second assessment. The hospital wouldn't have behaved that way if she was rich or insured."

I shook my head. "But she took her own life. It wasn't the hospital's fault—"

"Listen to this," he said.

I stopped breathing to make sure I could hear his next statement.

I heard a loud bang. I jerked the phone away from my head, but it was still so loud that my ears rang. "What was that?" I asked.

"Me, carrying out my promise. That was a small sample of my explosive potential." He chuckled softly. "The emergency room will need a makeover."

CHAPTER FIFTY-ONE

Friday 4:38 p.m.

"I WILL FIND YOU," I screamed and realized I was talking to the dial tone.

I looked at Ben. "Any trace on the call?"

Ben tapped away. "Cell phone from Vegas, near UMC. Certainly a burner, but I will check."

Officers called into headquarters to report the bombing, seconds after local news stations interjected "Breaking News."

The fishbowl's screens danced to life with videos near UMC. The Messenger was not joking. He had destroyed part of UMC's emergency room entrance. He intentionally damaged the outside of the building, creating a more sensational image for television. It resembled a war scene, with rubble and smoke among the ruins and shattered windows.

I clenched my fists and vowed to catch The Messenger if it took me forever.

Charlie patted my shoulder and announced, "Send any

available officers to University Medical Center and sweep for another bomb."

We would need a hundred officers to search UMC's giant complex, and we were still searching bank buildings and executive residences for explosives.

Charlie broke my thoughts and pulled me back into the present. "I will contact the UMC administrator and tell them to divert all incoming patients to another hospital immediately."

"What about the patients that are already at UMC?" Sandy asked.

Charlie hung his tired head. "We don't have the manpower to move them."

What about Robin and Elaine?

I knew department policy was not to tell anyone about a bomb threat to avoid a panic. But this was my family, my brother Robin and Elaine, who I now felt closer to than ever. I couldn't be silent. I had to tell her even if it meant losing my job.

I took my cell phone into the hall and whispered, "Elaine—"

"Donna, what happened? Was that an explosion?"

"Yes. How's Robin?"

"He's still unconscious."

I could hear the desperation in her voice. I had to tell her the truth. "You know the case I've been working on?"

"Yes, the bomber who injured Robin."

I exhaled to regain my composure. "Well, he has called in threats to UMC." I paused so Elaine could take all this in. "You should leave the hospital immediately."

"I'm not going without Robin, and he can't leave." Elaine's disposition told me this matter was settled, nothing more I could say to influence her. "Besides, you're going to catch this guy. I know you will."

I wished I shared Elaine's confidence. Leaving Robin in the hospital was the hardest thing I ever had to do.

"Everyone shut up," the captain announced. Ben increased the volume on the channel 3 feed. "We just heard reports that hospitals have been threatened by the bomber targeting Vegas hotels."

Freak. We needed more help.

Captain Creek called the Governor's office—they would dispatch the National Guard to the area hospitals. Patients who were mobile would be moved to the hospital at Nellis Air Force Base, north of the city. Of course, all these plans took time—time we did not have.

CHAPTER FIFTY-TWO

Friday 5:15 p.m

SANDY LOOKED AT ME, the exhaustion showing on her face. "This is hopeless. Between the banks, the hotels, and the executives' homes, we were already overwhelmed. What if he's trying to mislead us again? Maybe the bomb is at another hospital. We must find him to put an end to this. Where do you look for a damn snake?"

"He could be anywhere," Ben replied.

Captain Creek lit his cigarette, but no one complained. "I suppose I could put out an alert to look for a bald man with a cell phone."

I shook my head. "That won't improve the situation."

Sandy, Helen, and I looked for patterns in the bombs, regions of the city, neighborhoods of the CEOs—no patterns. The Disco Divas could solve this mystery. I believed in us. The Messenger had called in bomb threats to all the casinos on the Strip and all the ones downtown—no patterns. The maps of the explosions included Second United's downtown branch, the bus station, and the home of Mr. Oliver, his co-conspirator—no patterns. We reviewed the maps of the city, dotted with our searches. These sites *must* show a pattern. So, where was it? I reread the file on my desk about the cheated investors from Second United. My brain jumped into gear. Holy crapola. I dropped the files onto the floor.

Captain Creek approached me from behind, the heavy odor of cigarette giving me an advance warning. His normally unlit cigarette was lit, and he was puffing away. I wanted to complain, but the indoor smoke was way down the list of priorities. He looked at me. "Wyznecki, get to the hospital. I want you to oversee that search. Find the other bomb before he levels UMC."

"Let me look for him," I offered. "I have an idea."

The captain puffed another cloud toward me. "Donna, go to the hospital. We need you at UMC."

"No. I have to find him," I replied.

"Donna, report to UMC or consider yourself fired. We don't have extra bodies. We sent officers to all the local banks, the shopping malls, the Fremont Experience, all the casinos on the Strip, the national guard at the airport, and now the hospital. We are operating way beyond capacity. I need someone there I can trust."

"But I—"

"Dammit, Wyznecki, do as you are ordered."

I stomped out and drove Robin's fancy new car alone, my rump still aching, my pride stung. But I would catch Mister Toupee. At least I hoped so. If I guessed wrong, I would look stupid as bombs destroyed Robin's hospital and multiple banks around the city.

My phone buzzed. It was John-Boy.

"I want to take this guy down. I cannot believe Captain ordered me to stay."

I understood his anger. He wanted ten minutes alone with Higgins. So did I. Higgins had blown me up—twice!—my tush was still sore and my head still pounded from the most recent explosion. And Robin . . . and Archie . . .

I drove nearly double the speed limit, weaving in and out of traffic, followed by horn blasts and rude gestures. I was cussed in English and Spanish.

"I should be there. It's my job," John-Boy moaned. I imagined his broken ribs rubbing together.

I decided to confide in him. "I know where he is," I told my ex.

"Tell me! I'll have a team meet you there."

"I'm not one hundred percent sure, only a guess. I'll contact you if I find him. Keep searching for him. Every second counts. Be sure and tell the captain that—"

My phone slipped from my hand and landed on the floorboard, near my feet. On instinct, I reached down to grab it.

My body was jolted again, and the world turned black.

CHAPTER FIFTY-THREE

Friday 5:24 p.m.

I FELT like my entire body was in a vise. The pain was so intense I could not open my eyes.

"Are you hurt? Are you hurt?" I heard overlapping voices.

"Just help me get up," I said. Once upright, I could assess the scene. Robin's fancy car was half on the sidewalk, one tire bent horribly out of alignment, the windshield cracked, both sides very scraped, the rear-view mirror gone, and the air bags deflating.

Men circled the scene. "Terrible, just terrible," one of them said.

I sat on the curb, waiting for the world to stop spinning. I did a quick check of my body for injuries. I was still a little numb from the shock, but I didn't feel that anything was broken. A couple of cuts and aches. The other two drivers were bumped and bruised, but no one seemed critical.

"Awful . . ."

"Terrible . . ."

"What a shame . . ."

The gathering of men each offered their brief comments. Upon focusing, I noticed the men were not commenting about the injured people, they were enthralled with Robin's damaged sports car, with the price sticker in the now shattered window. What was it with men and their toys?

A uniformed officer arrived, and I gave a quick summary. "Accident was my fault."

The officer called in for an accident detail, but I didn't know if we had anyone available. Once he quickly confirmed that no one was critical, he said, "I'll need you to write out a statement. First you can talk to your union representative if you wish."

"Listen, I'm working on The Messenger case."

He nodded.

I explained the Reader's Digest version of my theory as to where The Messenger was hiding. Then I pronounced, "I must find the bomber. Sorry. I will do the statement later."

The first responders gave me a couple of quick bandages for my scrapes and insisted that I go to the hospital to get checked out, but I needed to leave, now.

I stood and could not get my balance. I was afraid I had a brain injury—until I noticed one of my heels had snapped off. Great, just great. Now my dependable date heels were broken and looked beyond salvage. Freak, they cost a fortune. At least to me. I didn't have any backup shoes in Robin's car, so I had to proceed barefoot.

I took a step towards Robin's car, as if I could have driven it in its current condition. Maybe I did have a concussion.

I waived down a taxi and told the driver it was a police emergency.

My cabbie drove like a demon, but once we got close, I had him slow to the speed limit, and he carefully guided the taxi into a spot. I didn't want to alert Higgins. If I was correct, he would be on guard, looking for anything out of the ordinary. I couldn't storm the building like the opening scene of *Star Wars*. Weapons would attract attention. I had to appear like a regular woman going to a meeting—a regular woman wearing no shoes, battered by a recent auto accident. I assured myself it made sense, even though I knew I must have been a sight.

I entered the sprawling Southern-inspired building, the snake pit, and greeted the receptionist.

"Welcome to our law firm. We're personal injury specialists. How can I help you?"

I flashed her my best smile. "Would you know if this man is in today?" I showed her my digital photo of Higgins.

"You know you're not wearing any shoes?"

"Yes, I broke my heel. One of those days."

She stared at the photo. "I don't think this person works for our law firm. Are you sure you have the correct address?"

"I believe he works for a different business that has an office upstairs."

"Let me check." The receptionist reached for her telephone.

I grabbed her hand before she beeped Mr. Higgins.

I held up my index finger to my mouth. "No sound please. Las Vegas police. This man is wanted for a violent crime." The blood drained from her face. She had no idea she worked near a monster.

"How many people are downstairs?" I asked.

"Ten," she whispered.

"Round up everyone and shuttle them out of the building, quietly."

My voice sounded deceptively confident, like I was a brave soldier about to charge up the hill facing enemy fire. But I wasn't confident, I was scared silly. I hoped no one noticed my hands trembling.

I hoped Higgins was afraid of dying.

I limped and padded up the elaborate staircase. My butt stung on every step. It must have taken a lot of car wrecks to pay for this place. When I was near the top, I took out my pistol. I entered the second-floor landing with gun chest high, ready to fire. A secretary, her arms loaded with paper files, walked by. I put my finger to my lips and whispered an explanation. The woman dropped the files and bounded down the stairs far too quickly, but I was past the surprise stage now anyway.

I silently guided the second-floor workers out of the building. Higgins's office was down the hallway to the left. Without a sound, I padded barefoot to Higgins's open office door.

I whispered to myself, "On three. Ready . . . one . . . two . . . three . . ." and I darted into Higgins's office, gun drawn. The office was empty. Nothing in the small closet except a police uniform and a pool cleaner's uniform on hangers. Higgins' disguises. No one was under the desk.

I looked at his setup. Mr. Higgins had a powerful surveillance system. Four computer monitors showed split screens of video cameras across Vegas, outside the building, and local television stations—a mini version of the fishbowl.

Whistling came from the hallway. I pressed against the wall beside the door. Higgins walked in with a steaming mug of coffee in one hand and two doughnuts in the other.

I slid up behind Higgins and placed the barrel of my pistol to the back of his head. "Don't even think about it, you dirtbag. You move one inch, and I will splatter your brains all over the ceiling." I had heard that in a Clint Eastwood movie. It was the best I could do at short notice.

"Oh, hell. You've got to be kidding me, Little Donna."

"Not one inch," I repeated.

"You won't shoot me, Little Donna, and I will never tell you where the bombs are."

I couldn't take being called "Little Donna" again. I fired a shot into the ceiling.

Higgins froze. He had doubted me. I was glad Higgins couldn't see me because I scared myself. I had fired my weapon weekly at the gun range, with earplugs and sound suppressing walls. Here, without either, it was ten times as freaking loud.

I eyed my handiwork. A nice hole in the ceiling plaster appeared above Higgins's head. Someone from the top floor spied me through my recent remodeling effort. "Sorry about that. You should leave."

Rapid footsteps indicated they took my advice. One of them must have pulled the fire alarm. The buzzing sound made me panic, but the surprise was over anyway.

"I can't believe this," Higgins said. "Little Donna found me?"

"Yes, I caught you, and *Little Donna* is going to haul your sorry butt to jail." I smiled, quite proud of myself. "First tell me about the hospital bomb."

"Not so fast," Higgins said. He tossed the coffee cup towards me, reached into his shirt pocket, and removed what looked like a garage door opener. The movement was so small and so fast, I couldn't react. Besides, I wasn't comfortable with shooting him in the head. His steaming coffee ran down my left pant leg. Freak! It's not bad enough he blew me up twice—he had to spill coffee on me twice too?

"What is that Higgins?" I asked. "Another toy?"

"A detonator."

"For what?" I asked.

"For the bomb over the doorway."

I turned and looked. Higgins wasn't bluffing. The device

was huge. It held at least ten sticks of dynamite and was coated in two-inch nails, several hundred of them. This was Higgins's doomsday device.

"Let me go, or neither of us leaves here in one piece."

I flashed back to the scene at the bank after the wire shrapnel had damaged everything and saw Archie's face, frozen in death. This time he had used nails, lots of big nails. Neither of us would survive.

CHAPTER FIFTY-FOUR

Friday, 5:45 p.m.

I HAD TO INTIMIDATE HIGGINS, get him to disable this bomb. I pointed the warm barrel of my pistol towards his face. "Higgins, I don't trust you."

He snickered under his breath. "You don't have a choice— Where are your shoes?"

The carpet was very thick and comfortable. It probably cost dozens of car wrecks. I was tired, exhausted really, and my eyes were burning and sore. Then I remembered the discussions with my Disco Divas in the fishbowl. Would Higgins risk his own life? No, he wouldn't, not his own precious life. Anyone who wore a toupee was too vain to risk his own life. I had to take the chance. "We already found the first hospital bomb. How many did you leave?" This was a big bluff, but it had to work.

"Did I say there was more than one?" His coy answer perturbed me.

I had one last strategy to try. I closed the door and sat in a chair to Higgins's side. I lowered my pistol. "Go ahead."

"What?"

I took his top doughnut. "Is this cherry icing?" I took a big bite. "No, it's strawberry. Great. I love strawberries. Go ahead and blow us all up, *Baldy*. First, please promise me all your toupees are in the room, so they'll be blown up as well. Are they here? In this room?"

"What? No, my *hairpieces* are not here. They're at home."

"Well, crap. I hate to think someone else is going to have the embarrassment of wearing that dead rat on his head. Totally unconvincing by the way. But go ahead, blow us all up, Mister Clean." I took another big bite. "These doughnuts are good. Where did you get them?"

Toupee Man was wide-eyed with confusion. "The doughnuts?"

"Please tell me the name of this bakery before you blow us up. I usually prefer chocolate, but this is making me reconsider. Is the bakery's name on the box? Do you have a break room? Is that where the doughnuts are?"

Higgins looked confused. "I will blow us up. I will do it. I *will*." His voice sounded less defiant.

"Wow, these are good. Fresh and tasty." I smiled. "I must find out the bakery before I leave. I'm sorry. I interrupted you. Go ahead, Kojac."

"Don't push me. I'll do it," he replied, almost an apology.

"Then do it already, you putz."

Higgins's bluff wouldn't work. Once he realized it, he surrendered without a fight. He placed the detonator on his desk. I had to ask. "Why did you do this, Higgins? For your foster mother? Really?"

"She was the only person who was nice to me in my entire life. She was so caring and gentle. And that damn bank treated her like garbage, then threw her out in the street." He teared up. Was Higgins human after all?

I got nose to nose with him. "Tell me where you hid the bomb at the hospital."

"Hard pass."

"Oh, you're going to talk Higgins. Where is the hospital bomb?"

"Lawyer."

"What?" I wanted to slap him.

"Lawyer," he repeated. "I want a lawyer. I. Want. A. Lawyer. I WANT A LAWYER."

I did not have time for this. I pushed his rolling chair to the doorway and pulled his nail-covered device from the wall.

"Be careful with that," Higgins warned.

"I will," I smiled. "Where is the hospital bomb?"

"No comment."

"Where. Is. It?"

Higgins didn't say a word.

I took the nail-coated bomb and placed it on Higgins's . . . lap.

"That might kill you, or it might just blow off your . . . lower half." I smiled and reached for the detonator.

"You wouldn't."

"Don't bet on it. I'm exhausted, emotionally drained, and my rump hurts all the time. And I'm hungry. I'm going to get another donut or two. Will I be safe in the break room if your bomb *accidentally* goes off? I'm asking for a friend." I took two steps for the door when Higgins broke his silence.

Tears streamed down his face. "You don't understand the first thing about me, Little Donna. The hospital bomb . . . it . . . it doesn't exist. I just said that to create panic, so you wouldn't have time to find all the others."

"So there never was a bomb at UMC?"

"I'm not a monster. Hurting sick people is not me."

"Except of course the one at the ER. Okay, Higgins, time to come clean. Where are all the bombs?"

Higgins laughed. "Why tell you? I'm sure you found some, but I'm confident you didn't find all of them."

"Maybe if you tell us, it can help your case," I said. "Reduce your time in prison."

"Help my case? I've killed people. I killed a cop. I'm going to jail forever. Nothing you can do."

"You might stop someone else from dying."

His defeated face turned into a scowl. "Anybody involved with Second United deserves to die."

I had no reason to trust Higgins, but I thought he was telling the truth. "Where are the rest of the bombs?"

"No comment, Little Donna."

I eyed his computers. All screens were locked. No password. Higgins had installed a thumbprint reader. Awfully high tech for a bottom feeder like him. I tried with my thumb. No luck. "I need your thumb."

"No way a tiny woman like you can force me—"

I jerked open his top desk drawer. A nice pair of scissors caught my eye.

Higgins laughed. "Gonna stab me? I don't think so."

"No," I said. "I need your thumbprint."

"Not going to help, and by the time your backup gets here, it will be too late."

I smiled and snapped the scissors open and closed. "Higgins, you worm, you don't understand."

He gave me a puzzled stare.

I snapped the scissors open and closed again. "I don't need you to help. I just need your thumb, and I really don't care if the rest of your disgusting body is attached to it or not."

After I snapped the scissors again, he became more cooperative. With the screens unlocked, I pushed his chair away. So many files on his computer. Which one? I didn't have time for this, and I didn't really think I could or would torture him, as tempting as that was. What would he call his list of bombs?

One file jumped off the screen at me, called "Mother's Day."

The two-page list was detailed. Higgins worked countless days on planting these bombs all over Vegas. Some addresses were familiar from our searches. I emailed the details to the fishbowl. Everyone would work on the list.

"I want credit for every single one, and I want everyone to know why I did this. That bank deserves it and much worse. Nothing more than predators, taking advantage of a single woman with a houseful of kids."

"But this? Explosions? That didn't harm the bank. You harmed people, real people, who didn't have anything to do with your foster mom." I had one more demand of Higgins before I brought him to jail. "Who helped you?" Higgins's stare turned cold. "Who is helping you? Someone on the inside of the investigation? Someone in Vegas Police?"

Higgins leaned forward and whispered, "You'll never find out." Then he smiled and said, "Lawyer. I want a lawyer."

CHAPTER FIFTY-FIVE

Friday 6:31 p.m.

I BOOKED Mr. Higgins into jail, my second arrest as a detective, and I made sure his last view of freedom was me. I could really use a double-double from In-N-Out Burger to soothe my aching stomach. Of course, with two orders of fries and a vanilla shake.

I moved into the press briefing room. Television cameras, reporters, and bright lights filled the room, an impromptu victory lap. I was half-thrilled, half-scared. Had I fixed my hair? What was I wearing? Oh my God, I was still barefoot. Sandy retrieved my normal day flats from my desk drawer.

"Thank you," I mouthed.

Sandy replied with a wink.

At least one problem was solved. The constant *click, click, click* of cameras unnerved me.

The captain thanked the Disco Divas as a group, and individually mentioned me, Sandy, Lynn, and Helen by name, along with John-Boy, Ben, and a special mention of Will Ignacio, Archie, and the three other officers for the extreme sacrifices they made. The press conference concluded quickly as the reporters sprinted out to make sure their stories were delivered first. If it wasn't Breaking News, it wasn't news.

I sat in the fishbowl when Mayor Steve Shale appeared. I was surprised to see him. His entourage followed like disciples.

"Detective Wyznecki, I wish to thank you."

I never expected to hear him thank me. "Thank you," was all I could say, still shocked.

"Your bravery and timeless action will not be forgotten."

Maybe Steve Shale wasn't a jerk. Maybe.

"My wife and I got you a token of appreciation." Shale's wife stepped forward and handed me a giant key to the city.

I was surprised and only said "Thank you" once again.

Wife number five looked at me with a bright smile. "The key is made of chocolate. Your friends said you might like it."

"Chocolate? Now you're talking my language."

You know, I kind of liked her, but I wouldn't make a big commitment since she might not be around long. I supposed Shale was decent, for a politician. I held my chocolate key over my head like a prizefighter's belt, to great applause from my fellow officers. I hope that didn't mean I had to share. This was chocolate, my chocolate. *There is no "we" in chocolate.*

It was twenty minutes until my blind date. I wasn't in a date mood, or any kind of mood really.

I called the number of my nameless admirer to cancel again. Ugh. I finally have someone interested in me, but after all this, I'm not first-date ready.

He answered on the second ring. "Donna, please don't tell me you want to cancel again."

"I hate myself for saying it, but yes, I do need another raincheck."

"What's wrong?" His voice showed genuine concern.

"You see all the news about The Messenger? Well, that case is over."

"Then how about we go celebrate?"

I hung my head. "Sorry. No. I still have a family crisis."

"Is there anything I can do?"

"Give me a rain check until tomorrow?"

"Consider it given. See you tomorrow."

This day was only half over. Now, to Robin's hospital room, so my world could end.

CHAPTER FIFTY-SIX

Friday 7:25 p.m.

I WALKED past the damaged emergency room entrance that was now covered in police tape and plastic sheeting so the ER could remain operational.

Robin's room. He had been in this damn hospital room for so long that I thought of this as *his room*. Several crayon drawings from the kids decorated the walls, and get-well cards were poised on the windowsill. Elaine's neatly made cot pressed against the back wall. Gloria and Elaine talked in hushed tones as they leafed through magazines. I went to Robin's bedside and held his hand. His slow, rhythmic ventilator breathed in harmony with the soft beeping monitors.

My brother was about to die. My whole family crowded in: my parents, the Wyznecki kids, assorted spouses and significant others, Elaine, and their two kids. We were shoulder to shoulder, but no one complained.

A nurse poked her head in and gave us a stern look. "This room is over-crowded. Could some of you wait in the hall?"

"Go away," was all I said. The nurse raised her eyebrow but left without another word.

We grabbed each other's hands, and Mom led us in a quick prayer. I was never terribly religious. Mom went to church every Sunday, and I tagged along about half the time, but it seemed more like a routine than a calling. Maybe I had changed. Two prayers in two days—I was practically a nun.

This was the end. I hoped Robin still had some fight in him. Dr. Pike nodded to a nurse, who turned off the ventilator. Robin took two slow breaths then stopped. My heart sank. The monitors beeped a piercing tone as his heart rate dropped. Tears ran down my face, my vision blurred. Robin's blood pressure dropped, and his oxygen level tanked. The monitors seemed deafening in this tiny room. The nurse silenced each one. His body showed no movement. I willed him to breathe so strongly, I thought my forehead might burst. Robin never moved.

The soft sounds of crying broke the silence. Elaine turned away and hugged her sobbing kids. Maybe we shouldn't have exposed the kids to this. Would hearing that your dad died be any better? This was a terrible, terrible day, and no attempt at emotional distancing would make a difference.

My siblings had talked about how Robin would have wanted this moment. We had agreed on what to do, but now it seemed too difficult. I was supposed to start, but my voice betrayed me. I nodded to my oldest brother, Barry, who did my part, protecting me, as big brothers always did. Barry sang softly and slowly to start. "I know your eyes in the morning sun, I feel you touch me in the pouring rain."

Maurice and my sister, Gloria, joined in. We continued with "How Deep is Your Love," Robin's favorite Bee Gees hit, and mine. The song represented happier times. Elaine smiled with tears streaming down. "Please, everyone join in. For Robin." We did.

Dr. Pike moved in close to listen to his heart. The monitor was a flat line. I knew what Dr. Pike would hear. Nothing. My brother was gone. We sang together, half-singing, half-crying.

Dr. Pike listened to Robin's chest, straining to find any sign of life. Then he whipped his head around to see the monitors as they all jumped into action. Robin had a pulse!

It was weak, but he still had a pulse. He was a fighter. Dr. Pike told us this might happen, a spontaneous reaction. The human heart cycled a few times like a last-ditch emergency reaction built into your body. Then Robin's body convulsed like he had gotten a blast of electricity. We turned the kids' heads away. This was the worst part, the very end.

Then it happened. Robin inhaled once, long and slow. Dr. Pike had also warned us about this, the death rattle, a last gasp of air the body demanded even when dying. We covered the children's ears, but I didn't think it adequately protected them from this horrid scene. Robin was motionless. What were we supposed to do now? We were clueless. No one had prepared us for the next step. Tears blinded me.

Then, I don't know how to describe it—a miracle, an answer to prayers—Robin inhaled again. His body shook lightly as he exhaled. He inhaled again while we all stared, dumbfounded. On his fourth shaky inhalation, Dr. Pike announced, "He's breathing again, on his own. He's going to make it."

Robin mumbled something, and I pushed through the crowd to get close, inches from his face. *Please be all right.* "Talk to me." I moved closer. "Robin, what is it?"

He spoke a little louder. "Two donuts. You have two donuts left."

Tears sprang from my eyes. Robin was alive. The family collapsed into a giant group hug. Today was a day for miracles.

CHAPTER FIFTY-SEVEN

SATURDAY WAS no day of rest for me. Despite my chocolate key hangover, I had to organize files from The Messenger case. We generated a lot of paper, and if Higgins didn't plead guilty, we would need all this for his trial. Four bankers boxes and two empty donut boxes later, I moved back to my desk.

Someone kicked the back of my chair. I turned my head to see Soames walk by. "Sorry, dwarf," he said. "I'm headed up to the barbeque dinner on the roof. You could go, but you must be at least this tall to ride " Soames held his hand about chin high.

"A short joke. Very original. I hope you choke."

"Tell your hot friend if she's still interested to call me."

"I think she would rather run through a Turkish prison naked."

He left and the room brightened up. I gathered my notes into one big folder. One handwritten note stuck out. *Messenger says I don't know what's going on right in front of my face.*

Strange comment from Higgins. What did he mean? What did I not see right in front of me?

Ben was away. I went to Ben's station, which consisted of six monitors and three keyboards. Which one had Shale used with his special password to access the DHHS files? I tapped a few keys. Still logged in. I looked through Higgins's background files and the foster mother's information. Something about that relationship bothered me. I glanced around. Ben was nowhere in sight, so I kept digging. Then I found the answer. Someone else had a relationship with the foster mother. Someone with advanced techie skills. Someone who had access to the investigation in real time. Someone who had an axe to grind. How could I have missed this? He really was right in front of me, just like The Messenger had said. I must have been blind. I printed my new discovery. I texted the Disco Divas to come to the roof and help me capture The Messenger's conspirator.

Ben appeared, another one of those disgusting energy drinks in hand. "What's up, Donna?"

Higgins did have inside help all along, and I hadn't seen it. How could I miss something so obvious? Now, the decisive moment. "Ben, can I borrow your gun?"

Ben furrowed his brow. "My gun? Sure. Why?"

"They took my primary gun when I was being sued for excessive force. They took my backup gun for the little stunt of shooting a hole in Higgins's ceiling." I smiled, but inside I did cartwheels in panic.

Ben reached into his desk drawer and handed me his police issue revolver. "Still shiny and new. Only fired it once at the range. Give it back when you're done?" he asked.

"Sure. Can you follow me up to the roof for a second?"

Ben didn't suspect anything, or he wouldn't have given me his gun or followed me to the roof. I tucked Ben's pistol into my back pocket where it bumped my sore rump, still tender. Ink pen injuries were the worst. Ben and I took the elevator up to Captain Creek's informal office, the roof, where the officers still celebrated the end of Mister Toupee's carnage. We didn't get many cases like this in Vegas, and we were thankful it was over.

Shale's office had sent over a BBQ buffet from John Mull's Meats & Road Kill Grill for the entire police force and the roof seemed the best place for it. Besides brisket, we had hot links, pulled chicken, ribs, pulled pork, and my favorite, burnt ends. I was in carnivore heaven.

Soames loaded his plate like it was the last dinner before hibernation. Cigarette smoke drifted in the air, but the rooftop winds blew it away. I waited for the crowd to thin, so I could make my confrontation. The captain smoked, which he shouldn't do, but that was a fight for another day.

My phone buzzed. It was Elaine. "What's up girl?"

"Robin wants to talk to you."

"Great. I love hearing his voice."

"Hey, sis. I was wondering. Where's my car?"

Freak. "I'll have to get back with you." I'd probably need to go into witness protection.

The Disco Divas arrived, breathless. I pushed my hands down to indicate *slow down.*

I approached the person who helped The Messenger terrorize Las Vegas. With tears in my eyes, I asked him, "Why?"

"Why, what?" he replied, no indication I had discovered his secret.

"You never told me you grew up in foster care, John-Boy."

"I didn't think it mattered."

"You were in the same foster home as Higgins, at the same time."

John-Boy slumped in his wheelchair. "I never talked about those times with anyone."

"Why did you help him, John-Boy?"

"She was the only person who cared for us when we were

young, the only one." He cried. "And what that bank did to her . . . inexcusable." Anger rose in his voice. "That bank should be burned to the ground and the earth salted so nothing can ever grow there."

"I understand, John-Boy, but this was wrong. You had to know this was wrong."

"He took it too far . . . was just supposed to damage the buildings." John-Boy looked down. "I'm not sorry. That bank deserved everything they got and much more. They threw Momma Rose into the street like she was garbage."

"This wasn't the answer, John-Boy. People are dead. Archie, that boy at the bank, dozens hurt, Robin . . . I was . . ."

John-Boy cried. "I'm so sorry. I never meant to hurt you or Robin or anyone. I don't suppose I could ask you to forget this, could you? I mean, Higgins is in jail. It's over."

"People are dead. I can't just look away."

"Are you going to arrest me?" John-Boy asked. I pulled out Ben's pistol.

Helen and Sandy withdrew their own firearms.

I inhaled deeply, then said my familiar refrain. "You have the right to remain silent . . ."

My third arrest as a detective.

"John-Boy, sorry, but I will let Helen book you. I have a hot date tonight."

A NOTE FROM THE AUTHOR

The author, M. Ludlum, was diagnosed with Multiple Sclerosis (MS) in 2019. MS is currently an incurable degenerative disease of the central nervous system (brain, spinal cord, and optic nerves). MS disrupts the flow of information within the brain, and between the brain and body resulting in mobility issues, fatigue, pain, and vision impairment. No one knows exactly what causes MS. Research is ongoing to identify the cause of MS and one day find a cure. Advances are being made every day. It is likely too late for me. Perhaps this will help the next generation.

A portion of the proceeds of each book will be donated to MS research.

If you would like to help in this fight, two very worthy MS charities are:

Race to Erase MS - https://www.erasems.org/

National MS Society - https://www.nationalmssociety.org/

ACKNOWLEDGMENTS

A novel is a project of love and dedication that requires a village. I have many residents of my village I wish to thank.

Writing is a lonely process. A special thank you to my dear family, Kara, Bailey, Justin, and Shan, and other family and friends for the many times I have needed solitude to complete this project.

Along the way, I have received invaluable advice from Amy Brewer, Melanie Hemry, Betsey Kulakowski, Barry Friedman, Lisa Gardner, Amy M. Le, Susan Kite, Rita Kae Koontz, Dee Britt, and many others. If I forgot your name, my apologies.

I have had incredible support from my amazing editor, Lara Bernhardt, who showed tremendous patience to a writer who could not remember his punctuation rules.

And an enormous thank you to Will Bernhardt and the whole crew at Babylon Books (BabylonBooks.net) for taking a chance on me.

I would also like to show my appreciation to several writers organizations, including WriterCon (WriterCon.com) and the Oklahoma Writers Federation Inc. (owfi.org). If you are interested in starting a writing project, the best advice I can offer is to get engaged with a group of writers in your area.

FOR FOODIES

Detective Donna is a foodie (as is the author). The award winning, local restaurants mentioned in the book (while used fictionally) are very real and absolutely delicious. On your next visit to Las Vegas, check them out. Tell them Detective Donna sent you.

In alphabetical order:

Blueberry Hill Diner

blueberryhillrestaurants.com/

A breakfast staple for Las Vegas. Family owned and operated since 1966 with four locations across Las Vegas, two of which operate 24/7 to deliver comfort food around the clock.

Dona Maria Tamales

donamariatamales.com/

Famous for tamales, authentic Mexican food, and Margaritas. Family owned and operated since 1980 with two locations in Las Vegas.

Golden Steer Steakhouse

goldensteer.com/

An old-world steakhouse, famous with celebrities since 1958. (Scenes from the movie, *Casino* were filmed there). Reservations required.

John Mulls Meats & Road Kill Grill

johnmullsmeatcompany.com/

A third-generation family business, famous for Las Vegas style BBQ, offering a variety of meats in the Market, prepared meats in the Road Kill Grill (limited hours, 11-6, closed Sundays), and catering for large or small gatherings.

Lindo Michoacan

lindomichoacan.com/

Gourmet Mexican cuisine, the largest selection of Tequilas, and gaming, operating since 1990 with three locations in Las Vegas and one in Henderson.

Pizza Rock Pizza Kitchen

pizzarocklasvegas.com/

Located downtown, featuring gourmet pizzas and Italian dishes, and a large assortment of beers in an artistic atmosphere.

St. Honoré

ilovesainthonore.com/

Featuring classic and signature couture doughnuts, beignets, shakes and pizza.

NEXT IN THE DISCO DIVAS SERIES

Political season has started in Las Vegas. Detective Donna Summer Wyznecki hopes to guard a senator, an ambassador, or a former President, but is relegated to watching Penny, the kindergarten daughter of the mayor. Confined to a hotel suite, Donna and Penny enjoy cartoons and room service. While Penny loves this, Donna is bored beyond words. Without warning, Penny collapses and Donna feels the room spinning. Donna wakes up to find a room full of officers and Penny gone. Donna is blamed for screwing up this simple assignment. When ransom demands are made, Donna and the Disco Divas jump into action. Donna must redeem her credibility, rescue Penny, satisfy her insatiable hunger for all things donut and taco related, navigate her fledgling romance with a blind date, and deal with her eclectic, disco-themed family. Figuratively and literally, Donna's plate is full. Can Donna disco her way through all this? Sit your paisley bell-bottom pants down and watch.

Make suggestions about the title, cover design, and all things Disco Diva at: LudlumBooks.net

ABOUT THE AUTHOR

Marty Ludlum is an award-winning author of the Disco Diva series. Marty's goal as a writer is to make the reader shoot wine out her nose at least once every hour. "If the reader is not laughing, I have failed, and I don't plan on failing," Marty likes to say.

Marty is a Professor of Business Law at the University of Central Oklahoma, having taught there for sixteen years. Marty has spoken to numerous groups around the world about legal issues, as long as donuts are offered. When not writing, Marty enjoys traveling with college sweetheart, Kara, Netflix, reading, hot tea, spoiling grandchildren, Tommy, Zailinn, and Lola, and is always searching for another great Mexican restaurant.

Find info about Marty's novels at LudlumBooks.net.